# Faerie War

## TITANIA ACADEMY BOOK 4

# Faerie War

## TITANIA ACADEMY BOOK 4

### Samaire Wynne

Black Raven Books

This is a work of fiction. All of the geography, characters, organizations, and events portrayed in this novel are either products of the author's imagination or are used fictitiously.

## Black Raven Books

Faerie War.
Copyright © 2020 by Samaire Wynne. All rights reserved.
Cover illustrations copyright © 2020 by Melody Simmons
Printed in the United States of America.
For information, including permission to reproduce selections from this book, write to
publisher@blackravenbooks.net or to
Black Raven Books, P.O. Box 3201, Martinsville VA 24115

The text was set in 12-point Californian FB

ISBN-13 9781948594431

First Edition: September 2020

10   9   8   7   6   5   4   3   2   1

Dedicated to the readers who've followed Holly's story this far. Don't worry: there's lots more to come.

# Faerie War

Chapter One
# Double Date

"Can you believe us?" I whispered as I applied lip gloss, leaning forward to look in our dorm mirror.

"No," Liesl giggled. "But I am so excited my hand is trembling." She wiped the edge of her lip for the third time.

"Here, let me help," I took her lip gloss from her and sat down on her bed, patting the blanket next to me. "Sit."

She sat down, wiggling herself in anticipation. I held her chin lightly with my hand, palm up, and tried to approach her face.

"Okay, I think I see your problem, Li."

Her smile faded. "What is it?"

"Stop wiggling!"

She grinned and held still for me.

"Relax your face," I instructed. "Close your eyes."

I touched the lip gloss applicator to her lips, and applied it evenly.

"This is a nice color for you," I said. "Very rosy." I finished and handed it back to her.

She glanced in the mirror. "You got it perfect, thanks!" She glanced down at the tube of lip gloss. "Yeah, I picked this up last year at the faerie marketplace. Been waiting for a chance to use it ever since."

I stood up and held my new top up to my shoulders. "Think this will do?"

"Of course, Holly. Blue is your color," Liesl grinned.

Aspen and Tundra, my two arctic wolf familiars, snored in the corner.

"Lazy bums," I murmured affectionately.

"Do you think Jack will kiss me?" Liesl said in a dreamy voice as she adjusted her hair in the mirror.

"God, I hope so," I answered. "Although we'd have to reapply your lip gloss," I laughed.

"Worth it," she said, puckering her lips into a pout in the mirror.

"Definitely," I answered.

As we were about to leave, I turned to my familiars.

"Aspen, Tundra: poof!" and they'd both vanished, returning to the magical familiar realm where they naturally existed when they weren't with me.

I'd trained them last fall to obey the command "Poof!" and return. It was a quick, one-syllable way to get them to go.

*Hey, sometimes it has to happen fast.*

I wondered about the magical familiar realm, and had asked my favorite teacher, Professor Farryn about it, and been told that was "a whole new class. Please wait for Year Three. Thanks for asking. Bye."

*Oh, well.*

We finished dressing and were out the door in ten minutes.

The sun was setting as we walked down the stairs and out the Academy doors.

Christmas had been fantastic. Father had spent a week at Titania Academy, and then we'd gone to Liesl's house for a week, and her family had put us up in two separate guest rooms.

Father and I had stayed in a tree house, and I'd loved it so much I hadn't wanted to leave.

The Oak King Faction hadn't been seen or heard from since last September, when Liesl and I had gone to the Elfen lands and spent a few unintentional weeks there. Father had destroyed the Oak King Faction hideout we'd found, after discovering it had been abandoned.

We'd tried to rescue the Oak King, and had almost made it. Almost.

I still had mental scars from that time. Not from being tortured and imprisoned by the Elfen Council. No, from our failure to rescue the Oak King.

The poor king had been drugged and drained of energy and seemed near death.

We'd tried to rescue him, with the help of new halfling friends; we'd gotten him out of the dark estate and into the woods.

But we'd been caught. Shot at. Captured.

And the poor Oak King, the brother to my father, the son of the rag woman — who we later found out was the queen in disguise — was recaptured and whisked away by the Faction to who-knows-where.

I'd felt horrible.

My poor uncle!

And Liesl and I, along with new friends Laura, Tam, and Lucy, had been caught and transported to the Elfen Council prison.

*Elfen Council prison. Now there's a phrase I would never have guessed I'd say. Who knew I'd end up in such a place?*

My father had rescued me after I'd inadvertently summoned him by rubbing the holly charm he'd given me (which I will never take off from around my neck). Then we'd gone back to the dark estate where The Faction had last been seen with the Oak King.

But we'd found it deserted.

Father had stormed through every room and found nothing.

He had contained his anger, for the most part, until we walked away from the castle. Then he'd waved his hand without even looking back, and the whole massive stone and wood structure had been flattened.

To the ground.

My father, the Holly King, had smote the castle.

The whole thing had been reduced to a pile of knocked-over rubble that wasn't more than a few inches in height.

*There's no coming back after that, lol.*

We got word a month later, from the halflings via Laura's father, that the pile of rubble was gone. They'd cleared it away and tossed it all into the sea.

*Good riddance.*

But the Oak King was gone, and we had no idea where he was.

The Faction had disappeared into thin air. No trace.

Father had scouts looking everywhere, but there had been no clue so far.

So celebrating Christmas with the Holly King himself was a fantastic way to help us forget our troubles, if only for a little while.

Liesl's family guest tree house had been incredible, and Father and I'd had more fun than ever there.

But now, back at Titania Academy, with classes about to start, we were reconnecting with old flames and new.

Jack had seen Liesl the first day back, and had asked her out.

Liesl had blushed crimson, and had said yes, but only if it could be a double date with Chance and me.

Jack had said, "Of course." I think he was just relieved she hadn't said no. Apparently Jack had been a skinny, short, pimply boy in Year 1, and had shot up seven inches over the summer. He'd been working out as well, Liesl told me.

He was shaping up to be quite the hunk, as anyone with eyes could see.

Chance and Jack were both waiting on the front lawn.

"Oh my God," Liesl murmured. She looked beautiful in her dress and pink sparkly high heels, which made light slapping sounds as we descended the outside stairs.

Jack and Chance were both dressed up, and in the fading light of dusk they looked good.

Really good.

I swallowed, feeling a tingle of excitement in my stomach.

*Don't throw up, Holly girl.*

I reached the walkway and took a deep breath, closing my eyes for a moment. Cool air was the best antidote to overactive butterflies in your stomach.

*OMG. What if faerie folk could really have butterflies living and flying around in our stomachs?*

I giggled and put my hand to my chin, remembering at the last minute not to touch my mouth or I'd smear my lip gloss.

"What's so funny, gorgeous?" Chance asked as he and Jack walked up to us. He smiled and put his hand out to touch the back of my waist as he leaned forward to kiss my cheek. "Never mind, I don't care. You look beautiful," he murmured.

Jack stood a few feet away, staring at Liesl. He'd only really seen her during classes or on lunch break or stuff like that. This was the first time he saw her dressed up.

This was their first date.

Jack's cheeks were red, and he looked like he might faint. There was a silly smile on his face.

We all looked at him. Liesl smiled demurely.

After a minute, it was obvious that the boy needed help.

"Jack," I said, "don't you think Liesl looks nice in her new dress?" *Come on, dude, let's get the evening going.*

"Uh," Jack cleared his throat, and then segued into a coughing fit that had me concerned.

Chance pounded Jack's back for a minute, holding the guy's arm. He bent his head close to Jack's, and I thought I heard Chance whisper, "Get it together, man."

Jack recovered and straightened. If his face had seemed blushed red before, it was flaming red now.

He looked ghastly.

I glanced at Liesl and she had an amused look on her face.

"Um, er... Liesl, you look... really nice," Jack said.

*Really nice? She looks fantastic, dude. Heck, I'd date her.*

I looked down at my feet to hide my grin of amusement.

"Okay." Chance patted Jack on the back once more. "Shall we proceed to the café?" He turned and took my hand, lifting it to his mouth and kissing it gently before leading me forward.

We followed the path as it arced around the quad, and stopping about a hundred feet on.

The new café had been created to boost student morale, and heartily encouraged by the Fae Folk Academy Council.

The neat dirt path that curved around the front of the school had been altered at one spot: A flat stone pathway branched off into the woods to the café. Lit tiki lights, their flames flickering in the night air, marked the beginning of the path, on the edge of the dirt Academy path.

Flowers lined the flat stone pathway on either side, glowing in the moonlight. These were moon blossoms, indigenous to the Faerie Lands. They looked like white pansies; they soaked up the sunlight throughout the day, and glowed at night with a beautiful light. Their white floppy petals softly glimmered and twinkled in the dying light. They made a perfect, gorgeous and romantic accent, guiding us along the pathway.

The path was just wide enough to allow two people to stroll side-by-side if they knew each other well.

Chance held my hand as we slowly walked to the café, Jack and Liesl behind us. The night was cold, but the interspersed tiki torches that had been put up to augment the moon flowers helped to warm the pathway.

We reached the café and were met by a faun in full form, dressed in a jacket and holding a folded white cloth over his arm.

"Mr. Mac Craith, we received your reservation. Your table is right over here, if you'll all follow me?" He turned and led us to the table, and I had my first close-up view of a faerie faun ever.

His fur was a light golden brown, and his hooves were a darker brown, and they looked glossy.

*Wonder if they're polished? Probably, probably...*

The fur on his body covered his lower half, and was

actually longer than I thought it would be.

*I can't see anything.*

I blushed.

*Stop that. Be nice.*

The waiter's jacket was black, and fitted to him. His head looked mostly human, but he had soft, furry goat ears that grew downward from the sides of his head. Short, goat horns extended from the area above his ears, and they curled in a Fibonacci sequences around and around until they ended in small points, like seashells. The horns were polished and very handsome.

His hair looked human, except it cascaded farther down than it normally would have, curling into what might have been called the sides of a beard, had it not been on a natural faun. As it was, it just looked like gorgeous faun sideburns.

His tail flipped a few times as he walked, and the underside of the little furry appendage was creamy white.

He needed less than a half-minute to show us to our table, but I took all this in during those few seconds.

"You're staring." Chance bent as he walked to whisper out of the side of his mouth.

"I can't help it," I whispered back.

"You're going to love fall classes," Chance murmured.

*What does that have to do with ogling a forest faun?*

"Here we are," the waiter said, pulling out a chair for me.

I sat, and he tucked it into the table as I lowered myself into it. Then he turned to seat Liesl.

Chance and Jack seated themselves, and we were there.

At the Faun Café. *For realsies!*

I'd been wanting to visit ever since I'd heard of it last fall.

Jack had asked Liesl out and planned to take her here, but with the craziness of our Elfen Lands trip, and the craziness when we got back, our plans had fallen through. So it was really good to be here.

The table was covered in a white cloth, and the plates were exquisitely carved from a light wood, with ivy vines and grapes etched into the edges. I studied the plates alone for a few minutes.

The flatware was carved from quartz. "Straight from the Elfen Lands, Miss," the waiter murmured as he surreptitiously filled my water glass.

I smiled and touched the fork with my fingertips. It was beautiful, and reminded me of all the white quartz I had seen in the Elfen Lands last fall.

The faun waiter passed out small menus, then retreated.

"Hmm, let's see what looks good," Chance murmured.

The menu was varied, listing many faerie delicacies, some which I could not for the life of me recognize.

*I don't want to order something embarrassing, so I'll stick with what I can identify. … Wait, what are these?*

I leaned over to Chance and pointed at one of the items.

He murmured, "Those are a kind of savory portobello mushroom, grilled with herbs; they're very good."

I glanced at his face, and he nodded and winked.

*He's not putting me on, is he?*

He wasn't. I ordered the grilled portobello mushrooms, which arrived shortly: a rectangular plate with five circles spread on it, each the size of a small hamburger patty. I cut a small piece with my fork and knife and placed it in my mouth; I closed my eyes as the flavors exploded, delivering an incredibly culinary sensation.

I moaned.

I opened my eyes to see both men staring at me with indecipherable looks on their faces.

I blinked.

*Note to self: Don't moan at the dinner table when on a date.*

I smiled and murmured, "it's very good."

Chance grinned and laughed.

"Told you." He winked.

Liesl and Jack were eating their meals and talking

softly, and I noticed a small smile on her face.

I really wanted her first date with Jack to go well, so I smiled, too.

After about ten minutes of silent eating and appreciative sounds over delicious flavors; of murmuring back and forth and smiles exchanged, Chance spoke.

"You three are Second Year spring term, so you'll be starting on one of my favorite classes ever: Hereditary Magic." He grinned and sat back.

Jack grinned. "My grandfather used to teach that class, back when I was a baby. He loved it."

"Oh, your grandpa taught at the school?" asked Liesl.

Jack nodded.

"He retired ten years ago. Now he travels with my grandmother."

I slowly shook my head.

*I've missed so much, not growing up in a Fae Folk family.*

I turned to Chance. "That class sounds incredible. I can't wait to start it." I smiled sweetly. "In fact, I can't wait to see you in your true form, Chance," I blew him a kiss as the waiter brought a table to cook our desserts.

Flaming fruit crepes, prepared at the table.

The faun flipped a crepe over a mesmerizing blue flame.

"Sir," I asked, "How is the flame created?"

"With Grand Marnier and Cognac, Miss," the faun

waiter replied.

It was beautiful and delicious, and I decided then and there to eat at the Faun Café as often as I could.

Chapter Two

# Classes Begin

The next morning, Liesl and I awoke so excited we could hardly contain ourselves.

I actually fell out of bed.

"I can't believe the list of classes for spring semester," Liesl said.

"I know! I'm not happy about all the plots and conflicts in the Faerie World, but I *am* happy the High Council okayed the Academy's request to attend advanced classes," I said. "This year is going to be unreal." I grinned and leaned over.

Aspen and Tundra had been sleeping on the floor next to me. Aspen heard me and jumped up as I leaned over;

her muzzle met my mouth with a sloppy wolf kiss.

I jumped back. "OH URGHH! WOLF SPIT!" I wiped my mouth repeatedly, then jumped out of bed. "ASPEN, I DIDN'T WANT YOUR KISSES!" I rushed to the bathroom to wash my face and mouth.

Liesl laughed. "Speaking of kisses, last night's ending was especially nice, don't you think?"

"Mmm Hmm," I said, then grabbed my toothbrush to clean my teeth.

*I don't think I'll ever feel clean again.*

We hurried to dress and go downstairs, eager to start our first class of the day.

At breakfast, Renée had Jade, her magical rabbit familiar, on her lap.

Chance and I munched bacon and eggs, as Liesl ate her omelet.

"Okay," Chance said, swallowing his last bite, "These are your new classes, Holly and Liesl." He handed us papers, then read off his own copy. "You are going to love these."

I took mine eagerly and scanned the list.

*OH MY GOD.*

"First off is *Advanced use of Shifting and Concealment*," said Chance. He looked at me. "Holly, you're already started on some of this, so you can help Liesl a bit after class, right?"

I nodded, grinning. "Absolutely." I winked at my roommate. I had been using concealment magic for nearly five months now, and I was good at it, if I did say so myself. "Liesl and I are going to ace that class, I'll make sure of that."

"Excellent," Chance said. "Now, next on the list is, um ... *Fellowship and Friendship Between Adversaries.* That's basically diplomacy. An extremely important set of skills to learn." He looked up at us and pointed his finger. "I'm sure you're going to get perfect grades in that class, aren't you, ladies?"

We nodded solemnly.

We'd heard of this class. Fellowship was a new course, taught by the headmistress, Professor Ó Baoghill herself. She'd designed it with the foresight that, no matter what conflicts the Faerie World might experience with the Oak King Faction, we'd have to work hard to build new bridges after they were over — within both the Fae Folk and Elfen lands. Reconciliation after conflict.

Professor Ó Baoghill had told us that the inhabitants of a land were responsible to heal it after a conflict. Our actions and attitudes would be what mattered. It would be up to us.

"Okay, next up is *Advanced Glamour*," said Chance. "Now, this is not a class on *How to Woo My Crush Against Their Will in Ten Easy Steps*, so don't get any funny ideas in your head."

Renée snickered.

I made a face.

Last fall, an extremely impressive Elfen Lord had tried to seduce me with his advanced Elfen glamour, and it hadn't ended well. Not at all. He'd been compelled to do it, when the Oak King Faction had kidnapped his wife and daughter and threatened their lives if he didn't do it. Still, overall, it just hadn't been cool.

No way.

It had been forcing his will on an innocent — and underage, if I might add — schoolgirl, namely me, and Chance had recognized it for the deplorable act it was, right from the beginning.

"Okay, so, yes, the *Advanced Glamour* class will focus on things like changing your appearance so you won't look like yourself," Chance said. "Changing not only the color of your hair and your eyes and skin, but changing your features entirely."

"Sounds like it could tie into the concealment class a bit," said Liesl.

"It definitely could, in the future," said Renée. "It very well might," she winked. "You never know."

*Hmmm.*

"Chance," I asked, "You're in Third Year, so have you already mastered this class?"

"Yes, I have indeed." He grinned at us. "But Renée has perfected it even further. Especially considering her Fourth-Year classes."

I turned to look at Renée, and she winked at me.

"Will you show us...," Liesl started to ask.

"No," Chance and Renée answered at the same time, then laughed and high-fived each other.

Chance shook his head. "We're not allowed to show the younger students, or even tutor them, before they have the class."

"Yeah," said Renée. "Bad things can happen, trust me."

*I don't even want to imagine...*

Chance consulted his paper. "Next on the list is *Chemical Magic.*" He looked up at us.

Liesl nodded. "Been there, done that, a little bit at home when I was younger," she said. "Best to learn in class, trust me." She lifted her shirt and revealed a two-inch scar on her side, up by her ribs. "I was ten years old."

I blinked.

*Whoa.*

"But... I still don't understand," I murmured, looking at Chance.

He smiled. "I sometimes forget you're more familiar with the human world. The *Chemical Magic* class is what they would call *Potions Class* in the Harry Potter books."

*AHHHHH.*

I nodded, completely understanding. I glanced at Liesl's side as she lowered her shirt. "So, the scar is from...?"

"Beaker exploded, splashed out, hit me full in the face, but I had on goggles and a mask. Got me a bit on the side, some of it soaked through. Hurt like the devil himself came to visit, I swear, girl..."

And that was it. I dissolved into a giggling fit and fell over sideways. Thank goodness Chance was there to catch me.

A few minutes later, I sat back up. "Okay, okay," I took a deep breath. "What other classes do we have, Chance?" I looked at him innocently.

"Well," he said, giving me a look, "The next one on the list is... *Beginning Flying.*"

*Oh, my God. I am going to have So. Much. Fun.*

Renée shivered. "Ohhh, be careful in that one," she said.

Chance nodded. "There's always a handful of new students in the beginning class that break bones during the first week." He looked at Liesl and me and waggled his finger. "Be very careful."

"How are we to be careful, if we've never done it before?" asked Liesl innocently.

I snickered, because Liesl had told me of a time when her uncle had gone flying at night after he'd just broken up with his girlfriend. The man had been drunk as a skunk and had flown into a tree. "Broke his wrist when he fell," Liesl had said. "Never lived it down."

"You pay attention in class and follow all the safety rules, that's how," said Chance. "Pretend you're taking your first driving lessons."

"I've never learned how to drive a car," I said solemnly. "That's something they teach you when you older than I am, in the human world." I blinked at Chance, trying to look as innocent as I could.

He playfully shoved my shoulder, saying, "Cut it out, you know what I mean. Just be careful," he grinned.

He laughed.

"But what if the medic is cute?" asked Liesl innocently.

*Oh my God...*

Jack's father worked as a healer at Titania Academy, and he'd told us that's what he wanted to do after he'd graduated.

Chance stared down Liesl, waiting until she looked away. He shook his head, and although he wore the slightest smile on his face, his voice was serious when he spoke, "Liesl, please. Be careful. Follow all the safety rules. Don't take a chance."

"Flying, huh?" I murmured. "Is this similar to, like, levitating?"

"A bit," said Chance. "Well, maybe more than a bit."

"Okay," I thought for a moment. "Are students safe from injury if we follow all the safety rules and precautions to a T?"

"No," Chance said grimly. "But you're much less likely to be injured if you follow them, and don't goof around. Take the class seriously."

"Okay," I said meekly. I didn't want to get hurt. I would follow all the rules.

"One more thing about the Flying class," Chance said, studying the schedule. "You've got it right after lunch, so be sure to eat lightly or you might find yourself throwing up all over the lawn." He looked up and grinned.

"Seriously?" Liesl said.

"Yes, I'm deadly serious," Chance nodded.

"Tell them how you know about this," Renée smirked.

"Never mind how I know, I just know," said Chance. "Trust me. Have a light lunch."

*Weird.*

I nodded. "Okay," I murmured.

"Will do," said Liesl.

Chance consulted his list once more. "Okay, yes, this last class was one of my favorites in Second Year. It's called *Hereditary Magic and Honing*. You'll be working on your true forms and studying how your subconscious instinct has masked your form since birth." He looked up and grinned. "And Holly, there's a ton more to this class than faun butts."

I sputtered. "I was *not* looking at the waiter's butt! I was studying his form, and his... his fur and hooves, and... everything."

Chance smirked.

"Actually, I was fascinated by our waiter as well," said Liesl. "I haven't been that close to a faun in true form before."

"Really?" Chance looked surprised.

Liesl nodded, her face solemn.

"*Anyway,*" said Renée, "one thing about Hereditary you'll be surprised about is how much the class is about yourself. A lot of us never gave much thought to how we looked in our true forms. It can be a surprise."

I thought about this. I knew Chance was of Faun heritage, and that Renée was of Melusine and Woodland Pixie heritage, and that Liesl was of Sylph heritage, but I had no idea what my heritage would come out as.

I turned to Chance. "What... how...?"

He put his hand up to stop me. "Already ahead of you, Holly," he said. "Since your mother is half human and half Elfen, and your father is The Holly King, who is of royal faun and Tylwyth Teg heritage, no one knows what your true form will look like."

*My ... the what...?*

I blinked and stared at him. "What?"

Chance chuckled and patted my arm. "You'll find out. You're both going to find out why I loved that class so much. Really, you're in for a treat."

Chapter Three
# Beginning Flying

It was right after lunch, and Liesl and I headed out to the front lawn for our *Beginning Flying* class. As we descended the front stairs, The Holly King appeared in the courtyard.

"Father!" I exclaimed, running to hug and kiss him.

*I'll never get tired of this.*

"Holly, my sweetness, how are you? And Liesl: How are both of you doing?" The Holly King said in a jovial voice. "I'm here for an administrative appointment with your headmistress, but I'm early.

"This is our first day of Year Two Spring Semester classes, and they've been marvelous!" I said.

Liesl nodded, "Up now is *Beginning Flying*."

"Oh, that's a fun one!" Father said. "Mind if I stick around to watch?"

"Sure!" I said with enthusiasm. I never got to spend enough time with Father.

Liesl grinned. She loved Father as much as I did.

*Wellllll, maybe nearly as much.*

With a last hug, I walked after Liesl to the grassy area where other flying students were gathering.

Our professor was a small woman, nearly as short as I was. She sported long, dark hair, pulled back in a ponytail, and had on traveling clothes.

I looked at the teacher as we walked. "I love her outfit," I murmured to Liesl beside me. "Don't you?"

Liesl nodded in agreement.

The professor was dressed in dark brown leather, her top was covered in a jacket made out of what looked like leather, with about a million buttons running up and down the front, reaching down almost to her knees. She wore matching brown, form-hugging pants that ended in dark brown riding boots, which came up past her knees. The knee area looked slightly padded.

Completing her ensemble was a short dark-green traveling cape that fell lightly off her shoulders and fluttered slightly in the breeze.

"Everyone gather closely; we're going to go over the

safety rules," she called out. "My name is Professor Cherrystone, and I will be your teacher for *Beginning Flying* class this semester."

We all moved in closer, sitting on the grass in a semicircle around her, listening raptly.

She spent a good half-hour going over the safety rules.

*Wow, they are really serious about this.*

"And last but not least," Professor Cherrystone said, "is learning to fall safely. Now, no matter what precautions you take, you are going to fall. One day, when you least expect it, your concentration will slip, and down you will plummet. There's not a thing you can do to prevent falls one hundred percent of the time, so you must embrace the reality and try to mitigate the results."

The next ten minutes were taken up with a stern lecture on how to fall, when to use magic to try and save yourself, and when to allow your faerie subconscious save you.

"How do you think an infant Fae Folk reacts when dropped from a great height?" Professor Cherrystone asked. "That's right, they don't act. They react. Their innate subconscious kicks in, and their downward velocity slows, until, hopefully, they float down to the ground." She looked at all of us. "Let your mind act without thinking, and it will save you every time. Allow your instincts to take over if you are in trouble."

Professor Cherrystone put her hand up and waved.

A man came forward holding a baby. The man looked dark and handsome, and the baby he held was fast asleep.

*Oh, no...*

"To demonstrate, I have brought my husband and baby to class today," Professor Cherrystone said. "This is my husband, Manuelo, and Cassidy. Cassidy was born just before Halloween, and is not quite three months old."

The man walked up to our teacher and handed her the baby, who was sleeping so soundly she didn't even move.

"Now, gather round. Everybody look." She bent down and showed little Cassidy's sleeping face. "See how she is utterly asleep, oblivious to just about everything."

We all looked.

*Yup, real baby. No tricks up teacher's sleeve, no wires, nothing.*

I had a bad feeling about this.

"Now," said Professor Cherrystone, "The reason I am using such a young child for this demonstration, is that a Fae Folk's instincts will take over if they fall, and in a young baby, these Faerie instincts are strongest of all." She bent to kiss the baby's little forehead, then handed her back to her husband, who took the child and stood next to Professor Cherrystone, waiting.

"Now, look closely," the teacher said. She nodded to her husband, who took a deep breath, closed his eyes, and concentrated.

Professor Cherrystone's husband, Manuelo, began to slowly rise into the air, about a foot every second, until he was at least seventy-five feet up.

The class gasped as he floated there.

"He will now demonstrate the fall," Professor Cherrystone said.

I held my breath.

I couldn't watch.

*Oh God oh God oh God...*

Manuelo held the baby out from himself, turned her sideways a few degrees, and let go.

There was a collective gasp from the class as the baby fell, and I think not a few of us had mini heart attacks.

I think I was the most scared.

The baby fell, her blanket slowly unraveling from it. We heard one outcry from the little mite, which sounded almost like a cry of outrage.

*How dare Daddy drop me?*

About forty feet up from the ground, after falling at full speed until then, the baby's descent slowed considerably. By the last ten feet, she was floating gently downward. Cassidy reached the grass at a placid pace, and serenely lit on the grass blade, and sank an inch as her weight settled onto the ground.

The class erupted in cheers as Manuelo drifted back to the ground, landing next to his child and picking her up.

He carried the baby back to Professor Cherrystone, gave her a kiss, and walked back into the school.

She smiled at him and waved, then turned back to us. "I promised him he could visit with his old professor and have a brandy if he came and helped me," she chuckled. "But see?! What you witnessed is something that will save you every time. Every Time! All you have to do is let your instincts take over. Let your subconscious rule."

I turned to Liesl. "That. Was. Amazing."

Liesl nodded.

"Okay, now," Professor Cherrystone clapped her hands, "Are you ready to try this yourselves?"

Most of the students cheered, a few chirped up that they'd already been flying at home for years, and one or two students stayed quiet.

I was not sure what to think.

"Now, everyone stand up, and space out," said Professor Cherrystone. "You'll want to be at least ten feet from anyone else."

We spread out, I gave Liesl a hopeful smile, then moved away. We stood on the spongy green grass, the sunshine pleasant and cheerful on our heads, and waited.

Professor Cherrystone spreads her arms out and waved her hands a few times. "Relax," she said, moving her head about, stretching her neck. "You need to relax. There, good. Now, close your eyes and just listen to the sound of my voice."

I took a deep breath, and closed my eyes, listening to Professor Cherrystone.

"Clear your mind. Take slow, deep breaths, think of the blue, blue sky. Think of the gentle white clouds drifting through the air. You are light, light as a feather caught by the breeze, lifted up, up, up, lazily drifted up into the air," Professor Cherrystone's calm voice came drifting to me, and I felt more relaxed than I had in a long, long time.

*I wonder when we will get instructions on how to begin flying?*

"Now," the professor continued, "Think of yourself as a drifting bit of flotsam, a feather, a light dust bunny, carried up into the air. Feel the gentle breeze under you. It lifts you, higher, higher, higher."

It was so relaxing I couldn't believe it.

*This is like meditation.*

"Now, students," Professor Cherrystone's peaceful voice came. "Take slow, deep breaths, feel utterly relaxed and calm. You are happy and light and airy on the breeze. Now slowly open your eyes."

I didn't open my eyes immediately, I was so happy

being so relaxed.

I heard some of the students gasp in surprise and became curious, so I opened my eyes.

I was in the air.

We all were.

I must have been about fifteen feet up. I glanced over and saw Liesl about five feet higher than I was.

"Listen to me, now," said Professor Cherrystone. "Stay relaxed, stay light, stay calm and peaceful. Try not to become rigid, or tense. Try not to become..."

*Too late.*

I was staring at the ground. At the nothing that was between the grass and my dangling feet. I could feel myself tense up. Suddenly, I dropped about eight or ten feet, hard as a rock. I instinctually closed my eyes, maybe in fright, maybe because of her instruction. I'm not sure. But I think I stopped dropping when I closed my eyes.

I took deep breaths and tried to regain the utter calmness I had during what I was not calling the meditation.

I heard Liesl cry out, and opened my eyes.

I was about six feet off the ground. Liesl was off to my left. She was on the ground, clutching her arm, looking stricken. Her familiar, Snowbear the snowy ermine, was balanced on her shoulders, chattering away in concern.

"All right, all right," Professor Cherrystone had her

arms and hands spread, trying to regain control of the class. "Do not panic!"

I looked around and saw that maybe a dozen students had dropped a bit, as I had. Liesl was the only one who had fallen all the way.

"Listen to the sound of my voice, students," Professor Cherrystone called out. "Gently exhale, and as you do, blow the air out forcefully, but not too forcefully. Try it, this will help you come slowly down."

The students began to drift lower, and I saw several medics rushing to Liesl's side. Then I saw Father come running to my fallen friend, and I could not look away.

The Holly King was a big man, a very big man. When he laughed, it was just like that poem, his belly jiggled like a bowl full of jelly.

Father was running to Liesl's side, and while he moved fast, faster than I thought he could, he jiggled like the biggest bowl full of jelly I have ever seen.

Womble-womble-womble-womble-womble!

I took a deep breath, inhaling slowly, and gently blew it out, pursing my lips in an O, blow out the air in my lungs slowly but forcefully, as I experimented with Professor Cherrystone's instruction.

Sure enough, I began drifting lower and lower and lower, until my feet touched the ground.

The grass was spongy and uneven, and I wasn't

prepared, I guess.

I fell.

"Oh!" I let out, and I dropped to my bottom.

Instantly, I scrambled to my feet and ran to Liesl's side.

Father was already there, as was Professor Cherrystone. One of the medics touched Liesl's arm delicately, feeling down its length.

"It's broken," the medic said tersely, waving for more assistance.

"Let me?" Father said gently.

The medic looked at The Holly King, then nodded. "Certainly, sir." The medic backed up a bit.

Father knelt next to Liesl, and gently patted her hand. "Does it hurt, young lady?" he asked.

Liesl's face was very pale. She nodded tightly. "Yes, sir. It hurts bad."

The Holly King nodded, and bent to cradle Liesl's arm between his two hands. He closed his eyes briefly, and Liesl's arm glowed for a few seconds, then the light faded and Father opened his eyes again.

"Better?" he asked Liesl. Liesl just stared at The Holly King, dazed.

He bent forward, gently cupping the back of Liesl's head, and lightly kissed her on the forehead. Then he sat back and waited.

Liesl's color began to return. She looked down at her arm, and seemed to come out of her daze.

She slowly flexed the arm, then moved it again, and again. "It... it's healed. It doesn't hurt at all," she said.

The Holly King grinned. "Good. That's what I was going for."

He got to his feet and stretched out a hand to help Liesl up.

Liesl took the offered hand, and allowed herself to be pulled up. As she got to her feet, her head seemed to clear.

"Thank you, sir," she said, and hugged The Holly King. "Thank you."

Chapter Four

# Hereditary Magic and Honing

W e had dinner together with Father and Chance and Renée and Professor Farryn, the headmistress, and Professor Cherrystone, and Liesl was holding court. We were all gathered in Professor Farryn's quarters, and the cooks had brought us shepherd's pie. It was deep and dark brown, and delicious.

"Least you have a nice, hot dinner in you, m'dear," said Professor Farryn. "That must've been a frightening occurrence."

"It certainly was," Liesl said. She glanced at Renée and

Chance. "Now I know what you meant, Renée."

*So true, so incredibly true.*

Chance nodded. "It sounds like a fun class, and it is, except for the dangerous parts."

I'd gone with Chance into the forest and brought back wildflowers for Liesl, and they sat in a small vase next to her as she ate. Several other collections of flowers sat nearby, all from well-wishers.

"It's always hard the first time, my dear," said Professor Farryn sympathetically.

"And don't worry, Liesl," Professor Cherrystone patted her hand, "I will absolutely have you in private lessons. We'll start tomorrow after your last class. You'll have several practices before our next class with the other students."

"You're going to love private lessons, Li," I said. "You learn so much one-on-one with a professor." I grinned at her, then at Professor Cherrystone, who nodded, smiling.

"Very true, very true," said the headmistress. "I sometimes wish we could just teach by private lesson, all the time."

Liesl finished her shepherd's pie and put her plate aside, then turned to The Holly King. "Sir, I want to thank you again for healing me."

"It was my pleasure, young lady," Father said.

"And when you kissed my forehead," Liesl went on,

"All the pain vanished, as if it had never been there!"

The Holly King smiled warmly.

I knew from personal experience how Father's kisses melted pain away: He'd helped me several times.

"This should actually be a kind of celebration," Professor Cherrystone said. "Firstly, I am personally ecstatic that Liesl's injury was a mere broken arm. I can remember back to several cracked ribs, and a couple of broken necks! And secondly, Liesl, it was such incredible luck that the king was there to heal you! I think that is the first time that has happened in a decade." She looked to the Holly King for confirmation, and he nodded.

"I feel very lucky," said Liesl. "And electric. The healing kiss buzzed in my head like some kind of... I don't know how to put it. It was crazy!"

I remembered Liesl's dazed look.

"That is a side-effect to my magic," Father said quietly. "It imbues the receiver with good luck that'll stay with you for months, I'm afraid. Never been able to separate it out from the pain relief," he chuckled.

Liesl face split into a huge smile. "Thank you, sir!"

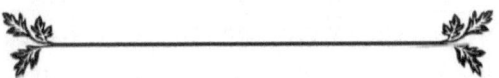

The next morning, we headed to the first class of *Hereditary Magic and Honing*.

"I wonder what Honing means in this regard?" I asked.

"Oh, it means we're going to get very good at magic that is in our DNA," Liesl said. "Like, subconscious magic." She smirked. "Not like flying."

Liesl's arm was completely healed, and she seemed to have no lasting ill effects.

Last night's dinner celebrating her recovery seemed to be just the right kind of family magic to cleanse her mind of any residual unhappy memories of her fall.

I bumped against her as I walked. "Could have easily been me that fell. I had no idea flying would be so tricky."

Liesl huffed. "I know! It's like it's the most jittery of all the magics we learn." She flexed her arms out sideways and back. "Seems okay now. Thanks to your father."

I smiled.

We filed into the classroom, where we would learn all about our true forms. I was very excited about this class, if only to find out exactly what I would look like.

A Fae Folk's true form was said to be a very private thing, and so I felt very shy about anyone seeing my true form. It was almost as if they were going to see me naked.

Since it was the first time I would know myself, it made me all the more apprehensive.

"Don't worry," Liesl whispered. "I think the class is going to be mostly on history and heredity, and they said no one's compelled to share their true form, not if they don't want to."

We sat down at a table next to each other.

There were six tables in the classroom, each with ten chairs.

I looked around. We were early.

"Is this a large class?" I murmured to Liesl.

She shrugged, looking at all the chairs. "Looks like it might be."

We waited as the other students straggled in and got seated.

By the time it was scheduled to start, the class was full. Very full.

But the professor still had not shown up.

The students whispered among themselves, and I leaned in and murmured to Liesl, "Have you heard anything about who is teaching this class?"

She shrugged and shook her head, "No, I'm really curious."

As the clock struck the hour, every student fell silent, waiting, expectant.

We waited and watched the door.

Suddenly, we heard the clopping footsteps of our professor approach, four at a time. He entered the classroom in his true form, which was of centaur lineage.

He was massive. Easily seven feet tall. His equine half's coat was coal black, brushed to an extreme degree, and shiny.

His tail was held at a proud arc, and reached all the way to the ground. His hooves were polished black.

His equine chest was enormous, broad and muscular. The equine fur grew up his torso to varying degrees in different places, stretching all the way up his sides to his rib cage.

His human form began at his hips and was well muscled, from what I could see. He wore a snugly fitted jacket over his torso, the sleeves of which went down past his wrists and ended an inch or two down his palm.

His face was proud and serious.

He walked into the classroom and to the head of the class, then turned to face the door.

From the door, in walked a second figure.

This Fae Folk was half the size of the centaur, and was a faun. He was big for a faun, and his light brown fur covered a muscled torso and chest, and stretched down to heavily muscled goat legs, and large, polished hooves.

He wore a snug jacket that was a match to the jacket the centaur wore. One could almost say it looked better on the faun. Or perhaps the faun was better proportioned.

I could see that this faun was larger and more muscular than the faun who had been our waiter when we visited the Faun Café. His arms were strong and muscled, and ended in shoulders and chest and a proud ... *wait.*

With a shock, I realized the faun was Chance.

I fell out of my chair with a loud crash.

Liesl glanced down and reached her hand out for me. "Get up, you ninny!" she whispered. I scrambled back up into my seat and sat looking at both the Fae Folk at the front of the class.

Chance's face was the same as always, but slightly bigger, and his expression was very serious. He looked out on the class with an almost severe expression, and did not say a word.

The centaur professor waited until the student hubbub settled down, then spoke.

"True forms," he said in a deep voice, "are very personal to each Fae Folk. We are, in essence, faeries, of every kind imaginable, and we are brought together at this school," he waved his muscular arm to indicate the actual walls, "Titania Academy, in order to learn together." He lowered his gaze back to the students. "We instinctually change into our mundane forms in order to maintain privacy, in order to maintain uniformity, and in order to lessen distraction." He walked a few steps to the side, then back again, and his centaur steps clopped like a horse's hooves, loud and strong.

He continued: "The true form that each of us is born into varies greatly, not only from heritage, but also from family history." He paused to think. "You cannot judge a person on what they look like in mundane form, any more than you can judge them in their true form." He waved his hand to indicate Chance.

"Do you see my friend here? He was one of my most honored students last year, and he has become a great friend now, after he has learned all I have to teach him about hereditary magic and how to best hone it. Do you see him?" The professor paused, expecting an answer.

After a heartbeat, the class replied, "Yes."

"Would you say he is a smaller or larger person than I am?" The professor asked.

"Smaller," the class replied.

The professor raised a finger, "Ah, but I told you a minute ago that you cannot judge a person based on what they look like in their true form. Witness." The professor closed his eyes and adopted a look of deep concentration.

Chance, in faun form, also closed his eyes, adopting a similar look of deep concentration.

They both shimmered, and the air around them shimmered as well. The sight of both of them seemed to blur, then disappear.

In their place stood Chance, appearing taller than he had in faun form, and a man whose face looked very similar to the centaur's face, but who was half a head shorter than Chance. In fact, he was pretty darned short in general.

He was middle-aged, with a receding hairline, and very stocky in body. He was still muscular; he was just short.

He stepped forward to speak.

"You cannot judge a person on what they look like in mundane form either." He turned and shook Chance's hand, a deeply respectful look on his face, thanked him, and bid him goodbye,

Chance, fully dressed in his mundane form, which I had come to know as his human form, walked out of the class. Right before he passed outside the door, he turned and caught my eye, and winked solemnly.

Then he was gone.

"Welcome to *Hereditary Magic and Honing*," the man said. "I am your teacher, Professor Leighton, and I would like to welcome you to our first class."

The students erupted in comments, half-asking the professor a bunch of questions, half-talking among themselves, chattering about what they'd just seen.

Liesl and I were doing the later.

We turned and touched our foreheads together, and whispered.

"Can you believe what we just saw?"

"That was Chance!"

"His faun form is gorgeous!"

"And the professor, he is so huge as a centaur, I can't believe it."

"And then he shrunk down so much when he changed to mundane form."

"If he stayed in human form, no one would ever suspect how massive he actually is."

"I can't believe it."

"I can't wait to see Chance out of class, I'm going to ask him to transform again, just for me," I squee'd.

There was a banging from the front of the class. "Order! order! Settle down, people," said Professor Leighton."

It was hard, but we finally quieted down.

*This is the most exciting class I have so far. And that's counting the Flying class!*

"Okay, everyone settle down and take your seats, so we can continue," Professor Leighton said.

He had a deep, booming voice, pretty much the same voice he'd had as a centaur. It sounded extremely odd coming from the short, stout man the professor was in his mundane form. Because of this, it was very, very cool.

"Now, sorry to start the first day of class with a demonstration, but we thought that would be a rapid and concise way to introduce you to the concept that forms cannot be judged." He took a breath, thinking. "Now, many of you know Mr. Mac Craith from outside of class, or from years past. In our True Forms, he and I looked very different, and he looked like a smaller person than I did in my True Form. But the instant we transformed, the roles were reversed. This is an important lesson: Size matters not. Remember that. You know what? Write it down, too. Size Matters Not." He waited as we all wrote this in our class notebooks.

"This semester, we will not only be learning all about our True Forms, but about our families, and our history," said Professor Leighton. "We will be practicing our transformations, until we hone the process to perfection. This is not the kind of magic that we practice that often; therefore, we often get rusty at it. Some may have hardly ever done it. Well, that's why we need to practice, practice, practice. And we must always remember: Size Matters Not. What did I just say?" He put his hand behind his ear and leaned forward, and the class responded.

"Size Matters Not," we all said in synchronicity.

"Now, no more demonstrations for today, but a lesson for you," Professor Leighton said. "Are you all familiar with the headmistress?"

We nodded that, yes, we were familiar.

"Professor Minerva Ó Baoghill is our headmistress. She is a very formidable and powerful woman, is she not?" Professor Leighton asked.

"Yes," we all said.

"And she is taller than I am, is she not?" Professor Leighton asked.

We nodded yes together.

"Well, does anyone know that Professor Ó Baoghill is of Sprite ancestry?"

We all stared. I didn't understand. Professor Leighton waited.

Liesl leaned to whisper, "Sprites are small, really small." I lifted my face and met her eyes, astonished.

"How small?" I whispered.

Liesl held up her hand, her thumb and forefinger about four inches apart.

*Holy Moly!*

"That's right," Professor Leighton said, after seeing realization dawn on most of the students' faces. "In her true form, our headmistress is small, yet powerful. In fact, believe it or not, she's one of the most powerful Fae Folk here at Titania Academy."

I blinked and tried to picture a small faerie the size of a flower.

I didn't think I would ever have the opportunity or the bravery to ask the headmistress to change into her true form so I could see for myself, but I suddenly felt insanely curious.

Professor Leighton was talking again.

"Now, who has already seen themselves in their true forms, at one time or another? Raise your hands," he asked, raising his own hand in the air.

Most of the students raised their hands, including Liesl, and I suddenly felt intensely self-conscious.

*This is just like first term.*

Two students toward the front of the class had not raised their hands, and Professor Leighton called on them now.

"Can you explain how you haven't seen your true forms, even at home?" he asked them.

"Oh, at *home?*" said one of the students, and he hastily raised his hand into the air.

The students laughed out loud.

He grinned and shrugged, and said, "I thought he meant only at school!"

The other student who'd not raised their hand looked at their feet, shy and embarrassed.

Professor Leighton came to their table.

"Mr. Haggerty, you've not ever seen your own true form?" the teacher asked.

The young man shook his head.

"I see," said the professor, turning back to the front of the class. "Well, we shall all be able to learn the magic necessary, and we will get quite good at it, because you have the top teacher of Hereditary Magic in the land," he nodded and smiled. "And that's me," he winked.

"Now," he turned to the front.

"Professor? Professor?" A student near the front of the class called out. "You forgot one more student who's never seen their true form."

Professor Leighton turned around. "Oh? I forgot someone? Who?"

I felt a chill go down my spine.

"Holly Ó Cuilinn, that's who," the student called out, and swung her arm to point back at me. "She has never seen her true form, because she's not really one of us!"

The class erupted in chaos.

The chill I felt down my spine turned to ice as I stared into the face of the student who'd pointed at me.

It was Jessica, the girl who's nose I'd bloodied on my first day at Titania Academy, for bullying Liesl. She looked different, older and thinner, and her skin was deeply tanned, and her hair was darker, too.

But it was her.

"Silence! Silence! People will you puh-lease settle yourselves down?" Professor Leighton demanded.

Liesl swung to whisper. "We need to tell the headmistress. Jessica is..."

"...part of The Oak King Faction," I finished, my face blanching white.

*Oh, my God...*

Half the students were aware of this. Did they even realize who this was?

I didn't think so; they weren't acting like it, so I took a chance.

"That's Jessica Penner," I called out, pointing right back at her. "She's part of The Oak King Faction! She's supposed to be in Faerie Council Confinement! Grab her!"

If the class was chaotic before, it was pandemonium now. Sixty students started screaming and reaching for Jessica, who turned and vanished into the crowd.

"Where'd she go?!" Liesl called out. "Grab her!"

The stampede to where Jessica had been was dangerous.

Liesl and I were shoved and pushed and, at one point, Liesl was almost knocked to the ground. I grabbed her at the last minute, as she dropped to one knee, knocked by the crowd.

I no longer cared about Jessica. This class was now a frenzied crowd and was turning into an outright mob.

I held on to Liesl's arm as I pushed my way to the left,

toward the door. Luckily, most of the tide was rushing in the opposite direction, trying to see or find or stop The Oak King Faction student member who was so incredibly dangerous that the whole student body had been informed and cautioned against.

I finally pushed my way to the door, shoving students aside right and left.

At one point someone cried out, "Hey, she hasn't seen herself in true form. Should we grab her? Is she a fake like that tall girl said?" and Liesl got so angry she spun around and in a raging growl yelled out, "She's an orphan! She grew up in the human world! LAY OFF!"

I felt a secret thrill at her words, and as we both nearly fell out the door of the classroom, I turned and murmured, "Thanks."

As we started to run down the corridor and down two flights of stairs to tell the headmistress about Jessica sneaking into the Academy and making a deliberate spectacle in the class we were in, Liesl said, "Anytime."

We ran like the wind to the headmistress' office, and burst in without knocking.

Professor Ó Baoghill was in the middle of a conference with an aged teacher I hadn't had before.

"Miss Ó Baoghill!" Liesl said, out of breath. "Jessica Penner is on the campus! She was just found in our class when she tried to get the students to gang up on Holly again!"

"WHAT?" the headmistress came around her desk and walked straight up to Liesl.

Liesl was red-faced and out of breath.

"Miss Becker, are you sure?" the headmistress asked.

Liesl nodded wordlessly, then caught her breath and finally spoke. "I am very sure, Professor. She is here. Inside the castle."

The headmistress swung around to the aged teacher she'd been meeting with. "Will you excuse me, Professor? I must attend to this very serious matter."

He nodded, but the headmistress had dashed out the door, not waiting for his reply.

We heard her calling to her secretary, giving orders for the castle to be sealed tight against intruders.

Liesl and I ran out after her.

I could not believe the Oak King Faction would be so bold as to sneak into Titania Academy, our stronghold.

Chapter Five
# Leaf Warden Sprite Faerie

The headmistress assured us that she had sent the guardians of the castle to search high and low for Jessica, but that it was important that we return to class.

"Now that you're approaching your third term, your instruction is more important than ever, Miss Ó Cuilinn, so I must insist you and Miss Becker return to class," the headmistress said. "And I have a very important task to attend to, so you must be off."

It was now an hour after Jessica had been spotted, and Liesl and I were headed to our last class of the day.

"They'll never find her," Liesl predicted.

"I know," I said in a low voice, glancing around as we

passed the center atrium. "I can't believe she snuck into the school, just to try and stir up trouble."

"What I want to know is: Does this mean the school is infiltrated by Oak King Faction students? I mean, are they spies or something?" Liesl whispered.

I made a rude sound. "Do they think we'd have meetings on how to get rid of them, right out in the open?"

Liesl laughed. "They very well might think that. Paranoid, those ones."

We headed into the third greenhouse, and found half the class already there.

"I thought we were early," Liesl said, looking around.

"Huh, well, let's find a good table." I scouted out clean seats toward the front, and made my way over, setting my bag down on the large wooden table where four other students were already seated.

Liesl consulted her list. "Hmm, Herbology. Taught by... Ohhh! Our professor is a Leafwarden! We're in luck: They are great Herbalists."

"Herbalists?" I asked, wishing I had a dictionary.

"Experts in plant lore," Liesl explained. "They have vast knowledge of plant lore, and know the secrets of plant life itself. Most of them are healers, too. Leafwardens can make remarkable salves and elixirs from plants. I mean, beyond just the general knowledge."

She turned to me. "Did you know a Leafwarden discovered the ancient cure for Malignancies when on a yearlong sabbatical to the outer southern reaches? I remember reading about it." She put her finger to her chin, trying to remember. "Oh, yeah. It was about thirty or forty years ago. It was a revolutionary discovery."

"Wow," I said. "Wait, what do you mean *cure for malignancy?*"

"Um, I think the humans call it cancer. Yes, I remember now." She giggled. "Can you imagine, though? Taking a yearlong vacation and spending it in some south American lab testing new plants? That's no holiday."

"Yes, but maybe that's what she found enjoyable, Miss Becker," said a high voice behind us.

We turned and I backed up in surprise.

In front of us was a sprite.

She was about six inches high, and had four long dragonfly-like wings that beat so rapidly they were a blur. She was dressed in green and brown and had an acorn for a cap. She hovered in the air at eye level as she addressed us.

I blinked in surprise.

Now that I was in more advanced classes, Chance had said I'd be seeing more of the Fae Folk in their true forms, so I shouldn't have been surprised.

But I couldn't help it.

"Oh!" Liesl exclaimed, clapping her hands.

"Thank you for that vote of confidence, Miss Becker," the sprite said, then turned and flew to the head of the class.

"Oh, oh! She's our teacher!" Liesl whispered excitedly.

My jaw dropped.

"Class! Class, please come to order," the sprite said. Her voice was high-pitched but loud, and it carried to the back of the classroom.

The other students fell silent.

"Now, I am a woodland sprite, and since you're all now in your fourth semester at Titania Academy, you're seeing us, the faculty, in our true forms, to better acquaint you with the adult Fae Folk world. I am your professor, and I am also a Leafwarden, as you may have noted from your class paperwork. In other words, I am highly qualified to teach you the venerable subject of Herbology, which has a long and glorious tradition of aiding the Faerie World and making us leaders in the fields of Medicine and Horticulture."

She paused to gather her thoughts.

We were riveted as she continued.

"Now, since this is your first day, I want to plunge you headfirst into the subject, so we will be making a tincture of nightshade, using the apparatus you see on the right." She gestured to a large contraption on the side of the classroom that covered most of a five-foot shelf running the entire length of the room.

"The instructions are outlined in your textbook, but I have never given much weight to printed directions. I prefer to rely on actual classroom demonstration," she said. "However, before I can show you how to prepare this particular elixir, I must transform into my mundane form." She paused and flew down the middle aisle of the class.

Every eye followed her.

"Now, I understand such a public metamorphosis often engenders mild chaos, however, I demand that my students behave with decorum at all times, including on this occasion." She spoke with quiet authority. "Therefore, I am setting the first of many classroom rules: Remain calm and in control of yourself, or I will fail you."

My jaw dropped open.

Liesl gasped quietly beside me.

"You may think I am being harsh," the sprite said. "But I believe that forewarned is forearmed."

She stared at all of us as she hovered in the air, her four wings moving at a rapid pace. "So, I ask you now, and I will only ask you once: Are you prepared?"

It was two heartbeats before I slowly nodded. Before we all nodded.

We were ready.

"Good," the sprite said. "Well, here goes."

And the sprite glowed with a bright light, right there in the middle of class. When the light faded, she had transformed and stood before us in human form.

It was Professor Ó Baoghill, our headmistress.

"I knew it," Liesl whispered under her breath.

I smiled, but stayed quiet and still.

The entire class did not move.

The headmistress slowly scanned the entire room and nodded, then walked back to the head of the class.

"We will be using our gloves today, and nearly every day here in Herbology class," Professor Ó Baoghill said, reaching into a bag on the side and withdrawing a heavy pair of gloves, which she slid over her hands one at a time. "You want to make sure each finger is securely inside and to the end of each fourchette, like so." She turned to us and held up both hands, now secured into the safety gloves.

"Each of you should don your gloves at this time," she said, indicating the bag on the side. "Mr. Swenson, will you please distribute them?"

A skinny, bespectacled student came forward, took the bag, and walked up and down the aisle, giving each of us one pair.

"Good, good," Professor Ó Baoghill said, "Now put

them on, each one of you, that's right, and make sure the fingers are completely filled." As she spoke, she walked up and down the aisle, looking at each one of us as we donned the safety gear, before returning to the head of the class.

She paused and took a slow, deep breath as the class finished and fell silent again, watching her.

"All right," Professor Ó Baoghill said. "Nightshade, or *Atropa belladonna*, as it is known in the science laboratories, is a simple, innocuous looking plant." She turned to a cupboard, unlocked it with a key from her pockets, and brought forth a medium-sized wooden box.

She used a second key from her keyring to unlock the box, then carefully opened the lid and reached in, withdrawing a small sprig four or five inches long.

"Notice the color and size of the leaves and blossoms," she said. "The blossoms will eventually grow into berries, on the live plant."

She held the sprig high for all to see as she walked slowly down the center aisle.

"The leaves are a dull green, and the blossoms a dark yellow to orange color as they age. The berries," she said, "are shiny and black, and about the size of cherries. So, rather on the large side, actually." She finished walking to the end of the aisle, and slowly turned, walking back to the head of the class.

She placed the sprig back into the box, then turned to us once again.

"The berries are sweet and alluring, and as such, have enticed children, in particular, to consume them. But this is a deadly mistake. Nightshade contains atropine and scopolamine in its stems, leaves, flowers and berries, and even in its roots." She took another deep breath, a serious expression on her face. "These chemicals cause paralysis in the involuntary muscles of the body, including," she paused for effect, "the heart. This is applicable to all animal life."

She tapped her gloves together. "Even touching the leaves can irritate the skin. This is why we wear gloves."

*This was actually interesting.*

"In the works of Shakespeare there is a legend," said Professor Ó Baoghill. "It's said the invading Danes were poisoned by Macbeth's soldiers with wine made from these sweet Nightshade berries. Entirely plausible, actually."

She turned to the large contraption along the wall. "Today we will be first boiling the Nightshade plant, then distilling the resulting liquid using this device."

She turned and indicated the box where the plant resided. "I will be passing out sprigs of Nightshade to each of you. Use your classroom flatknives to chop the plant into fine pieces." She retrieved the box and began carefully setting one sprig in front of each student. "The smaller the pieces are chopped, the better the outcome will be."

We chopped our deadly Nightshade into fine pieces, then boiled them in the classroom apparatus, checking the calibration of the thermometer, and filling the distillation flask before heating the liquid.

As the liquid began to drop from the condenser, we kept a keen eye on the thermometer reading.

"Careful there, Miss Becker, your temperature is getting too high," said Professor Ó Baoghill as she came to check our work.

In the end, we each had a flask of distilled fluid.

"Now, students," she said, "believe it or not, in centuries past, drops of this liquid were used by human women to dilate their eyes, to make them look more seductive. It was also at one time considered a medicine by the humans. In the end, these uses of Nightshade came to bad ends. It is only really valuable as a deadly poison. Who can tell me how Nightshade might be used in modern times?"

And the class discussion took off, becoming quite lively, during the last fifteen minutes of class.

At the end, Professor Ó Baoghill had each of us disinfect the gloves we'd worn before returning them to the holding bag, and we all gathered together outside the class door, discussing the lesson.

Liesl and I held back, waiting for the headmistress as she emerged last.

"Oh, there she is," I said, seeing the headmistress coming toward the door.

"Professor Ó Baoghill," said Liesl, "That was a great class!"

"Why thank you Miss Becker," said the headmistress. "And I hope you enjoyed seeing my true form? You younger ladies are going to be learning quite a lot this semester, especially about true forms of the fae."

"Professor?" I said. "I know it's just been a few hours, but is there any information about... what happened in the Hereditary Magic class?"

"Not yet, Miss Ó Cuilinn," the headmistress said. "Trust me when I say, you'll be the first to know when I have more information. Now, in the meantime, I think that, while staying vigilant, we can all enjoy our last day with your father. The Holly King leaves tomorrow for his biannual tour of the Faerie Lands."

Chapter Six
# Mark of Chaos

"Holly, come quick!" Chance ran up to us. "Hello, headmistress."

She nodded at him. "What is the emergency, Mr. Mac Craith? Have they found the intruder?"

He shook his head. "No, Ma'am, she seems to have disappeared. But a letter was left in the front for the king." He looked pained. "It was hung twenty feet up, on the clock inside the door, by some kind of joker, I think."

"Could be Jessica," Liesl murmured.

"Whoever it was is long gone, Chance said. "Professor Farryn retrieved it; he saw it was addressed to the king."

"This can't be good," I said, and we hurried off with

Chance.

The Holly King stayed in the V.I.P. guest quarters that had been built for whenever he stayed at Titania Academy.

Professor Ó Baoghill, Liesl, and I hurriedly followed Chance to the guest quarters at a run, and arrived in record time.

"Father, what is it?" I puffed as I hurried into his chambers.

"Holly, thank goodness you're here, daughter," he said. "I heard about what happened in the Hereditary Magic class. I think the same person delivered... this."

He handed me a white envelope address to him.

"May I open it?" I asked.

"Yes, I've already read it. It's not good," Father said as we sat together and I opened it and withdrew the letter inside.

My eyes scanned the words typed on the paper, then I read them again, more thoroughly.

"My God," I whispered, looking up at Father.

"What does it say, Holly?" Liesl asked, sitting on a nearby chair.

The headmistress and Chance also sat look at me expectantly, expressions of deep concern on their faces.

I read the letter a third time.

"It's..." I swallowed. Then, "Father, what is this mark?"

I asked, pointing to the top of the page.

The letter was typewritten in bold, and was brief. Above the words was a stamped mark that I had never seen before.

"Believe it or not, my daughter, that is the most troubling thing about this letter," The Holly King murmured.

My jaw dropped open. "More troubling than this... this... declaration of war!?"

Liesl gasped softly.

Chance lowered his head.

Professor Ó Baoghill looked stricken. "I was afraid of something like this."

"You knew this might happen?" I asked her.

"After what happened last fall," said the headmistress, "and when they stayed silent and hidden for these many months, yes."

I turned back to the letter. "I actually was hoping they would go away."

"Evil never goes away, Holly," said Chance. "It must be defeated, or it grows, like a cancer."

"Read it out loud, Holly," Father said, nodding.

"Okay," I said softly, clearing my throat. I gripped the paper, making sure my fingers didn't touch the stamped mark at the. top of the page, and began to read it out loud.

"We, the noble warriors of The Faction, hereby declare war upon The Faerie Council, The Holly King, The Elfen Council, and all their minions, invoking our right to rule the Fae Folk lands, the Elfen Lands, and all their affiliated territories, which have been cruelly subjugated by the Councils and The Holly King in their unlawful quest for exclusive dominion. We who have refused to yield to his tyranny now invoke our right, by ancient charter, to renounce our winter fealty to the Councils and The Holly King and assert our right to self-rule and our just duty to rule over the lands named in this declaration. Those who dare to stand against us will stand against our ancient claim, against our might, and will face a force of arms and magic the likes of which the world has never seen. You cannot hope to prevail, and should you defy us, you will be smitten from the earth like the plague that you are."

I lowered the paper and looked at my father, my jaw dropped open.

The Holly King took the paper gently from my trembling hands and turned it to face the others. He indicated the black mark at the top of the page.

"This is the sigil of an ancient figure from seven thousand years ago. He did his best to spread evil and chaos during his three hundred years here, before the forces of the Faerie Council subdued him. This was about the time the Faerie Council split into two, the two we know today. The lasting damage from the ancient one had a rippling effect, long after his death, and the chaos he instigated is the main reason that Faerie is split into two lands in modern times." He took a deep breath and glanced at the mark, then continued speaking. "I don't know how this group is claiming and using this mark, but I know it can only lead to sadness and devastation."

The headmistress raised her hand and spoke. "Sire, is this group the same as The Oak King Faction group that has been fighting us for the last few years? I can't tell from the paper... erm... the declaration."

Father glanced at the letter again, scanning it quickly, then nodding. "I think so, Minerva. Since we now know they've kidnapped and drained my brother, The Oak King, my guess would be that they are no longer hiding behind that name." He glanced up at her. "The Oak King is still missing, so I don't have any doubt that this... this 'Faction', as they're calling themselves now, has him at an undisclosed location and is still draining him. In fact, since they are no longer trying to keep up appearances, my guess would also be that, when the Spring Equinox arrives, the Faerie Lands are going to be in trouble."

*Oh, no.*

The Faerie Lands needed the power of the two kings, all year 'round. Their power brought life and magic to the land. I knew Father couldn't sustain the land for the whole year; maintaining the life force of the land for even half the year steadily drained each king, until they eventually were forced to enter magical slumber, or be lost forever.

"I am guessing both the Fae Folk Council and the Elfen Councils received a copy of this," The Holly King said. "We need to ramp up our strategy if we are to meet this threat head on. Minerva, I'm meeting with the High Council tonight, and it would probably be best if I address the students tomorrow."

The headmistress nodded; her face white.

"Sire, I can research and gather information regarding this ancient mark of chaos. I'm sure Farryn will be willing to help me on that, he has the largest antiquarian collection in the castle," Chance said quietly.

"Very good, Mac Craith, you do that," Father said. "Okay, I was hoping to have dinner with everyone one last time, but I must cut short my time here at Titania Academy, and hurry to the Fae Folk High Council, and thence to the Elfen Council." He rose to his feet.

I jumped up and fell into his arms.

"Can I go with you, Father?" I whispered, my words for his ears only.

He bent and hugged me for a long, long time, then nodded. "Get your things, quickly," he whispered back, before straightening. "I will be returning to the school in a day. While I am gone, please prepare the battlements, according to the plan we discussed last summer."

He nodded and I hurried out the door and ran to my dorm room.

Liesl ran after me, peppering me with questions, one after another. I answered as best as I could without stopping. After ten or twelve questions, she finally stopped and just hurried to help me.

In our room, stuffing a few things in my bag, I finally turned to her and gave her a quick hug. "I'll be fine, I swear, Li. I'll be with Father the whole time." I squeezed her one last time. "You've got to stay here, and help the headmistress prepare. You know the plan."

Liesl nodded, tears in her eyes. "I just can't believe it...war."

"I feel the same way. I can't believe they would do this," I said. "And I wonder what Jessica's visit has to do with everything. As much of a bully as she was, I can't picture her being part of a war."

"I think we're all going to be part of the war, now," Liesl murmured, wiping her eyes. She took a deep breath and straightened her shoulders. "We must be strong!"

I nodded, straightening as well. "We must be brave!"

We reached our hands out and clasped them together, lifting them outward to form a circle of two friends. "We must excel!" we said together.

The old school cheer was especially appropriate now.

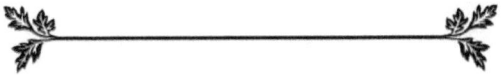

Chapter Seven

# The Lay of the Land

Father and I arrived in a meadow, and I gasped at its beauty. Birdsong filled the air as he led me forward through the field of wildflowers.

The temperature was cold, as if we were in the beginning of spring, and the flowers that grew fluttered in a slight breeze.

I stared at everything around me as I walked, amazed at the brilliance of the colors.

"Father," I whispered. "The colors are so... so bright."

He paused and glanced around us. "We are very close to The Origin here," he said, then began walking again.

*The what?*

I followed, not speaking again. The beauty of the valley made it hard to talk. I can't explain how, I just... it was amazing.

Father and I walked on a path made of coarse sand, edged with grey pebbles. The pathway led through the meadow for a long while. I wondered how far we would walk, and why we couldn't just arrive at the council chambers; I tried to ask my father this, but just ended up panting.

He grinned as he walked.

"This place makes it hard to talk, and hard to sleep, if you ever want to try," he said. "It was built with protections in place, and the walk we're on is part of that. We have several miles to walk, and while we are here, we are being watched."

"Were these protections put in place by the High Council?" I asked.

"Ah, no. They were put in place by me," he winked.

*Hmmm.*

He chuckled and explained. "The Faerie Council chose their headquarters very close to where I slumber, because of the protections. The Fae Folk High Council took the building when the split occurred."

"The split?" I asked.

He nodded as we walked. "After the chaotic one made war upon the land, the Faerie Council split into two: the

Fae Folk High Council and the Elfen High Council. The Elfen departed for the northern reaches, and made their home there, and that is where the Elfen High Council building is." He walked and thought for a few minutes.

I said nothing, not wanting to disturb his deep thoughts.

"The place where you and the others were held and tortured last year was razed. The new Elfin High Council erected a new building, not wanting to occupy the same space where so many bad deeds occurred," he said.

*Ahh.*

"We're nearly there," he said.

I looked around us as we walked. We had come over a slight rise, and now the path dipped and brought us down to another part of this vast meadow. But I could not see where any building was.

*I guess I will see it when I see it.*

The Holly King walked on through the huge meadow of wildflowers, leading me up a second rise and down again to a small hill. I think we must've walked more than two miles altogether.

As we got closer to the hill, I could see a door set into the slope.

Father walked straight to the wooden door, and opened it, beckoning me in.

I ducked through, and he followed me, and we

continued down a well-lit flight of stairs made of light tan bricks. We descended five or six flights, pausing on each landing to rest a few seconds, because going down so many stairs was dizzying. We finally arrived at a second door, which looked much like the first.

We opened it and entered, and I stopped to take it all in.

The Fae Folk High Council chambers were a massive three-story-tall library.

I stood there just inside the door and raised my eyes to survey the multistory bookshelves. I slowly turned to take it all in.

"Good God Almighty," I whispered.

Father paused and glanced up and around us, "I guess I'm so used to it I never stop to look at it anymore." He smiled. "But Holly, we really have to go, we're on a tight schedule, to put it mildly."

We walked through the center of the massive, book-lined room, our footsteps silent on the thick carpeting. Here and there, I saw comfortable-looking couches and chairs where people were sitting, reading books.

*I wonder who they are?*

The Holly King led me to the other side of the huge library, and into a smaller room, where the council was waiting.

There was an especially comfy-looking sofa near the

door to the interior chamber. Father led me there, picking up one of the many pillows that lay next to it.

"This is the place I sit when I'm early and need to wait for my turn to speak," he said.

"They make the king wait?!" I asked, astonished.

"No, I make me wait," he said. "Sometimes I need to gather my thoughts."

"Ohh, that makes sense," I smiled.

"You should wait here for me," The Holly King said. "Is that okay?"

"Sure," I replied. "Is it okay to touch the books?"

He grinned. "They belong to me, so yes."

He disappeared through the door, and I turned to the books. There were so many I wasn't sure where to look first.

"Try the books right next to the door," a voice said. I looked and saw no one, then I glanced toward the suggested bookshelf and saw him.

It was a sprite, and now that I had seen my headmistress in her true form, I felt proud that I was able to immediately identify him. I wandered over to the bookshelf.

"Hello," I said quietly. "My name is Holly." On impulse I curtsied.

The sprite bowed deeply at the waist, his face serious. "Pleased to meet you. I am Mr. Dewberry, one of the librarians in charge of the collection." He stood on the middle shelf, at shoulder level to me, and strolled along the width of the ledge as I examined the books.

The library had many classics; I decided on one, and took it from the case.

"Thank you, Mr. Dewberry," I said, turning and walking back to the sofa. I sat and found it very soft and comfortable, and I sank into the deeply plush cushions with a sigh.

The book in my hands was very old, judging from the aged leather binding and parchment-colored paper inside, but it was in fantastic condition.

I had become a lover of books ever since losing my way in Professor Farryn's private library some months ago.

I opened the book and began to read.

It was the story of a lost man who traveled to distant lands, and how he found people and animals of unusual sizes, philosophies, and behaviors. I swiftly became lost within the pages.

It was several hours later when Father finally emerged.

I stretched and yawned, and my stomach growled.

"Sire, the young lady is wonderful," the sprite librarian said from the shelf ten feet away.

The Holly King glanced over at the little man.

"Thanks, Dew, I'll take it from here." He turned to me, sighed and smiled. "Ready to go, Sweetheart?"

I closed the book, drawing my hand across the front cover. "Yes," I hesitated. "Father? Do you think I could borrow this book for a while? Just until I read it?"

He nodded, still smiling. "Of course. I know you'll take good care of it."

I tucked it safely into my bag, happy.

"Is your work here all done?" I asked.

"Yes and no," he said. "The meeting is over, but there's a ton of work now to do."

I stood with difficulty and stretched. "Not an easy sofa to leave," I remarked.

Father glanced down at the cushioned seat, "No," he chuckled, "it is not." He turned and saluted the sprite librarian, "Carry on, Sir," and then turned and led me out of the building.

I was sad to go.

"My dear, we must now travel to the Elfen lands," The

Holly King said, as we walked back along the path through the meadow of wildflowers.

It was late in the day, and blue butterflies hovered over the blossoms, leisurely sipping nectar. For just a moment, I wished I was one of them, drinking the wildflower ambrosia.

"I wonder if we'll see Laura and Tam and Lucy," I said.

"At this point, anything is possible," Father said.

As I walked, I held my hand against the firm square shape of the book in my bag. Its presence was reassuring.

We walked all the way to the end of the path, several miles, in companionable silence. The sun was just beginning to set as we neared the end.

"All right," The Holly King said, taking my hand, "Are you ready?"

I nodded.

"Close your eyes."

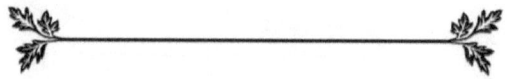

Chapter Eight

# Attempted Meeting with the Elfen High Council

We arrived in the Elfen lands at dusk, just outside a plain-looking building next to the forest.

"Okay, let's go in together, shall we?" Father said. "I'm sure there will be a place for you to wait."

He opened the door and led me in.

We entered onto a long hallway that ended in another door. There were tables and chairs placed along the length of it, and the corridor was empty.

Father and I walked to the end of the hall, and I sat at a table to wait.

"I don't know how long I'll be," he said, glancing

down at me as he stood at the door, one hand poised to open it.

"No problem," I said, pulling out my borrowed book. "Take your time."

He nodded and disappeared through the door.

I'm not sure if I should have said that, because if I thought the waiting at the Fae Folk Council headquarters was long, it was nothing compared to the wait here at the Elfen Council headquarters.

For the first few hours I sat contentedly, reading my book. Then I got up to stretch and decided to walk up and down the length of the room for a bit of exercise. I walked down to the outside door, opened it and peeked out, and saw that night had fallen.

I walked back to the table where I had left my book, open to where I had stopped reading.

I sat again and looked around. The long room was well lit, and must have been equipped with some kind of vent system, because although there were no windows, the air wasn't stale.

I picked up my book, and had begun reading again when I heard a loud thump come from inside the room Father had disappeared into.

I blinked, turning to stare at the door.

Everything fell silent again.

*Should I go in?*

I thought about it for a minute, but then decided The Holly King could handle just about anything.

*He's so powerful.*

I remembered how I'd inadvertently called him to me when I was held by the old Elfen Council, and how he'd blasted them against the wall, and freed all of us.

*Yes, Holly, but what about how The Faction kidnapped The Oak King and drugged him and drained his power? Supernaturally powerful beings can be defeated, I think we can all agree on this.*

I sat there holding my book, lost in thought. I felt conflicted. I was just one young Fae Folk girl, still in school, still learning. I didn't feel very powerful at all. I felt small and slight and weak.

Another thump sounded from beyond the door. Then several more.

I stood up.

Suddenly, the whole building shook with the force of an explosion, and the door was blown off its hinges.

I was knocked to the floor, and showered with rumble.

My head rang as I tried to stand.

Dust was suspended in the air, and I felt a tickle at my head. I put my hand up to touch it, and it came away bloody.

I groaned and shook my head, then scrambled to my feet.

Whatever had happened, I had to get out of there.

I turned to the doorway and, stepping over the chair that had been knocked to its side, I called out. "Father? FATHER?!"

No answer.

No sound at all.

I blinked, trying to see inside.

Suddenly, the lights went out.

*Great.*

*Wait, I know how to deal with this.*

I muttered a few magical words, and suddenly Aspen and Tundra, my arctic wolf familiars, appeared out of nowhere next to me.

I looked down at them. "Why didn't you come to me when the explosion happened?" I whispered.

Tundra looked up at me and fixed me with an expression of cynicism. If a wolf could have a sardonic look on her face, Tundra managed it. The message was clear.

"Okay, okay, I won't send you away as much," I whispered. "I was just worried about you getting hurt."

This got me an even more extreme expression, this time from both of them.

"Sorry," I mumbled.

These wolves were magical and had been assigned to help me when I got into trouble, I remembered.

*Yeah, I really shouldn't be sending them away anymore.*

Something told me they could not only read my thoughts, but also my feelings, because each of them gave my hand a brief but warm lick from their wet tongues, then turned to face the source of the explosion.

I took an unsteady step into the room.

The air here was doubly thick with dust hanging suspended, plus smoke.

"Wolves," I whispered, "Find the King."

They immediately took off into the room.

The rubble on the floor was so thick that I decided I'd be better off using my hands to help pick my way through it, so I bent and scrambled over several large chunks of ceiling that had fallen.

This room was even larger than the waiting room behind me, and I wasn't sure where to start searching.

The wolves were nowhere in sight.

I heard a woman groan nearby, so I made my way over to a large pile of rubble.

"Hello?" I called tentatively, and was rewarded with another groan. I began picking through the debris, throwing pieces of wall and table aside, until I finally uncovered a struggling figure.

A hand reached up and grabbed my arm, and I hoisted the dust-covered figure up.

"Laura?!" I said, recognizing my friend.

Laura coughed and put up a finger, "That's me, all right."

I helped her out of the rubble, and she stood unsteadily next to me.

I searched her, looking for signs of injury.

"I think I'm okay," she said. "I was behind a few others who shielded me from the blast."

"Your arm is bloody," I said, looking around her side. "And part of your leg." I reached out to touch something on her sleeve.

"Yeah," she glanced at her side, "that's not my blood." She saw what I was staring at, and bent her head to look closer. "Ewww," she shook her arm, and a piece of flesh fell off and dropped to the ground. "Wow, that's definitely not mine."

*Urrggghhhh.*

"So there're others under all this stuff?" I asked, trying not to throw up.

"I think so." She turned to look at the wall where the door had been. I had just come through it and hadn't noticed it was splashed red with... blood.

I took a deep breath.

*Focus, Holly.*

"Laura, help me find my father?" I asked.

"Oh, he probably went through there," she pointed at the far side of the room. "He was chasing them when the blast went off."

*Huh?*

"Okay," I started to climb over the debris to get to the other side of the room. "Tell me what happened while we search?"

We both climbed over pieces of wall and ceiling and roof as we made our way to the other side of the room, as Laura explained what had happened.

"Well, the new council was here, we got the letter from The Faction declaring war. Bunch of asses, if you ask me," she said. "Anyway, the new Elfen Council is made of locals, in case you didn't know. Da and Mother are on it, as well as my uncle and a bunch of neighbors. There aren't too many left who wanted the job, we found out. Everyone is too afraid of that Faction group." She hopped over a large bit of roof that had come down onto a table in the middle of the room.

"So, your whole family is on it," I said. "That's good. Right?"

"Yes and no," said Laura. "It's made us kind of a target. We've gotten threats and things, delivered right to our front door. Last week it was a dead chicken."

"What?!" I was so surprised I stopped climbing for a second and just stared at her.

"You heard right. Some wonderful person came in the middle of the night and killed one of our chickens and stuck it on a pole right next to our front door," she said grimly. "Ran the poor thing through, right onto the pole. There was blood all over the ground."

I shook my head. "What is wrong with people? That chicken didn't do anything to them."

"I don't think they care," Laura said. "I think they were trying to scare us. None of us heard a thing, and there was no note or message or anything. Just dead livestock."

A chill ran through me.

"Laura, how are Tam and Lucy?" I asked.

"Oh, they're safe. Mother and Father keep them very close; someone's with them at all times," said Laura. "In fact, we now all sleep in the same room. Remember the center room where the fireplace is? We set up all our beds there."

"Wow." I said softly.

"Yeah, they took the threats seriously," she said, a slight grin on her face, "and I don't think they were too happy when we all snuck out."

"Yeah, I can understand that," I said slowly. "Parents..."

"Well, anyway, we're all sleeping together in the main room, and eating together," Laura said. "And when I go to school, they walk me there, and Tam and Lucy are never left alone. Tam's just about had it, but I think he understands. He hasn't taken off on one of his splits lately."

"That's a relief," I said, remembering when Liesl and I helped search for her little brother after he'd run away. "It's really not safe, what with this Faction on the loose."

"That's what Mother said when she chewed us out," Laura said. "Naw, Tam's been good. We've all been pretty careful." She fell silent, concentrating on climbing over a particularly rough patch.

We heard more groans, and went to the spot where they were coming from, lugging debris aside to pull whoever it was out.

Three more council members, bloody and scraped-up, but alive.

"Where were your parents and uncle sitting when the bomb went off?" I asked Laura quietly.

"They went after your father, when he ran after the two guys," she answered.

"And they all went out there?" I pointed toward the outer door, which was half buried in rubble.

She nodded.

"Let's go find them, then," I said. I looked over at the three people we'd uncovered. They were beginning to move aside debris from a fourth person. "They can handle getting the others out."

Laura nodded, looking worried.

We climbed over to the door.

It was open a few inches, and we had to clear a bunch of stuff out from in front of it before we could open it further.

"It's almost as if, some of them got knocked down but some of them got blown up," Laura muttered, glancing at a bloody spot. "There's no in between."

"Weird bomb," I said. "Was it in this room?"

"Oh, pffttt, it was strapped to one of the guys that came to speak to us," she said."

"What happened?" I asked.

"Five of them came in, on the pretense of negotiation," Laura explained. "But all they did was make demands. They basically parroted what was in the letter, they wanted possession of all the Elfen Lands! They claimed they had a right to govern themselves and not be forced to the rule of The Elfen High Council."

She made a rude sound.

"I don't think they understand how laws work," she said. "I mean, what about the tens of thousands of Elfen who live here that *don't* agree or belong to their little *Faction*?"

"Very true," I said. "Plus, they are bombing things and killing people to get their way. And kidnapping The Oak King."

Laura stopped and pointed her finger at me, "That's

right. What's the status with The Oak King, anyway?"

I sighed. "Still working on that."

We got through the door, and the next room wasn't as badly strewn with debris, so we were able to make our way swiftly out of the Elfen Council headquarters and out onto the grounds.

I looked around.

*Which way would they have gone? And where did my wolves go?*

"No way to tell which way to go," said Laura. "We're not far from the house; come on, it's dark, let's go there." She set off at a brisk walk, and I followed.

Another explosion sounded in the near distance, off to the right.

"They're still attacking," I said, ducking my head. "We need to take cover."

We hurried into the wood, and ducked behind trees, making our way to Laura's house this way, instead of using the gravel path that was out in the open.

Chapter Nine

# Too Many to Count

We arrived at Laura's house ten minutes later, from the direction opposite where the school lay.

"Let's be careful," Laura whispered, hiding behind a large tree and peeking out at the back door.

The house looked dark. The only light we could see came from the crescent moon and the fireflies.

"Do you think anyone's inside?" I said in a low whisper.

"Probably," answered Laura. "We blacked out the windows, so the little light we used wouldn't get out." She looked around. "Let's wait a minute."

We could hear more explosions going off, but it

seemed like each one was farther and farther away.

I crouched low behind a tree and studied the nighttime forest.

Normally, I heard owls hooting, crickets chirping, tons of frogs croaking, and saw fireflies blinking in and out of sight high up in the trees. And bats. I remember bats flitting in and out of the trees, catching insects for their nightly meal.

But this evening, nothing made a sound. No animal made an appearance. The forest was still and quiet. As quiet as death.

Another explosion sounded, this one maybe a mile away. The explosions were the only sounds.

*It seems the war has started in the Elfen Lands.*

I had thought we'd have more time: time to negotiate, time to prepare. I know Father had thought we had a little more time, or else he wouldn't have traveled.

*Actually, I'm not entirely sure about that.*

"Okay, let's go," Laura whispered, tapping me on the shoulder. We ran, both of us in a crouch, across the backyard and to the woodpile, then to the back door. Laura knocked three times, paused, then knocked three more.

The door immediately opened.

"Oh, thank God," Laura's mother appeared and pulled us both into the house, shutting the door firmly behind us and triple-locking it. "I was so worried!" Laura's mother hugged her in a tight squeeze, then called over her shoulder, in a stage whisper. "They're here!"

Laura's father came around the corner, followed by The Holly King, and Aspen and Tundra.

Father enveloped me in such a big hug that I could hardly breath.

"Oh, Holly! I'm so glad to see you!" He murmured.

"I'm fine, I'm fine, Father," I laughed, happy to be reunited with him.

Aspen and Tundra would not stop licking my hands. I bent and hugged them both. "Yes, puppies, you did good, you did so good!"

I heard a shriek and a shush, and Tam and Lucy came running to jump on me.

"Hello, you guys!" I laughed quietly. "Long time no see!"

We all gathered in the main room. Candles covered the tables, giving off a flickering light and throwing shadows over the walls.

The windows had indeed been blacked out, with several coats of black paint. It looked thick.

Laura's uncle saw me looking over at the windows.

"Took me four coats of paint to get them completely blacked out," he said. "Can't be too careful."

I nodded.

Laura's mother handed out small, singular shepherd's pies to Laura and me, and I took mine gratefully. The golden-brown crust was fragrant, and I stuck my spoon in and lifted a steaming bite of carrot, peas, onions, beef, crust, and gravy into my mouth. It was the best thing I'd tasted in a long, long while.

*I love home cooking.*

I sat and ate while listening to the adults discuss everything.

Off in the distance, I could still hear bombs going off.

Lucy came and sat in my lap and fell asleep, her thumb in her mouth.

"Is your Academy safe?" The Holly King was asking.

"The Academy?" Laura's father laughed grimly. "The Academy is mostly rubble. They took that out this afternoon." he shook his head. "To destroy a place of education..."

"Were any students hurt?" Father asked.

"A few were, but it happened in a series of explosions; the first bomb went off outside, so we were able to evacuate," Laura's father said. "No serious injuries, just cuts and bruises. Light trauma. The students were all sent home on indefinite leave, until we get this figured out."

"We'll start repairs tomorrow, I'm sure," said Laura's uncle. "If they'll give us a chance," he looked to the side as another explosion sounded in the distance.

I finished my pie and was handed a mug of warm cider, and I sat, sipping the sweet drink and listening.

Aspen and Tundra lay on either side of me, surrounding Lucy and me with warm, furry protection.

The adults spoke in whispers, their heads together, while we kids lay quietly in the dark house, the candles flickering, the forest silent around us, and the thought of war heavy on our minds.

The fire crackled in the fireplace.

I think I dozed off.

The next thing I knew, I heard a massive explosion, and then screaming, right next to me.

I opened my eyes to chaos, my heart thundering in my ears, beating a mile a minute.

The candles were out, but I could still see, because the roof was gone and the moonlight shone into the main room.

*The roof was gone!*

Lucy had her hands tightly around me, and Aspen and Tundra were pressing up against me, and I could see no one else.

Another bomb shook the ground, and we were showered by flying things. Dust and debris flew up into the air.

A third explosion went off, very close. My face was hit

by splattering hot things, blinding me. I shut my eyes as they burned.

*We have to get out of here. NOW.*

I grabbed Lucy with one hand and turned and began to crawl out of the house, which now lay in rubble around us.

"Father? Laura?" I called as I scrambled away.

At first, there was no reply, then, a hand grabbed me around the waist, and I was lifted up and the owner of the hand ran with me, holding me to his side. I kept hold of Lucy with both arms. She was so light I fleetingly wondered if she was getting enough to eat.

I opened my stinging eyes and glanced at who was running with me and was met by a face full of soft, fluffy Father Christmas jacket.

Lucy stayed quiet, grasping me with both hands as I held her.

Father's arm was hooked around my waist, and he held me tightly to him as he ran into the trees. More bombs went off as he ran, and they landed almost at our feet; we were showered with all kinds of hard stuff.

I kept my eyes closed against the fiery material being rained down upon us. Some of it was dirt, some of it was sticks and boards and pieces of the house. Some of it felt wet, and I worried about that.

The Holly King ran into the trees and didn't stop

running until he was a mile away, and the explosions had been left far, far behind us.

He stopped, and he wasn't even breathing hard.

He stood in the dark night forest and turned, looking all around us, then gently set us down beside him.

Aspen and Tundra raced up to us then, and stood against us, looking back at the bombed-out land behind us.

I set Lucy on the ground and helped her to her feet, kneeling to check her face.

"You okay?" I whispered as my hands touched her cheeks and smoothed her hair. Her face was covered in smudges and dirt, but her bright eyes shone with a serious look out at me. She nodded silently. Her fists kept a tight hold on my coat, not letting go.

*I don't blame you, kid.*

I turned and saw Father had held Laura and Tam in his other arm as he ran to escape.

"You guys okay?" I asked.

They both nodded.

The Holly King was still scanning the forest with focused eyes. Finally, he turned to us. "I'm taking us all back to Holly's school," he said. "That okay with you, Laura? Tam?"

They both nodded thankfully.

We had no idea if their parents or uncle had made it

out.

We couldn't go back to check.

Explosions were still going off near what was left of the house and school.

Too many explosions to count.

Chapter Ten

# Back Home Again

A day and a half after we left, Father and I arrived back at Titania Academy, with a few scars and three extra Faerie Folk.

Our feet landed on the front steps of the Academy, and I stumbled a few inches. My father's hand grabbed my elbow to steady me.

"Thanks," I murmured, looking around. "What time is it?"

"It's an hour before dawn," Father said, wiping blood off his hand. "Come on, let's stop by the infirmary and get that cleaned up."

My arm had several gashes in it, and the blood was

drying already. Crusty and black, it mingled with the dirt on my arm.

Laura and her brother had cuts and scrapes that needed to be cleaned and bandaged.

Lucy seemed okay, but I wasn't completely confident she wasn't hurt.

We entered Titania Academy and climbed the stairs to the infirmary.

Some hours later, after getting cleaned up and bandaged, we sat in the med bay in beds alongside each other.

The headmistress, Professor Ó Baoghill, and Professor Farryn, stood quietly talking to Father as he lay in a hospital bed.

Lucy had her own bed, but insisted on sharing mine.

Father looked huge and barely fit in his. He insisted he was not hurt badly, and would heal magically much quicker than normal, but the healer, Mrs. O'Bambury, would hear none of his excuses.

"Sit!" she pointed to his bed. "You will stay in bed until I am satisfied you are well enough to leave my care!" She said imperiously, daring The Holly King to cross her again.

Father got into bed, meekly, and rested there a while.

It was about eight o'clock in the morning, and we had all been brought trays of breakfast. My plate held a huge omelet with bacon slices next to it, and my stomach rumbled as I ate.

Lucy was given a bowl of brown-sugar porridge, upon request, and was eagerly eating steaming, dainty spoonfuls of the light-brown cereal.

Laura and Tam had eggs and bacon; they'd asked to try the typical Titania Academy breakfast.

Father was eating a hearty steak, sausage, eggs and biscuits with gravy, and a large whole-cooked fish. His tray was full of food plates, and he was busy wolfing it all down.

Aspen and Tundra had refused to leave my side the whole time. Mrs. O'Bambury had said their presence was fine, and they had been brought large bowls of raw deer meat and bone marrow. They were eating slowly, savoring the delicacy before them.

"Holly." Chance came trotting into the room, followed by Liesl and Renée. He skidded to a halt next to my bed, bending to give me a hug.

Liesl came and squeezed my hand, then gave Lucy a hug.

Renée smiled and looked relieved. "I'm Renée. I'm Holly and Liesl's friend. We heard what happened," she said. "I'm so glad you all got out."

Liesl went over to Laura and Tam and gave them hugs. "I'm sorry your parents and uncle are still missing," she said softly.

"Oh, I have no doubt they got to safety," Tam said confidently. "If you think me and Laura are good at survival, we learned everything from them." He nodded firmly.

Laura smiled at her brother. "Yeah, Tam's right. Heck, they might even show up here."

"Father got us out magically, but everyone else has to walk, or take a unicorn carriage," I said.

Mrs. O'Bambury bustled in with a huge jar of midmorning tonic and a handful of spoons.

"All right, now, visitors are okay, but stay quiet and calm. We don't want to excite the patients too much."

She began going from bed to bed, and each of us was made to swallow a large spoonful of the dark syrup.

"Mmmm, elderberry!" squeaked Lucy, licking her lips after receiving her dose.

"Sire?" Laura asked The Holly King.

"Yes, young lady?"

"The attack on in the Elfen Lands, the bombing of the council headquarters and the Academy and our house: Do you think they'll keep up the attack?"

The Holly King looked thoughtful for a few moments.

Tam stared at him, and stayed very still, waiting for his answer.

"I think," Father said, "that we cannot know for sure, but it does seem as if they are determined to destroy all that they can. The Faction made a show of asking for a negotiation, but it was just so they could get inside the Elfen High Council headquarters to bomb it from the inside."

"Suicide bomber," Laura whispered, looking angry. "I think most of the council members were killed."

"And they likely attacked Elfen Lands first because there is more wilderness, less defense," Father said.

"Sir, there is less defense because the Fae Folk High Council doesn't give us much," Laura said quietly.

"You're absolutely right, Laura, and that is something we need to correct," said The Holly King.

"It may be too late," Laura whispered.

"Well, I dearly hope not," Father said quietly.

Two days later, we were all pretty much healed up, thanks to a special salve supplied to Mrs. O'Bambury by Professor Farryn.

"My grandmother swore by this. Just try it," he said. I have never seen a wound healed so fast.

My arm looked like it hadn't even been torn open by shrapnel.

We all gathered in the evening in Father's special Holly King quarters: all of us, including the headmistress, Professor Farryn, and all of us students.

I held Lucy in my lap, as usual. She never wanted to leave. Although she did sleep in quarters set up for her to share with Laura.

The Holly King took a deep breath. "Okay, I have gathered you all here to talk about something of grave concern: I am extremely troubled by this dark sigil they're using." He held up the letter the Faction had used to declare war on everyone, and tapped his finger on the paper, pointing at the mark at the top of the page, but careful not to touch it.

The design was made up of black spikes that curled around one another in a backward fashion.

"I recognize this, and it frightens me. Yes, me. I am The Holly King, and this frightens me to death," Father said. "The dark faeries that used this mark have not been seen in over seven thousand years. Not since the time of the Dark Wars."

Professor Farryn gasped, his sharp intake of breath loud in the quiet room. The Holly King nodded in agreement with his sentiment.

*If Doctor Farryn is horrified, this has to be really, really bad.*

Father continued, "The Dark Wars were a time in the distant past when the Faerie Lands were all united against a common enemy. This was before the Faerie High Council split into the two lesser councils: Elfen and Fae Folk. The Dark Wars happened in an age long past, when the Faerie Lands were still considered one, not Elfen nor Fae Folk, but One: Faerie."

He took a deep breath before continuing.

"We were united against an enemy worse than any that had come before. A dark, chaotic figure who demanded rule over all our land. It was a horrible, deadly time in our history. But this was thousands and thousands of years ago. This dark, chaotic being was thought to be defeated. Lost in the misty past."

The Holly King turned the letter over and looked at the dark sigil with a deeply worried expression.

"The sigil here on this declaration of war is the evil one's sigil: the mark he and his dark faerie followers used so very long ago," Father said. "They would put this mark upon every evil deed they did. It could be found burned into the wood of every stump in every forest they burned down. It was found carved into the flesh of every corpse they left behind, and there were thousands."

I began to unconsciously breathe fast. My heartbeat quickened.

*Ohhhh, God...*

"I am frightened for the Faerie Lands, all the lands. If this sigil is used here to mean that this dark chaos has returned to our land, we are in deep trouble," said The Holly King. "I have no idea what they think they're playing at by using this symbol, or if they even know all the history connected to it, but judging from their actions of the last several days, especially deep within the Elfen Lands, they are serious about the dark chaos. They are embracing it."

"Sire," Chance asked in a quiet voice, "Can you tell me, where did the dark chaos eventually die? Was it in a battle? Which area of our lands was his final resting place?"

The Holly King took another deep breath. "Chance, I wish I could be certain. I believe the history books say the final battle in which the Faerie Forces defeated this madman took place somewhere in the northeast. We are not certain. It was so long ago. But what we must do is take this threat seriously. Whether The Faction is somehow connected to this ancient chaos, or they are simply emulating it, the threat is incredibly dangerous.

They will try to lay waste to the entire land of Faerie. They may even go beyond Faerie borders."

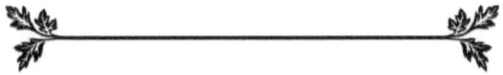

Chapter Eleven
# Game Plan

An icy chill ran down my spine.

"Father, what do you mean, this may go beyond Faerie borders?" I asked.

He looked at me, a grim expression on his face. "The last time a war this devastating happened in our land, it spread into the human world. The Dark Wars, as we call them here, when we fought the dark chaotic one, spilled over the borders into the human realm and caused several natural disasters and hundreds of deaths. They had no idea what had hit them."

I swallowed hard. "And what...?" I asked in a small voice. "What would happen now if this war spreads like that? Now, in modern day?"

Father looked at me, an indecipherable, haunted look on his face. "It would be devastating," he said. "They would not understand where or who it was coming from. It would probably touch off a nuclear war."

It felt like ice water was washing over my whole body. *World War III.*

We ate dinner in Father's room while we talked and brainstormed and strategized well into the night.

In the end, we agreed that one thing had to happen or we were lost.

"We need to get Oak back," Father said. "Not just because of the magic with which he imbues the land for half the year, not because they've kidnapped him, drugged him, and tortured him. And not because he's my brother, and my mother and I are beside ourselves with anguish at what's happened to him. No, the main reason is that they are draining him of his power. His power regenerates. They are using his power for the war. That's how they are creating the weapons. The exploding bombs, the fire bombs, the water bombs, and the air bombs."

"Without The Oak King, they will wither, like a weed when the water is withdrawn," said Professor Farryn slowly, almost dreamily.

"Exactly," Father said.

*The Oak King... find and rescue The Oak King...*

I had tried to do just that last autumn, with the help of two other teenagers, and half a dozen halflings.

I had failed.

*If you fail at something important, get back on that horse and try, try again.*

This time, I would have far more power behind me. I would not fail this time.

"I'll do it," I said, raising my hand.

"You'll need an army," the headmistress said.

"Not necessarily," said Father. "First things first: We need to know where he is and what kind of forces are holding him. From what I witnessed in the Elfen Land, The Faction has drained a massive amount of power from him. They've constructed so many weapons that they were dropping bombs indiscriminately, as if they had ten thousand of the things. Twenty thousand."

"They may have spent all autumn and winter draining him," Liesl said, thinking out loud. "They may have drained him completely. They may have..." She stopped speaking, looking pale.

The Holly King put his hand up. "We've got to find him. He cannot be killed in this way, but he can be drained so completely that he enters a thousand-year slumber from which he will not awaken, not for... well... a thousand years or more." He sat back, looking ill. "It's all conjecture, it has never happened, but..."

"But you don't want to test the theory," the headmistress said sympathetically.

Father nodded. "As we all know, the Faerie Lands were borne of Titania, and she bore The Oak King and me. The life of the Faerie Lands resides in us. If The Oak King were to be drained to such a degree... that he fell into a... magical coma, for lack of a better term, the land would suffer greatly. The land might begin to die."

"Sire," said Chance, who had remained silent and thoughtful until now. "Perhaps if we were to send reconnaissance teams throughout all the territories, they might be able to gather information on what is happening with the land and with the flora and fauna. We might be able to track any changes, and use this information to locate The Oak King."

"That is a brilliant idea, my friend," The Holly King said. "And I have an idea who we might send. We need magic, and we need to be able to gather information from every animal and plant, everywhere. The only beings that would be able to do this as quickly as it needs to be done are the familiars."

*The familiars!*

I reached down to touch Aspen at my feet, and she looked up at me, her eyes true and her heart full. Tundra lay next to her. She had fallen asleep waiting for something to happen, and her legs were splayed out sideways as she'd stretched in a dream.

I knew they could read my thoughts and feelings.

When I whispered, "Tundra," her eyes opened, her head came up, and her ears wiggled. In an instant she was up, and had her chin on my knee next to her sister's, and they were both ready for whatever The Holly King ordered.

Snowbear lay curled on her side across Liesl's shoulders like a fur neck wrap. Liesl smiled and made a light kissing noise, and the snowy ermine's eyes popped open. She flipped and crouched there, and began chattering, talking up a storm.

Chance whispered a magic invocation, and his hawk materialized on his shoulder, the noble animal majestic in her form. She dipped her head and push her neck up under Chance's chin, and he moved his head back and forth, rubbing her fondly.

Renée whispered a call, and her rabbit familiar, Jade,

materialized in her lap. Jade snuggled up against her, then began preening and washing herself, turning her head so her tongue could lick the fur on her back.

Professor Farryn uttered a magical call, and a huge white lion materialized at the little man's feet. He began to make huffing noises, and nudged his massive ear against Farryn's hand, and Farryn began to scratch him. The lion let out a soft moan of pleasure.

Professor Ó Baoghill tilted her chin up and chirped her magical call, and her familiar appeared. It was an enormous gold eagle, and it perched on her forearm, and leaned against her shoulder, chirping like a baby.

"I am not sure if there's room for my familiar," The Holly King rumbled with a chuckle. "There's barely room for me on this love seat."

"Oh, Father, do call her!" I pleaded.

"Very well, my daughter," he smiled and winked. "I can never refuse you." The Holly King whispered the magical invocation for his familiar to appear, and suddenly, it popped into the realm beside Father, and I gasped with delight, and clapped my hands.

The Holly King's familiar was a gargantuan polar bear. Her white fur was brilliant, and her nose was black as coal. Her eyes were wide and intelligent, and she leaned against The Holly King's arm fondly, making huffing noises.

The room was filled with the purrs, hums, trills and huffs of pleasure from all the familiars.

Later that night, near midnight, we all gathered out on the lawn in front of Titania Academy. Each of us had communed with our respective familiars, and explained with words and song and gestures what was unnecessary, because they could all read our thoughts and feelings.

They were all eager to help, every one.

More students had joined us, forming a group of twenty that The Holly King and Professor Ó Baoghill trusted implicitly. Most were upperclassmen who had already been sent on various missions. They knew to keep this project secret, for the safety of the animals.

At a signal from all of us, every familiar vanished, each dispatched to the outer reaches of the Faerie Realms. Their charge: to investigate, inquire, ask and sense, any change of the land, sea or air, in every corner of the realm.

"He could be anywhere," The Holly King said quietly.

"The Faerie Lands overlap with the lands of the human world. The Oak King could be anywhere."

I put my arm around my father's and leaned into him in a hug. "It will be all right," I whispered. "We will find him and bring him back. I feel it."

He lowered his face and kissed the top of my head. "I feel it, too, Holly."

Three days later, they were back.

We all gathered in the center atrium to meet together, and I was delighted and surprised to see Jess, the lacewing faerie, and Brendan, the dwarf both there.

I ran and hugged them. "You guys! It's really great to see you!"

"Well, we had to come," Brendan said. "We had to add our familiars to the mix, since they're both unique." He glanced at Jess and winked.

Jess grinned and nodded. "Absolutely right. My familiar heard about the exercise and insisted he join in."

Everyone was gathering, and the general hubbub in

the large room grew as more people arrived.

*This is way more than the initial group.*

The Holly King stood on a table so he could better see everyone. "Okay, we're just about ready for their return, everyone," he said. "Be sure to make plenty of room, now. Remember: Some of our familiars are larger than others."

We all decided to move to the edges of the room, so the animals could rematerialize in the center area.

Chairs and sofas were scooted back, and lamps and tables were moved aside.

Father put his hand up. "Everyone ready? They are all waiting, and they've given their reports to my team, so let's get them back to you, shall we?" He dropped his arm, giving the signal, and suddenly, the room was filled with familiars, large and small.

"Pavlov! I've missed you so much!"

"Cherry! Good girl!"

"Ribbit! Oh, Rib, I love you!"

"Gorse! Ha! Sweet!"

"Snowbear!"

"Tundra! Aspen! Good girls!"

"Willow!

"Ashley!"

"Cloud!"

"Flit!"

And on and on it went. Dozens of familiars had made

the journey; they had all wanted to help.

I was down on the ground, on my knees, hugging my wolves, squeezing my arms around their necks. I hadn't realized how emotional it would be. I'd missed them something terrible, but the added danger of their mission had my heart in my throat and tears in my eyes at their safe return. I knelt there, and I couldn't speak around my thickened throat. I rubbed my tears in their fur, and was finally able to murmur sweet words of happiness to my two arctic heroes.

"The best, you girls are the absolute best, I adore you. It was such a brave thing to do, so brave and so courageous. I love love love you two. Mmmmmmm," I kept up a continuous whisper of loving to them both, and they wiggled with joy at being reunited.

It was a long time before everyone settled down, in chairs or on the floor, and looked to where The Holly King was waiting to speak.

Father sat with his back to his massive polar bear familiar, who curled around the great king's torso and provided a soft place for him to rest.

Chance stood next to The Holly King. His hawk familiar was perched on his shoulder, wings partially outstretched, nuzzling the top of his master's head.

We quieted and waited for Father to speak, and while I was waiting, I scanned the room, curious as to what each person's familiar was.

I saw Brendan's first: a huge green-and-brown dragon the size of several school buses. He was crouched and purring in contentment, and Brendan sat on his head between his two enormous ears. I was surprised, I'd had no idea.

*I didn't realize dragons could purr.*

Close by Aspen and Tundra stood Jess. At first, I couldn't see her familiar, and I wondered how small it was. Then I looked at the small animal she held to her chest. I stepped closer and peered at what she nuzzled and murmured to, and she saw me looking and smiled and brought her hands down to show me.

Jess's familiar was a medium-size frog.

"This is Ribbit, my familiar. Rib, this is Holly," she said proudly. "Rib and I have been together for over a hundred years."

I blinked in surprise. It made sense that since familiars were magical animals, that they would have really long lifespans.

I touched my hands to Aspen's and Tundra's fur, glad they would be with me for my whole life.

Jess bent and kissed her familiar's back, and the frog croaked in pleasure. He put one foreleg up, and Jess touched her forefinger with it. "High five, Rib!"

"Rib is amazing," I said, smiling.

"Okay, everyone, settle down, settle down," The Holly King said, his arms extended, palms down, patting the air, asking for calm.

The crowd noise lessened a bit but was still somewhat loud, too loud to speak over.

A piercing whistle cut through the air sharply, like a knife.

"QUIET YOU LOT," Chance called in a booming voice.

The room fell so silent you could hear a pin drop.

"Good, thank you, Sir," The Holly King said to Chance, who bowed, then straightened and remained at attention.

"Now, the animals finished their quest for information about an hour ago," Father's voice boomed out loud and clear. "And they've all reported back in, and we've compiled everything they've told us. First things first. We have special congratulations to the familiar who traveled the farthest, the familiar who gathered the most information, and the familiars who found several pieces of evidence and brought them back."

*This is interesting.*

Aspen shivered with anticipation; I put my hand on her head and murmured to her, and she settled down.

I sat on the floor, my arms around them both, and leaned back against them.

"All right," said Chance, stepping forward. "To the familiar who traveled the farthest, and gathered the farthest-reaching reconnaissance for the mission, we have this gold medal." He held up a large gold disk, with a long blue ribbon attached. "To Zen, who flew for three-thousand, six-hundred and fifty-three miles. Congratulations!" He tossed the gold medal up into the air, and it flew over to Brendan's massive dragon, who bowed his head in thanks, with Brendan still sitting on it, as the ribbon settled over his head.

Everyone clapped and cheered loudly for the dragon, Brendan loudest of all.

"YAY! Yeahoo! That's right! He's so awesome!" The dwarf clapped atop the dragon's head.

The crowd noise died back down, and everyone look at Chance expectedly.

"Okay," said Chance. "Now we have a gold medal for the familiar who gathered the most information. This familiar spoke to more animals in the wild than any other, and the information this provided has helped us zero in on The Oak King's actual location." Chance held up another large gold disk with blue ribbon attached, and clasped in his hand was also a miniature gold disk and ribbon.

*This familiar must be smaller.*

Chance held up both and said, "This medal goes to

Rib!" He threw both gold disks high in the air and they traveled to Jess, who whooped and hollered and caught the larger one. The smaller gold medal and ribbon settled gently over Ribbit's head as Jess held him up, and he croaked in thanks, and waved his webbed foreleg briefly in the air.

Jess squealed in pleasure.

"Here, I'll put the big one around your neck for you," I said.

"No, it's not mine, I'll just put it in my bag; we can hang it in the tree house when we get home," She grinned, reaching and placing the larger medal under the flap of the old leather bag around her shoulder.

I nodded.

"Last but not least, we have a pair of familiars who were out gathering information, and came upon concrete evidence, and took great pains to bring the pieces back to us," Chance called out. He held up two gold disks in his hands. "With the help of this evidence, we were able to pinpoint The Oak King's precise location, working with the information from Rib. So, congratulations to Aspen and Tundra!" He tossed the two gold medals into the air, blue ribbons fluttering.

I gasped and shrieked in delight, "YEAH!!!!!!!"

The two gold disks floated over to us, and both my noble arctic wolf familiar rose to their feet and stood proudly as the two medals drifted down and settled on both of their wolfy heads.

Chapter Twelve

# Magical Quest

Father convened the last meeting that night, and the inner circle, as I had come to call them, was convened.

Liesl, Renée, Chance, Laura, and I sat in a semicircle on the thick carpet, each of us overstuffed from the supper we'd enjoyed with Father just a half hour ago.

I was extremely sad that Laura, Tam, and Lucy had been driven from their homeland, but I was very happy Laura could be here with us. Liesl and I had quickly integrated the three into Titania Castle life, and Laura had blended in seamlessly.

She'd had just one incidence of bigotry regarding her Elfen heritage. A young man visiting his sister, who was a student at Titania Academy, had made a sneering remark at Laura as our group had passed. The headmistress had been present and had immediately escorted the man out of the castle, and to the edge of the school grounds, and over his protestations had banished him from the property in perpetuity. It had been epic.

Professors Farryn and Ó Baoghill sat in the overstuffed leather chairs near us, and both sipped on small brandies Father had poured them earlier.

The room was cool on the outer edges, especially by the windows, as a late-winter snowstorm buffeted the castle; but a fire crackled merrily in the large fireplace next to where The Holly King sat.

The mood was jovial. The familiars were all back, and in one piece: Not one had gone missing or come back injured. The results had been better than expected, Chance had revealed, which surprised me.

I'd had no idea they'd expected injury or worse for the familiars. Chance had explained that yes, each animal had been briefed about the possible dangers, and each one had bravely been eager to take on the responsibility.

"Everyone," Father said, "We've learned that The Oak King is being held in Álfheimr. Very far distant. Thanks to all the information the familiars gathered, we learned of an area that is normally rock and dirt, but is now showing signs of unexpected and incorrect life. This land is very remote, in fact, nearly to the Arctic Circle, but the normally stunted and bare trees there are flowering. The artic grass is growing at an accelerated rate. Mushrooms are appearing in the soil." He sat back and took a deep breath, then continued. "Rib was not only able to gather information from every creature in the sea, but also every amphibian on the land. He made direct contact with one arctic Caecilian who had actually set eyes on The Oak King himself."

I gasped.

"How... how is this possible?" the headmistress asked, astonished.

"A rare and lucky combination of a very lost Caecilian and a Siberian Newt that Rib came across." The Holly King shook his head. "That familiar was able to do this much, I think, because he's extremely wise and he's been around for a very long time. Apparently, Jess encourages him to travel." Father smiled. "Very lucky for us that he was available and willing to help us."

"So The Oak King is in Álfheimr, Sire?" Chance asked, looking thoughtful. "That's... that will be difficult."

The Holly King nodded. "From the evidence that's been gathered, of unnatural surges in growth, we can tell that he's still drugged and that they haven't allowed him to enter slumber. He will be incredibly weak. Certainly not conscious at all."

I gasped and put my head down in sorrow. To not allow The Oak King to enter his magical slumber? This was torture.

Father continued, "And I've had new information from our Holly Army forces stationed in the outer reaches." He looked solemn and serious. "The Faction has begun their assault in the Fae Folk lands."

I gasped.

They weren't expected to enter our lands for some months; our tacticians had surmised that The Faction would remain in The Elfen lands until the spring.

"Oh no," Renée murmured.

"They are closest to the Highlands," said Father.

My blood froze, and a chill ran down my back as I looked at Chance. His family was near the Highlands.

He saw me looking and nodded. "They've already evacuated, along with everyone else in the area."

I looked stricken. I was glad Chance's family was safe, but for how long? This war was getting personal. My friends' families were being evacuated and threatened. People were dying. I felt myself move from feeling heartsick to feeling a growing anger inside me.

*We need to act and act now.*

Chance was speaking about assembling a rescue in the coming weeks. I got to my feet and lifted my chin.

"I will lead the rescue team, and we will leave at

dawn," I said in a clear, loud voice.

"I will go too," Renée's voice rang out not a second after mine.

"Me, too. I'm going," said Liesl.

"Pffttt, y'all aren't going without me. I'm ready to kick ass," drawled Laura. "Who else is going?"

Chance raised his hand and smiled.

Father's eyebrows rose, and he looked at Professor Ó Baoghill and smiled.

We got about five hours of sleep, after planning and strategizing late into the night.

Professor Ó Baoghill announced she would break a school rule and supply us with Bags of Holding, so we could take all the supplies we'd need.

The Holly King stated he would personally transport us to the edge of the sea. We would have to travel in human lands for a while, as a shortcut, to save a week's travel.

*I wish Father could transport us directly there.*

I actually asked him why he could not do this, and he gave a long, complicated answer which Chance summarized by saying The Holly King needed to conserve his power to fight The Faction and keep them from bombing the land, destroying trees and villages, slaughtering Faerie Folk right and left.

*This evil must be stopped.*

I fell asleep feeling angrier and more determined than I'd ever felt in my life.

It was barely not-dawn, the black sky had turned midnight blue in anticipation of the arrival of sunrise.

Liesl, Laura and I were packed and ready.

We didn't say much. Each of us knew how important my uncle's rescue was, and we were eager to get started.

I tightened once last buckle on my bag of holding, slung it over my shoulder, and looked up to see both of them looking at me expectantly.

I had been unofficially crowned the leader of the dorm. I nodded to them, and turned and walked out the door.

We headed down the stairs and to the inner courtyard, where Renée and Chance were waiting with Professor Ó Baoghill and The Holly King.

Professor Farryn came running on his short legs, taking the stairs rapidly, calling out, "Miss Becker! Miss Becker!"

We all turned, and Liesl stepped forward. "What is it, Professor?" she asked.

Doctor Farryn came to a halt in front of Liesl, and stood there panting for a moment. "Here, take this." Farryn flicked his hand, and a long, rough wooden branch appeared out of his palm. "You've been practicing enough in class, you should be able to make use of it in dire circumstances," he said, handing Liesl her practice magical staff from class.

Liesl grinned and took the weapon, flicking her hand and popping it out of sight. "Thanks, Professor."

"Now," said The Holly King, "I highly recommend having your familiars walk alongside you for as long as possible. They know the lay of the magical land you'll be traversing, and they'll be able to help a lot. So, don't just call them in an emergency, keep them with you all the time." He winked at Aspen and Tundra, who waited patiently beside me.

"Did they ask you to say that?" I whispered to him out

of the corner of my mouth.

"No!" he replied. "Besides, it's a good idea."

I grinned.

Professor Ó Baoghill came to Laura, who stood beside me. "Miss Greenleaf, as I understand Elfen are not normally assigned familiars as they enter their academy training, but Titania Academy would like to extend the offer to you."

Laura blinked in surprise. "You're kidding. Really?!" She grinned broadly.

"Absolutely," the headmistress replied. "This quest is of utmost importance, and having a familiar by your side will be invaluable."

Laura stood a little higher. "I accept," she said proudly.

"Very good. Come into my office for a minute so that we may assign one to you," the headmistress replied.

Laura and Professor Ó Baoghill left for a few minutes, and the rest of us were handed extra bags by the head of the kitchen.

"Take this. You might get hungry and need something fast," she said, handing each of us a small odd-looking bag. "A new kind of magic I've been working on," she said.

"What is it?" I lifted the bag to my eyes, then sniffed inside. It was empty.

"Blow into the bag," the cook said.

I did as she had instructed. A small biscuit appeared in the bag. I blew again, and two more appeared.

"It's still in the trial stages, but this adventure seems like the perfect way to test it," the cook said proudly.

"A biscuit bag of holding?" Liesl exclaimed with delight.

"Of a sort," Cook replied. "The biscuits aren't very good, because they're dry and in stasis until they're called into the bag, but it'll keep you alive," she laughed. "Still working on a jug of holding, for water. That one needs a ton of work."

"Thanks!" I said. "It'll come in handy," I tucked the empty bag into my larger bag, and munched on the biscuits.

"Good luck you lot, I have a good feeling about this." Cook waved as she walked back to the dining hall.

Tam and Lucy ran up. "So glad we caught you before you left," said Tam.

"Lucy." I bent to hug the little girl. The nanny assigned to the two children smiled from a few feet away.

"Holly," squeaked the tiny girl. I smiled, happy that Lucy had finally started to talk again. The shock of losing her parents had left her mute, although she'd shown no other ill effects.

She hugged me tightly, her small arms around my

neck and shoulders. Then she stood back and handed me a small white flower. "I picked this for you. For good luck."

I took it and threaded it through a buttonhole. "I shall treasure it always," I murmured, smiling.

She grinned.

Laura and Professor Ó Baoghill were walking back to the group. Laura had a brightly colored parrot on her shoulder. She was grinning broadly.

"The familiar chooses the faerie," the headmistress said, smiling.

"Awwww, he's so pretty," said Tam. He put his arms around his sister's waist. "Laura, be careful," he said in a serious tone.

I realized with a start that since Tam and Laura had been separated from their parents and uncle, they just had each other now.

Laura bent to hug her little brother back. "I will. I'll be fine. Don't worry, Tam." She patted her side, and I remembered she kept her sword there in an invisible holster.

I walked over to The Holly King and gave him a hug. "Be careful, Father. They are violent and they've already stolen one king."

Father hugged me back tightly. "I will be careful, my daughter, and you be careful, too," then he pulled back slightly to look into my eyes. "The council has put special protection on me. Don't worry, I will be all right."

I gave him one last squeeze and released him.

I took a deep breath and scanned the room. It looked like we were ready.

Turning to Father, I nodded. He nodded back.

And we left.

## Chapter Thirteen
# Stone Cottage Wait

We landed next to Loch Alsh, looking into an inlet facing east. Father had transported us in a white streak of fast traveling cloud that had deposited us into an old stone cottage at the edge of the lake.

"What's that noise?" Liesl asked.

The windows of the little house were thick and framed with old wood: They seemed to be locked tight against the elements. And yet the storm outside buffeted the windows, the wind battering the old panes, making them creak and moan.

I peered out the cloud glass. "Looks like quite a storm. Let's just sit tight here and wait for it to pass before we venture forth, shall we?"

Chance nodded. "The map says this is the Isle of Skye here, across the bay."

Laura pulled out a compass, studied it, then pointed to the right. "That way is north, so we've got to go east, is it?"

"Yes," Chance said, withdrawing a small map from his bag and studying it. "There's a bridge with a pedestrian walk along the side."

Laura walked to the door. "I'm just going to peek outside, see how bad it really is, k?" She pulled the door open a few inches.

It was a small, ancient wooden door, but it opened smoothly, without creaking.

*This cottage is frequently used.*

Laura stuck her head out the door. "It's not so bad," she called back over her shoulder. "I think it's mostly wind."

"Well, we've got our coats. Why don't we go?" I asked.

We stepped outside. The wind threw us back against the front of the cottage.

I was actually pressed against the ancient rough stone.

Chance said something, but his voice was carried away by the wind. He gestured to us, then ducked back in the door.

We all filed back into the cottage.

"Well, that was the shortest outing in the history of the planet," Liesl said. She reached out and pulled a spruce twig from my hood. "You've collected shrubbery on you, Holly," she said, grinning.

"Okay," Chance said. "New plan. We wait for a couple of hours."

"I'll start a fire," Laura said, walking to the stone fireplace at the other end of the cottage.

This hut was obviously used for wayward Faerie travelers, because not only was the fireplace clear and swept out, there was a neat stack of wood next to it.

"I'll bet there's a large stack just outside, too," said Laura, arranging the wood in the hearth. She stood back and extended her hand, palm out, then muttered a few indecipherable words of magic.

Nothing happened.

I blinked.

Laura turned to us, grinning. "I was just kidding. Anyone know a spell to make fire?"

Renée chuckled and stepped forward. She leaned down and blew onto the wood stack, and a small flame appeared in the middle of the pile. She blew again, and the fire grew and began to catch and crackle. Straightening, she turned to me.

"Holly, do you still have that wand the old woodsman gave you last year?" she asked.

"Uhh, yeah." I reached down and fumbled in my bag; it took a minute to find it. Finally, I withdrew my hand and raised my fist triumphantly, grasping an ordinary-looking stick.

"My stick," I said proudly.

"You already know it's magical, but they teach wand use in Year Three," said Renée. "One of the things you'll be able to do with it after taking the class is, start fires. It's something you have to take great care with, but it's hella useful."

I stared at my stick with new eyes, and nodded, putting it carefully back in my bag.

"I'm in that class, now," Chance said. "Renée is right. It's incredibly useful."

"Oh," I said, glancing at him. "Do you have a stick, er... a wand, too, Chance?"

He shuffled his feet. "Uh, no, not yet. You get one at the end of the class, in June. Right now we're just using the class wands to learn from." He looked at me and smiled.

"So," I said slowly, "if I have one now, and I haven't taken the class..." My voice trailed off.

"The class is important," said Renée. "Without training, wand wielding can be very dangerous." She gave me a pointed look. "In fact, the only reason he showed you how to get a wand was because you were in such dire straits. It was an emergency."

"Just be careful with it, Holly," said Chance.

I nodded. I was already aware.

The fireplace blaze was going well, and we sat around it, throwing twigs from the wood pile into it.

There was something mesmerizing about looking into a fire, I found it almost hypnotic.

I suddenly thought of something. "Chance, Renée, if we're now in the human world, and about to cross the bridge over to the island, when do we cross back into the Faerie world?"

Renée chuckled. "We already are in the Faerie world. Where do you think this cottage is?"

Chance took a deep breath. "Holly, we're in a place where the two worlds overlap. We can use the bridge because in that space, in this cottage and the land around us, and on most of the island itself, the two realms overlap."

"I don't understand," I said, feeling like an alien. Not growing up in the Faerie Realm, some things were just alien to me.

"In places were the two realms overlap, people can cross from one reality to the other, because they occupy the same space," Chance said. "So, for instance, this cottage is in the Faerie Realm, so a human wouldn't see it. Humans nearby will see an old abandoned building instead. And the bridge exists in the human realm, but we can walk across it because we can step from our realm into the human realm, with magic."

"Will the humans see us?" I asked.

"Yes," said Renée.

*Huh.*

We sat there, watching the crackling fire, and the storm just got worse.

*Thank goodness the cottage is made of stone.*

It was hours before the wind died down. Laura had dropped to her side and lay there, watching the flames.

Liesl and I lay face to face and whispered, discussing the wand magic class. "I have a confession to make," she whispered.

I grinned.

"I have my great-grandmother's wand," Liesl whispered so quietly, she was practically mouthing her words without making a sound.

Her eyebrows popped up and down.

"It's back home, in my room," she whispered. "In the old chest I showed you last time you were there."

"I remember that chest," I said slowly. "So, have you done any spells with it yet?"

Liesl shook her head. "Oh, no, no. I'm keeping it just

to use after next year's class. I just have it. It was bequeathed to me after great-grandmother passed away a few years ago. It's in a velvet case, locked." She bent her head closer to mine. "Sometimes, when I take it out of the wooden chest, I can feel it humming through the case." She nodded significantly. "It's really powerful."

"All wands are really powerful, after that long," Renée said dryly from a few feet away.

We glanced at her, wondering what she meant.

"Your great grandmother probably had the wand for hundreds of years. It soaked up a lot of magic in that time. That's why it glows," said Renée. "Your stick, as you call it, Holly, will do that same thing in a few hundred years. When you're old and wrinkled," she winked at me.

*Wands soak up magic?*

I turned to Chance, who was chatting on the side with Laura. "Hey," I whispered. "Can I ask you about something?"

"Sure," he said. "What's up?"

"So, Renée said that old wands soak up magic? Have you learned about this?" I asked.

He nodded. "It's not old wands, it's all wands. Maybe she meant, after a Fae Folk is old, their wand will have soaked up a lifetime of magic."

"Does this make them stronger?" I asked. The old

woodsman had told me my stick would channel the magic within me. Channel and focus it.

"Yes, in a sense," Chance said. "The wands get better at channeling the user's magic. They've soaked up magic through the years, but also, they've become very accustomed to that user, so they channel better. That's why borrowed wands don't work nearly as well. I think that's why they have us use class wands at first. It kinds of dampens the magic, so when we're learning, we can't do much damage. But also, it makes us try harder to get a spell right, which is always a good thing."

I thought of my flying class. "Tell me about it," I said.

He grinned and nodded.

"Hey, y'all: The storm is pretty much over, let's go," Laura was at the door, listening, her ear pressed against the old wood.

We gathered our stuff, getting ready to head out.

"Should we put out the fire?" I asked, looking at the crackling wood.

"Why don't you put it out with your wand, Holly?" Renée asked.

"All right," I said, withdrawing my stick from my bag. *How did this magic go again?*

I pointed my stick at the fire, and closed my eyes.

*Think. Think. Water? Yes! Water water water water water.*

A thin stream of water shot out from the end of my

stick and hit the burning wood, and the fire went out with a hiss.

The steam blew back from the fireplace and hit me full in the face, spraying me with a bit of crackled charcoal and droplets of water.

I lowered my stick, backed up, and wiped my eyes.

"Here," chuckled Chance, handing me a small towel from his bag. I took it and wiped my face.

Renée leaned closer to me. "Next time, put it out with magic, and there'll be a lot less mess."

*Huh?*

I lowered the towel. "What? I thought I did put it out with magic?"

"No, you put it out with water," Renée said. "It's possible to use the wand to focus your own magic and put out the fire out that way. What you did was use the wand to focus your magic and produce a stream of water."

"I don't understand," I said, in a small voice.

"Look," said Renée. "There's still a small bit going."

I glanced at the fireplace. The water I'd sprayed on it from my stick had put out most of the fire, and the whole room was filled with steam and smoke. It was slowly clearing, and I could see a small bright flame on the side I'd missed.

Renée brought forth her own wand. It was made of

light-colored wood, long and slim. "Rowan," she said at my questioning look. She extended the wand and whispered a spell. The flickering flame in the edge of the fireplace fire immediately went out.

"How did you do that?" I asked, intrigued.

"Instead of thinking *water*, think: *Fire go out*," she said, smiling. "Try it next time."

*That's amazing.*

I looked down at my stick. It looked like an ordinary stick you'd pick up off the forest ground.

"You'll learn more in class next year," Renée said. "But what you should be doing instead of trying to overpower the thing you're trying to magic, is speak to it. Don't try to destroy, try to change the essence."

"Don't worry, Holly, you're way ahead of the game. I'm just now learning this kind of magic," said Chance. "The only reason you're even this successful is because you have more natural magic than most."

I nodded, still looking thoughtfully at my stick.

Renée's rowan wand had been stripped of its bark, and the wood was polished. I glanced up at her. "Would it work better if I polished it?" I lifted my stick in the air.

She shook her head. "It shouldn't really matter. In fact, if you took the bark off and stained and polished the wood, it might inhibit the flow of magic it pulls from you. I'd let it stay natural, for now at least. Next year when you get to that class, you can ask the professor about it."

I nodded, giving my stick one last squeeze and then carefully tucking it back into my bag.

"Liesl, Holly, you still have your magical staffs?" Chance asked.

We nodded, yes, we had them tucked away.

I called to my wolf familiars: "Aspen, Tundra, you two go out of sight while we cross the bridge, I don't want the humans to notice you." Both wolves winked out and disappeared.

"Okay, let's head on out."

Chapter Fourteen
# Bridge to Skye

It was still early afternoon when we made our way, single-file, on the dirt path from the cottage down to the road. The hillside was thick with lush green grass growing in tufts and bulges on the moor.

The road was paved, and modern cars traveled along it. I glanced back the way we'd come and saw the cottage was no longer there.

"Come on, stay to the side of the road," said Renée, leading the way.

We walked nearly a mile, then came to the arching bridge that led to the island. It was completely modern, and had a wide pedestrian path that ran alongside the car lanes, on the right.

We walked up the curling ramp until we reached the top, and looked out across the water.

Chance glanced at everyone. "Ready?"

We started across. The bridge was long, and I wondered how far it was. As if reading my thoughts, Renée said, "It's less than a third of a mile, so we should be able to walk it in a few minutes."

We walked and were soon over the water. Cars and trucks sped past us, and the view was amazing. I had to remind myself to keep walking a few times, when the scenery had been so epic, I had stopped to gawk without realizing it.

Quite quickly, we were approaching land again.

"Is this the end?" I asked.

"No, we're not even halfway across," said Chance. "This is just Eilean Bàn, the little island halfway across."

*Ahh.*

On the island were a few crofter's cottages and a stout white lighthouse right next to the bridge that was so cute I wished we could stop and visit.

I stared at it longingly as we passed, my steps slowing as I gazed into the top narrow window.

*What was that?*

I could have sworn I'd seen a shadow flit across the window. A shadow in the shape of a... I wasn't sure. But it wasn't human. It wasn't a dog, either, or a cat, or even a monkey.

Liesl stopped, looking at the lighthouse with me. "What do you see?" She asked.

"I don't know," I said slowly. I peered at the window intensely, but nothing else appeared.

*Maybe I imagined it.*

"Renée? Chance?" I called out. "Are there any magical beasts on this little island?"

Renée smiled and said nothing.

"There are magical beasts everywhere in the Faerie Realm, Holly," said Chance. "And this land overlaps the Faerie Realm, so you may see the lighthouse the humans built, but you may see a magical beast of some sort from our realm."

I wondered if the beast had crossed over into the human world, and asked Chance.

"Not normally, no," he said. "But many times, especially in older buildings, there will be a corresponding build in the Faerie Realm in the same spot, so that as we look, it appears that something from the Faerie Realm is in a human building, when it's actually not.

I watched the lighthouse as we walked past, intrigued. I wondered what building was there in the Faerie Realm that corresponded with the lighthouse.

*Might be another lighthouse.*

I smiled as I walked.

We crossed the small island of Eilean Bàn, and the bridge took us over the water again. I could see the larger island ahead of us, a few hundred feet away. We appeared to be over halfway there.

The sky was still stormy grey, with clouds rushing across the expanse. It looked like they were late for some appointment and were hurrying to make it on time.

I felt a few raindrops on my face.

A couple walked toward us from opposite direction, returning from visiting the Isle of Skye, our destination. They opened umbrellas as they passed us, their heads down against the rising breeze.

"Think we're going to get soaked?" Chance asked, glancing back at me from a few steps ahead.

Before I could answer, a wave of rain whooshed against us so hard it knocked Liesl against me.

The rain was so ferocious it was like a solid wall of grey, I couldn't see through it at all.

Liesl and I had been straggling at the tail end of the group, and Chance, Laura and Renée disappeared behind a wall of rain coming down so hard it was like a solid curtain.

It was so loud my ears roared.

I grabbed Liesl's coat, holding on to her, as the wind

lashed against me and tried to blow me over the walkway railing.

Liesl gasped, and grabbed the metal poles to hold on.

I looked back, trying to see what had become of the couple who had just passed us, but they were gone, whether over the railing into the sea, or down the path to Eilean Bàn, there was no way to tell.

"Holly!" Liesl screamed right against my face. "Hold on!"

The roar of the storm was so loud and had come upon us so fast, that even though she screamed an inch from my nose, I could barely hear her.

I let go one of my hands that had grabbed Liesl's coat, and reached and hooked it around the metal pole of the bridge. When it was secure around the cold metal, I moved the other hand to the pole railing. Liesl held on next to me.

We crouched down low, trying to stay steady. It was as if the wind was trying to grab us and throw us over the railing and into the sea.

I could see the water from my position, through the metal poles of the railing, and it was not only stormed-tossed, it looked churned-up.

"Hold on," Liesl mouthed.

There was no sign of Chance, nor of Laura or Renée. They were just... gone.

I had no time to mourn, I had no time to even think. I just held on to the railing for dear life.

The wind and storm howled, and lashed at us.

We were beyond soaked.

I felt my hands growing numb from the cold.

The cold of the pole.

I looked down.

The pole was ice cold, so cold the rain was starting to freeze onto it.

Amid the storm and frantic rain, I wondered about that pole.

*It shouldn't be freezing.*

The weather had been chilly, but not freezing. We'd worn medium-thick jackets, and I had a knit cap on my head that I'd grabbed and stuffed into my bag when the wind had started up.

I stared at the pole.

Then the sound of the storm subtlety changed, and a deep low moaning howl started up in the background.

Liesl grabbed me, pulling my head close to hers.

"We... we need to get off this bridge," she said. I could barely hear her.

The rain lashed at us from all directions as the wind moaned louder.

I saw Liesl's mouth form the words, *"Oh, no..."*

The wind became like a tornado, pulling us from our

crouch and dragging our grip on the metal railing, tearing our hands from the pole.

Liesl lunged and grabbed me around the waist, and I hooked my arms around her as well.

The wind lifted us up, slowly, our hair whipping around our us as we struggled to keep our heads tucked into each other's shoulder.

We were lifted bodily, still clutching each other, and drawn over the railing, as if the wind, like a living thing, wanted to take us into the sea.

Chapter Fifteen

# Storm Hag

We held on to each other for dear life, as the wind pulled us down into the water. I felt my legs buckle under me as I fell onto the rocks, landing in waist-deep water.

We fell sideways, into the bay, and I jerked up, spitting seawater out. We had landed just at the edge of the land.

*The wind must've pulled us forward as well as sideways.*

Liesl and I kept a hold of each other as we struggled to stand, but the waves lashed out at us at every attempt, throwing us back down.

After a few tries, we stayed down, half-kneeling in the

sea, holding on to each other, trying to keep our heads above the water. I knew the bridge must be above us somewhere, but when I glanced up, all I could see was grey rain and swirling clouds.

Wait.

Those weren't swirling clouds.

A dark figure descended next to us, cackling.

Liesl looked stricken, and held on to me for dear life.

The figure was out of a nightmare. She was dressed in deep blues, and black tatters, and dead fish. The rotting fish were strung about her haphazardly, as if for decoration.

She stank.

Her face was mottled pale white and moss green, her skin was wrinkled so bad it was falling from her face, and her eyes were white orbs dripping with green wetness.

She landed next to us on a large rock outcropping.

"O seall na lorg mi san stoirm agam," her voice rang out, sounding like a screeching wind.

"Oh, no no no no," murmured Liesl, her mouth right next to my ear. "Holly, we have to..."

"Ithidh mi gu math a-nochd," the voice rang out, then the thing began to cackle again.

"Holly, we need to jump into the sea, we have to try and get under," Liesl said hurriedly. She grabbed me bodily and leaned toward the deeper water, and took a deep breath.

*Why? Okay.*

I was in such shock and so frightened and disgusted by the creature I couldn't think straight. I took my own deep breath of air, and Liesl and I fell into the water, diving sideways head first.

I heard the creature's scream of anger as she saw her prey trying to get away.

Something clutched at my foot as I fell into the water, but I kicked out and dislodged its grip.

Liesl swam down as fast as she could, and I followed her.

I kept one fist's tight hold on the edge of her coat. I did not want to get separated from my best friend while under attack from this nightmare creature.

We swam for several minutes, down under about ten feet of water. I could see the surface of the sea, and a swirling dark figure passing overhead, back and forth, searching.

Just when I thought my lungs would burst, Liesl led us upward.

Our heads broke the surface, we took another big lungful of air and dipped back down. We were only in the air for a few seconds, and I didn't see the creature, but as I swam back down with Liesl, we could see the dark shadow flit across the surface where we'd just left, and I imagined the thing was angry.

We swam farther this time, and Liesl led me down lower.

We came up for air one more time, dipping back down quickly, and then Liesl led us directly down. We hovered a minute under the water, holding steady.

Liesl turned her face downward toward the bottom and made four chuffing noises. They came out as large bubbles, and I could hear a faint "chorrrr-chorrrr-chorrrr-chorrrr" come from her.

A screech sounded overhead, and I glanced up, and saw the flitting shadow of the creature had quickened its pace, and was zigzagging frantically over the water.

*Searching for us.*

Liesl held me still, and waited.

A minute later, a grey torpedo-shaped body rapidly approached, and bumped up against us.

It was a bottle-nosed dolphin!

Several more joined the first. Then several more. We were soon in the midst of a school of at least fifteen dolphins!

Liesl looked into the face of the first one, not blinking.

It seemed to understand her, because she turned to me and gestured that I should grab one and hold on tight.

She wrapped her hand onto the dorsal fin of the first

dolphin, and the whole pod turned and swam together, pulling Liesl and me with them.

We breached the surface of the water and rapidly dipped back down a few seconds later. The dolphin pulled us around and to the opposite side of the bridge, where the Isle of Skye had a beach. We were practically flung up onto the sand.

The crazed, mad, stinking creature rushed at us from the opposite side of the bridge, screeching the whole way, and the dolphins swam to meet her, chattering and scolding the whole way.

One dolphin jumped out of the water and hit the creature directly in the chest, bouncing it backward. It flew far, screeching in anger the entire way.

Liesl grabbed my sleeve. "Run," she said in a low voice.

We ran up the beach and onto some scrubby grass, our steps soaked and plodding. My bag banged against my hip as I loped, and my shoes made squelching sounds.

We ran up a slope until we were far from the water, then turned and looked down on the scene before us.

The pod of dolphins was herding the creature back past the bridge and away from us.

I coughed, and sea water came out of my nose.

"What...?" I coughed again.

Liesl pounded me on the back.

I sputtered and coughed a few times and spat. Finally,

I could talk again.

"What the heck was that?" I murmured.

"Storm hag," answered Liesl.

*What?*

"Wait," I said. "We studied those last year, didn't we?"
Liesl nodded.

"I didn't recognize it at all," I said. "The picture in the
book looked like a spirit floating in the air, not a stinking
monster wearing rotting fish."

Liesl shrugged. "Next time you visit my house, I'll
show you the book of monster pictures my uncle put
together years ago. Sometimes storm hags look like this.
In fact, I think the pictures they showed in class were
kind of romanticized."

"I guess so," I answered dryly. Well, as dryly as I could
in the half-drowned state I was in.

I reached down and wrung out the corner of my coat,
and water poured onto the grass.

"Where did the others go?" I asked. "Did the storm
hag get them?"

"I doubt that. Renée can handle herself just fine. Plus
Chance," Liesl said.

"But not Laura," I said, suddenly, looking into Liesl's
eyes. *Oh, no.*

"Okay," she nodded. "Maybe we should look for
them."

We walked toward the part of the island that the bridge let out on, calling our friends.

"Laura! Renée!" I called, long and loud. "Chaaa----ance!"

A few minutes later we spotted them, high up on a hill above the road, near the bridge. Renée waved at us, and they began hiking down to meet us.

After a few minutes, Chance ran the last few yards and grabbed me in a bear hug. "Are you okay?" He asked, breathless.

"I'm okay, thanks to Liesl," I said. My teeth were beginning to chatter.

"We need to get you inside," he said. "Come on, we found another cottage." He grabbed my hand, turned and grabbed Liesl's hand, and began taking wide, sweeping steps back up the hill.

A half-hour later, we were all in another stone cottage, just on the lee side of the hill.

Renée had pulled several blankets out of her bag of holding, and Liesl and I were wrapped on them, in front of a blazing fire, with our wet clothes hung nearby, already beginning to steam.

"Laura," I asked through my chattering teeth, "You okay?" I rested my hands in my wolves' fur; they lay on either side of me, trying to help warm me up.

The Elfen girl grinned over the rim of a mug Chance

had just handed her. Her hands were wrapped around the warm ceramic, the hot cocoa inside steaming up around her face, but she lifted one hand long enough to give me a high five.

"We did fine," Chance was saying. "The wind pushed us forward, and we ran off the end of the walkway."

"I can't believe a storm hag tried to get you," Renée said, shaking her head. "Thank God you knew what to do, Liesl."

Liesl nodded from her chair, her blanket wrapped tightly around her, as Chance handed her a mug of hot cocoa. "Of course, I knew what to do, every kid's read that story," she said.

"What story?" I asked.

Liesl rolled her eyes and gestured at me. "This is why I drink... cocoa."

I laughed.

"Holly, I'm so sorry you had to go through that," said Renée, "but I'm so glad Liesl was with you."

"Can you imagine what would've happened if Holly had been alone?" asked Chance, a stricken look on his face.

"What would have happened?" I asked.

Laura shuddered. "Holly, even I've heard that story. Everyone knows that fable."

"What fable?" I asked.

"Don't tell her," murmured Liesl between sips of hot cocoa. "Do not tell her."

Laura nodded in agreement. "Nobody."

"Okay, *now* you've got to tell me," I said.

Chapter Sixteen
# Little Blue

"I really don't think we do," said Chance grinning.

"Plus, Holly, do you really want to know what might have happened?" asked Renée.

"Yes, yes I do," I answered. "For my general Faerie education. For what I missed not growing up in the Faerie Realm. IN CASE IT EVER HAPPENS AGAIN," I finished loudly.

"We've got a long way to go to find The Oak King," said Chance.

"And an even longer way back," said Laura.

"Hey...," I said.

"We're going to find him, aren't we?" asked Liesl. "I

mean, I don't really want to go back without him. Imagine facing The Holly King and having to tell him..."

"EXCUSE ME," I said.

Everyone fell silent and looked at me.

"I know what you're doing," I said. "You're trying to change the subject so you don't have to tell me what almost happened."

"Holly, it's just a child's fable," Liesl said quietly.

"A fable that nearly came true," Laura mumbled, hiding her smile behind her hand.

"Tell me, or I swear I'll die of curiosity," I pouted.

"No, you won't," said Chance.

I huffed.

"Okay, okay," said Laura. "I'll tell you."

"Oh, my God," Renée snickered.

"Okay," said Liesl. "But just realize, you were never in any danger."

"How is that?" Laura asked. "Didn't you say the storm hag was talking to you? Right next to you?"

"So?" I said.

"So, in the story, that's usually the point of no return," said Laura. "If she gets that close to you, it's too late."

"What?" I said, feeling a little scared. "Why?"

"Okay," said Laura. "I'll just tell you the story. Okay?"

I nodded.

"It's a story told to little kids. Kind of to warn them

not to wander off near the sea during a storm," Laura said. "You're supposed to be okay when you've got a group of at least three, so it's weird this happened to you."

"Mmmm," said Renée. "We got separated from them, right before. Remember?"

"Oh, right," said Laura.

"Please continue," I said.

"Okay." Laura took a deep breath. "There was once a little girl with sea-green hair, who always wore a deep-blue coat. She lived with her mother next to the sea, in a cottage made of redwood. Her grandmother lived in a houseboat down at the water's edge, past a bridge made of glass, along the shoreline about two miles away."

"My mother always told it so the houseboat was three miles away," said Liesl.

"Shhh. It doesn't matter how far the houseboat was," said Renée, who had become engrossed with the story being told.

Laura continued. "Little Blue used to go down to the water's edge early every morning to help bring in the nets the fishermen had returned with the night before. She would keep one fish back each day, and after delivering a basket of fish to her mother, she would set off along the shoreline to bring a basket of fish to her grandmother, who was old and feeble. Along the way, Little Blue would meet her friend, Little Grey.

"Little Grey was a bottle-nosed dolphin who lived with his family in the sea nearby. And each day he would come, when Little Blue called him, and they would play together for some minutes, and Little Blue would, at the end, throw Little Grey the fish she had held back just for that purpose.

"Little Blue would call her dolphin friend with a low, chuffing noises, slapping the water with the palm of her hand and calling out to the sea.

"One day, the sky was stormy, and Little Blue's mother cautioned her, and told her not to go out that day. 'Little Blue, Little Blue, keep inside during strong weather by the sea, or the storm hag will grab you with the wind, and eat you up!' But Little Blue told her mother that grandmother would be counting on her basket of fish, and if the fishermen were not afraid, why should she be? So she put on her heavy, deep-blue coat, and set out toward the seashore.

"Wind blasted her face, making Little Blue's hair fly this way and that. But the girl pushed on, through the wind, down to the shore. She picked up the basket of fish for her mother, and began to walk back up to the cottage.

" 'Little Blue, be careful. Do not make the long walk to Grandmother's houseboat,' Little Blue's mother said, 'The storm is getting worse, the danger is closer.'

" 'Oh, mother, I will be just fine. Remember, if I am in need, Little Grey will surely help me,' replied Little Blue as she went out the door.

"The wind buffeted Little Blue as she grabbed up the second basket of fish, and the extra fish held back, she stuffed in her pocket. She walked along the beach, trying to hold her steps in a straight line as she went. After a while the storm got so bad, and the wind so strong, that it was as if the wind was attacking Little Blue. She tried to stay strong, but the rain buffeted her from all sides.

"After another few steps, the wind grabbed her second basket of fish, which was for her grandmother, and threw it into the sky. It was gone in an instant. Little Blue lay flat on the ground, trying not to let the wind carry her into the sky as it had the basket of grandmother's fish.

"After a few moments, Little Blue heard a howling sound, which turned into a cackling, which turned into a loud thump as something fell from the sky and landed on the ground nearby. Little Blue decided to look, to see if the basket of fish had been put back on the ground by the northern wind. But it wasn't the fish. It was a figure so dark and horrible that Little Blue hid her eyes again.

"It was the storm hag. It was coming to get Little Blue. It was coming to eat Little Blue. She now remembered her mother's cautions, and how she wished she had heeded her mother's warnings! The storm hag began to talk to Little Blue in the old language.

" 'Oh, look what I found in my storm!' the storm hag said, cackling in pleasure. 'I will eat well tonight!' said the storm hag. And Little Blue was so frightened she began to tremble. Little Blue tried to crawl away, but the wind buffeted against her and blew her this way and that. The wind blew Little Blue until her hands and arms were in the water. The storm hag continued to cackle and moved closer to Little Blue. Little Blue shook with fear, and her hands moved so much they slapped the water.

"Suddenly Little Blue had an idea, an idea which became her only hope. She crawled an inch more into the water, and put her face out and pointed her mouth out over the sea, and called. Little Blue called for Little Grey, to come help her. To come save her.

"Presently, the little bottle-nosed dolphin came and saw how Little Blue was cowed by the storm hag, who was about to eat Little Grey's friend. The dolphin raced away and called to her family, and the entire pod of dolphins raced to help Little Blue.

"By the time they returned to the beach, the storm hag was nearly upon the little girl. The creature was trying to lower herself down on top of Little Blue, to eat her up as she cowered on the sand and shook with fear.

"Little Grey and the other dolphins began attacking the storm hag, flinging themselves against her, then jumping back into the sea. Dolphins, as we know, can deliver a killing blow with their beaks. The storm hag was pushed back, away from Little Blue, and the dolphins pushed her all the way back to the deep sea, where she lives, hovering over the water in the form of a dark mist."

Laura sat back, pleased with herself.

I stared, open-mouthed.

"Tell her why the storm hag was trying to eat her by sitting on her," said Renée. "Go on, tell her!"

"I'd rather not," said Laura primly.

"I... think I can guess, thanks," I dryly, mildly grossed out.

Renée chuckled.

"Wait," I said. "Are you telling me that story was true?"

"As true as the human's story of Little Red Riding Hood, Holly," said Chance. "Maybe more true."

I felt thoroughly icked out, and more than a little freaked, as if I'd barely avoided being in a train wreck.

"So, storm hags are a real thing," I said.

"You saw her with your own eyes," said Renée.

"We both did," said Liesl.

"Storm hags," I said, thoughtfully. "So, they're kind

of... one of the monsters from the Faerie Realms? Like the Blackberry Wytch from last year?"

Laura nodded.

"I'm starting to see a pattern," I said. "Are all the evil creatures of the Faerie Realm in the form of old women?"

"Not by a long shot," said Liesl. "Wait till you meet a trow or a hobgoblin. Or an imp. Those are mostly male. Don't ask me why, I do not know." She winked.

"Okay, I'm going to heat up some stew, cook gave me so much it's incredible," Chance said, grasping his bag of holding and pulling out a small cauldron. He set the round black pot over the fire, hooking it on the metal arm fixed into the side of the stone, and swinging it out over the flame.

I had finally warmed up while Laura had told the fable. Liesl and I soon dressed back into our clothes, behind a blanket hung for privacy, and within the hour we were all settled with bowls of the thick beef stew Chance had heated for us.

It was delicious.

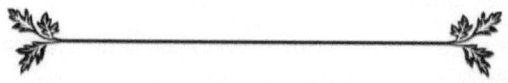

Chapter Seventeen

# The Wild Magic

By dawn the next morning, Liesl and I were completely recovered from our wet, cold, freaked-out-of-our-minds-scared adventure from the day before.

"I will forever have just a small bit of trepidation for the Skye Bridge," I confessed to Liesl as I followed her out the cottage door.

She nodded, giving me a *ohhh yeah, me too* look.

"Thank God for these cottages the Fae Folk Council has maintained all over this area," Chance was saying. "It would have been a cold, wet night without it."

"Well, I don't know about you, but I've got a canvas tent in my bag. A big one," Laura winked.

Chance smiled. "Now that's going to come in handy, I can feel it."

We walked on, up and down several gentle hills, crossing the moors. It was cold and drizzling, but I think I will forever not be the least bit bothered by gentle rain and mist, having just been through stinging rain and winds that tried to blow me into the sea.

"That storm, on the bridge yesterday," I asked. "That was not normal, right? That was... how do I put it ...?"

"Magical?" asked Renée.

"Yes, that," I said, touching my forefinger to my nose. "Magical. Right?"

"That storm was a product of the storm hag, Holly," said Chance. "We won't get a storm like that now that we're moving away from the sea."

"Well, that's good, I guess." I was thoughtful as I walked. "So tell us about the place we're hiking to, Chance."

"Well, we've got to go over this moorland, and through a thick, overgrown forest," he said. "And we'll be deep in the Faerie Realm. We're hiking through the crossed-over realms right now. Do you see what I mean?"

I looked over to the side as I hiked. This morning, far off in the distance, as I stood outside the cottage where we'd spent the night, I could see the bridge and the town on Eilean Bàn. And the lighthouse. Farther east, I could see the city buildings on the Scottish mainland.

*That's the human world.*

Turning now, looking forward and to my sides, toward the rocky outcroppings that Aspen and Tundra ran over, chasing a squirrel, I could see a sparkle of light, in the air, right above the ground. I had seen this before, on the grounds of Titania Academy, and in the forest surrounding the school. It was the magic of the land itself.

I looked closer at my familiars. Each of them chased a squirrel, and they were about two feet apart.

*Those were squirrels, right?*

Suddenly, one of the squirrels being chased stopped and turned to face the wolf. I think it was Tundra. It was hard to tell at this distance. But I could clearly see the squirrel, who suddenly raised itself up to its full height. It was about a foot tall.

*That's no squirrel.*

We had all stopped to watch.

"That's a brownie," I murmured. "Isn't it?"

"Mm hmm," said Liesl.

"Sure is," Laura chuckled.

*Uh oh.*

"Don't brownies... um... like to pelt people... um... with...," I mumbled, almost to myself.

"Yep," said Liesl.

The second "squirrel" turned to fight.

Both wolves stopped, their ear forward, their tails up.

There was a pause of maybe two heartbeats.

Then, the brownies began throwing pebbles at the wolves, fast. The first little rock hit Tundra square on the nose with a *zing*. Tundra yelped and turned to run.

Soon, both brownies were chasing the wolf that had just been chasing them, and they threw rocks at them as the wolves ran.

I smiled.

*Serves them right.*

We continued hiking across the moors.

The area had a stark beauty unique to Scotland.

We passed a huge cairn, with moss growing over the heavy stones. It looked like it had been there for thousands of years.

"Did humans make that?" I asked as we passed.

Renée shrugged. "Probably not." She glanced over at the twenty-foot structure. "Look at the base."

I looked closer and saw the bottom stones, half-buried in the soil, were glowing. I thought back to my first-year lessons.

Magic glowed. Magic sparkled. Magic usually made some kind of light, and by its very nature, could never be without some kind of mark.

The cairn was magical.

"So, probably not," I said as we hiked on.

"Probably not," Renée grinned.

"Chance, are you following one of the Old Ways?" asked Laura. "I've heard so much about them on these islands in the west."

"Yes," Chance answered. "Can you see the path?"

"No," Laura said. "Wait. Does it...? wait." She studied the ground we walked on. "No, I guess not."

Chance muttered a spell. Laura gasped. The grass of the moor lit up briefly, and the grass looked as though a thousand fireflies glowed from within its blades. It was gone in a few seconds.

I smiled as I walked. I loved magic. The more I was exposed to the different types of magic, the new places and the surprises, the more I loved it.

Even my experience with the storm hag had been exciting. I mean, she was scary and smelled like rotting fish, but being rescued by dolphins, barely getting away, and being saved by Liesl, it was the most excitement I'd had in a long while.

"Look," Chance whispered, pointing.

The sun was setting early, as it did in these winter months. Across the moors, down the softly sloping hill, about a mile off, was a forest. That was where Chance had been pointing.

Even this far away, I could see a few magical creatures

flitting in and out of the trees, and the trees themselves looked ancient and mystical.

"Race you," said Chance as he took off running.

"AH!" I cried out, laughing and running after him.

Liesl and Laura and Renée ran after us as we rushed forward to the trees.

I heard Tundra and Aspen each give a joyous bark and run after me.

As we entered the forest it grew darker and quiet. The trees grew close together, and there was a clear path through the deep wild wood.

The forest was full of life and sound. Animals called to each other across the treetops, and birds flitted here and there, curious about us.

As soon as we'd hiked fifty feet into the wood, the path turned downward, and the sides of the path ran high on either side of us, as if water had carved a path through the ground.

*Or animals.*

The light filtering through the trees turned blue and green as it traveled through the leaves and moss, making the most gorgeous colors appear at ground level.

The deeper into the wood we walked, the lower the slope went, until the sides of the pathway rose fifteen feet above us on either side.

As we turned a corner, we came upon a huge tree root

that had grown across the path, and it reached from the high side on the left, across to the high side on the right. It was gnarled and curled and covered with moss and fireflies. The effect was that of a canopy of wood above us as we walked underneath it.

As we came out the other side, we saw in the thick side of the root, a door.

My breath caught as I peered at the six-inch-high wooden door, and I saw that there was a small, maybe one-inch-square, stained glass window set into the wood at the top. It was blue and green and gold, and we could see a light glowing behind it.

I had the deepest desire to be small enough and knock on that door, and be invited in for supper.

Chance came to stand next to me. He grunted, "Mm hm, mm hm. Leprechauns," he murmured.

*Leprechauns?*

I leaned closer, trying to peer through the stained-glass window in the door, trying to see inside.

"I wouldn't do that if I were you," said Chance.

I glanced at him over my shoulder. "But... it's so cute!"

He shook his head and walked on.

I looked at Renée, and she lifted her eyebrows in an *uh oh* expression.

"Leave them be, Holly," Liesl whispered. "Come on, we've got a forest to cross and a king to rescue."

I nodded, and, with one more forlorn look back at the Leprechaun's door, I followed my friends.

The forest lights moved here and there, and most of them were fireflies.

But not all.

A few of the lights bouncing up and down under the trees were...

"Pixies," said Laura. "Very, very small pixies, but pixies nevertheless."

We walked on and came upon a massive tree that had been hollowed out, somehow.

"Struck by lightning," said Renée. "Fire burned out the inside. The tree is still alive."

The hollow of the tree was large enough to stand upright in.

Liesl and I took turns standing there and saying, "Abracadabra!"

The inside of the tree was home to dozens of fireflies, and a family of very tiny sprites.

"These are so much smaller than Professor Ó Baoghill," I murmured, reaching my finger out and tried to touch the nearest one.

"Holly, what would you do if a giant were to try to touch you with its giant finger?" Chance asked quietly.

I withdrew my finger just in time. The sprite I had been reaching for had just extended a long spear with a very sharp point.

I backed up.

Chapter Eighteen

# The Wild Apple Girl

We made camp for the night in a clearing we'd come across just as the last light of the sun was leaving the land. The glade was bright green with grasses and mushrooms, and a small stream trickled nearby.

"Okay, Laura," said Chance. "Can I help you set up that tent?"

"You sure can," she replied, digging in her bag of holding. "If I can only find it." Her whole arm disappeared into the bag, and she had a look of concentration on her face as she searched, her shoulder moving as her arm ruffled through the different contents of her magical pack. "Ah, found it!" She pulled her arm out of the bag, and as her hand appeared, it was triumphantly grasping a large bit of canvas, wrapped up haphazardly.

She tossed it on the ground and sat next to it, and was soon hard at work on the knots that tied it closed.

Ten minutes later, Laura stood again and flipped the canvas open. Chance grabbed an edge, and together they spread the large rectangle flat on the ground.

"Now," Laura said, leaning over and touching the top rivet, "if I can just reach..." Her finger tapped the button, and she retreated swiftly, falling back on her heels.

The tent began to rise slowly. By the time two minutes has passed, it was fully assembled, standing at least ten feet high.

*Amazing.*

Laura looked pleased at her contribution.

Liesl and I had gathered fallen wood in the forest around camp; we'd brought two large armfuls to an area Renée had cleared and ringed with rocks she'd found near the stream. We now set to work building a fire.

I wanted to try out my stick again, and pulled it out of my sack, but as I extended it toward the pyramid of branches, I hesitated.

Renée sat back on her heels, offering encouragement. "Okay, take a deep breath. That's it. Now relax. Point it at the wood. That's right."

My hand shook. *What if I set the forest on fire?*

"You're doing fine, but you're tense," said Renée. "You're liable to set the forest on fire if you're tense."

*Great.*

I closed my eyes and took a few deep breaths, trying to relax. Then, opening my eyes, I stared at the stacked wood waiting to be lit.

"Now, look at the wood as if the fire is already there," Renée said. "Now think, *fire: start.*"

I took a last deep breath and said in my mind, *FIRE: START.*

Flame shot out of the end of my stick, reaching ten feet out, and lit a bush on fire across the clearing.

"AH!" I exclaimed.

Chance swiftly had the bush fire out.

"Okay, that's good, that's good. That's a good first try," said Renée patiently. "Now, this time, we're going to look at the stacked logs, not at the end of your stick, okay? And dial it down, way down. Whisper it in your head if you have to. Now try again."

I looked at the stacked wood waiting to be lit. I forced my eyes to avoid the sight of my stick, which for some reason I naturally wanted to look at when I was doing wand magic.

*Look at the wood. Look at the wood.*

I thought in my mind, very quietly: *fire: start for me.*

A flame appeared in the middle of the stacked wood, and the wood at the base of the flame glowed red, as if it had been burning for a while.

"That's excellent," Renée said. "Really nice, actually. Good job, Holly."

I grinned.

We sat around the little campfire that I had lit, and ate and talked about different things well into the night.

After I yawned three times in short succession, I headed into the tent. Liesl and Laura were not far behind. We left Renée and Chance talking by the fire, and as I fell asleep, I wished for dreams to foretell the future.

Despite my wish, I passed a dreamless night, and woke up refreshed when Liesl nudged me.

"Holly," she whispered. "There's a girl lying in the grass nearby."

I opened my eyes, now wide awake. "A what?" I sat up.

"A girl," Liesl repeated. "And she's *green*."

I looked around the tent. Chance had fallen asleep next to me, and was snoring softly.

"Is it morning yet?" I whispered.

Liesl nodded.

The tent was so well sealed that outside light and noise couldn't get in, I'd found out last night. I hadn't been able to see the fire through the canvas, or hear Renée and Chance's voices.

"A green girl, you say?" I looked at my friend with a quizzical expression.

She nodded again.

*Okay, well, then...*

I nudged Chance's arm.

"Wake up, sleepyhead," I said in a soft voice. "Weird things are happening again."

"Msnbsyeappm...," Chance mumbled in his sleep.

I nudged him again, harder.

Nothing.

I bent to his ear and blew.

Nothing.

I swung my leg over and knocked it against his sock-clad foot.

Nothing.

I bent to his ear and said in a clear voice. "Chance, The Holly King is here."

His eyes popped open. He sat up, looking around, his

eyes bewildered.

Liesl and I waited.

He looked all around and then turned to look at me. "I'm awake. What's going on?"

"There's a girl asleep in the grass next to camp," Liesl said. "And she's green."

Chance blinked.

Renée was already pulling on her shoes. "I'll go look."

That spurred Chance to hurry. He grabbed his shoes and tried to put them on so fast he got the left shoe onto his right foot and had to start over again.

*I think there's some kind of rivalry going on here.*

We all finally emerged out of the tent and into the morning mist.

The fire was cold and black.

The air was brisk and moist.

The birds had started chirping to each other.

And there was indeed a girl, asleep in the grass, beside camp.

We all stood in a half-circle, staring down at her. None of us wanted to wake her up.

She looked to be in her teens, and was clothed in leaves and grass and moss, which seemed to cling to her skin as if it were part of the girl herself. Tufts of wild grass grew out of her shoulders and elbows and knees, and her skin looked like it was a soft, smooth kind of bark, like the bark of a fruit tree. Instead of hair, small branches and leaves grew out of the top of her head.

"What should we do?" whispered Laura. "Should we wake her?"

"I don't want to wake her, do you?"

"She looks so content asleep."

"What if she has to sleep?"

"Well, she wasn't here last night. Maybe she wants to meet us?"

"Why would she want to meet us?"

"Maybe she likes Fae Folk? You don't know."

"Well, someone should wake her."

Chance nudged the toe of his sneaker against the girl's leg, which, come to think of it, looked like a young tree trunk.

"Hey, hey, pssttt," whispered Renée.

The girl opened her eyes.

My eyebrows went up.

Where my eyes were white, hers were a light green. And the irises were tan.

*Weird.*

"Oh, hello," she yawned and sat up. "Good morning."

"Good morning," I said. *It pays to be courteous.* "Did you sleep well?"

"Oh, marvelously," She stretched her tree bark-covered arms high, yawning again.

I blinked.

When she stretched I saw that she had what looked like vines or roots or branches or something, growing up and down her torso.

*This girl is intriguing.*

She got to her feet. She was about four feet tall, and Liesl was absolutely right: she was green, everywhere. Even her toes, which I hadn't been able to see when she'd been lying down, because she'd tucked them into the grasses.

She bowed. "The forest is all a-twitter about your presence," she said. "Everyone is excited and guessing why you are here."

She ducked her head and giggled.

*What's so funny?*

"Uh, hello. We're here on a royal quest from The Holly King. This is Renée, Laura, Liesl, Holly, and I'm Chance," he stuck his hand out in greeting. "Pleased to meet you."

The green tree girl made a deep curtsy, spreading her leaf skirt as she bowed.

"I am The Wild Apple Girl, and I greet you," she said, smiling. "A royal quest from The Holly King, you say? That sounds magnificent!" She skipped around the grass and came to a halt before us again.

"I have a gift for you, then." She turned and skipped to a nearby tree. It was a large oak tree, gnarled and old.

The Wild Apple Girl flitted to the top and skipped away through the trees and was gone.

I blinked.

"Okayyyy," I said. "Guess she's departed, so..."

"She's back," said Liesl, pointing.

The Wild Apple Girl reappeared, smiling and with a small woven burlap bag in her hand. "Here," she handed the little bag to us, "These are seeds, for you to take back home when you return."

Renée took the bag and looked inside. "Oh, these are nice, thanks," she smiled.

The Wild Apple Girl curtsied again. "They are apple seeds. Plant them in a place that will get snow in winter."

"Okay," Renée said.

"It was nice to see you. Goodbye now." And The Wild Apple Girl was gone.

I stared at the bush leaves that still moved from her passage.

*Weird.*

"All righty," said Chance. "Let's eat and pack and be on our way. Who wants tea?"

Renée walked back to the campfire, looking into the bag The Wild Apple Girl had given her.

"You okay?" I asked her.

She nodded, but seemed in a daze.

"You sure you're okay?" I asked again.

Renée took a deep breath. "Yeah, that was just...weird. I've never met a Wild Apple Girl. I've heard of them, they're said to be very rare, lost to legend, really. I'm just wondering why she appeared to us..." Her voice trailed off.

"Well, when we get back, we can ask Professor Farryn about the seeds, maybe they're magical in some way," I said.

"Oh, I'm sure they are," said Renée. "I wish I knew how, though." she looked in the little canvas bag again, almost as if she was willing the seeds to reveal their secrets to her.

Chapter Nineteen
# Ancient Seer

As we packed up the camp and headed out, we passed the tree through which The Wild Apple Girl had disappeared. She was there again, high up in the branches, nearly indiscernible from the tree's natural foliage. We almost didn't see her except that, as we passed, she sang softly to us.

The Wild Apple Girl's song was ethereal and ghostly, but lovely. She sang softly of the wild beauty of the forest, the dangerous entanglements of intruders, and the fleeting fragility of life.

It was almost as if she was cautioning us.

We stayed listening, all of us stopped on the trail and

ringing the tree, for the few minutes it took for her to finish.

When the last note fell, she vanished. Try as I might, I could not see where she had gone. The tree looked gnarled and full of curling branches and brambles, but The Wild Apple Girl was gone.

None of us said a word, we just sighed in loss and headed back down the trail, pushing forward in our quest.

After a few hours of hiking, the forest hadn't changed much. The path took us higher, though, and we were now able to look out at the trees on either side of us.

"Uh oh," Chance said from the head of the line. We all stopped to see what had caught his attention.

A massive boulder, overgrown with ivy, was half-buried in the forest on the left side of our path.

The path dipped down and around the huge thing, and trees grew over and around it. Farther on, we could see a massive tree that had fallen across the path, stretching over the dip the trail took around the boulder.

Blue-green moss grew across the fallen tree, and tendrils of ivy covered everything, almost like a giant leafy cobweb. Mushrooms of every size, shape, and color grew across the ground in this area of the forest, covering almost everything that was not on the path. Some of the mushrooms practically glowed with an ethereal light of their own.

"Do you want to go around?" Renée whispered.

But Chance shook his head, then muttered a magical charm, waving his hand over the ground.

Our path was illuminated with a ghostly flicker, and it led directly along the side of the boulder.

"There's probably spiders in that ivy," I said. "And four out of the five of us have long hair. There's no way in hell I'm just pushing through that." I brought out my magical staff and walked to the forefront of our little expedition.

Chance shrugged. "Back up, everyone."

I glanced back at my boyfriend with a smirk. "I'm not going to light the whole forest on fire, you know. Have a little faith in me."

"I saw you start the campfire last night," Chance murmured.

"That was an accident, and I'm learning. I'm better now," I said. "Besides, I'm more skilled with the staff than a wand. You know that."

Chance shrugged and nodded, but still backed up a step.

I sighed, then turned back to the overgrown ivy blocking our path.

Thinking for a minute, I closed my eyes and gripped my staff, then tilted the top forward a few inches.

The ivy did not budge.

I tilted the staff a few more inches forward, muttering a magical command designed to enhance the staff's power.

The ivy began the blow back.

I lifted the staff an inch and brought the end down with a thump, and repeated the command.

The ivy pulled back, lifting from the path and wrapping itself around the tree trunk from which it grew.

I took a deep breath, secretly relieved.

Renée clapped.

"Good job, Holly!" Laura patted my shoulder, grinning.

I smiled at her, then looked over at Chance and lifted an eyebrow.

He bowed his head sideways, acknowledging my success.

We walked under the ivy, and around the boulder, as the path curved down and around.

Our steps took us curving to the left, and a recess in the embankment appeared.

A fire was lit, and an old, old faun was seated on some moss, about four feet up.

We stopped and stared, open-mouthed.

He looked at us with eyes that were white and cloudy. His skin was so pale it looked as though someone had brushed him with a white paint. Tangled white hair grew from around his antlers, which looked almost like branches. The antlers were long and overgrown, and indicated his deep, old age. Moss grew on the antlers and hung down, providing a little color in an otherwise pale individual.

Charms and trinkets were braided throughout his hair, and some kind of flat bone was tied to the center of his head, between the antlers.

His face was old and wise, and his broad brow and nose showed his kinship with the deer that share the fauns' bloodlines.

He looked ancient.

I heard Chance gasp beside me and glanced over at him. His face was pale.

"Kushim," Chance whispered.

The old faun shook his head. "That is not I," he said in a gravelly voice. "But approach, I have been waiting for you, children."

We all gathered in a half-circle around the old one's fire, which crackled and popped as we drew near.

"I have not had visitors in a long, long time," the old faun said. "This forest has been closed to most travelers for over a thousand years."

"The King sent us on a quest," Chance whispered.

"Ahh, yes. It was foretold that you'd come," whispered

the old faun. "You seek passage to Álfheimr."

He said it as a statement, not a question.

We nodded slowly, and he lifted his hand, throwing a powder onto the fire. Sparks flew up in a rush, and when they had flown a few feet high, they turned into small orange moths that fluttered to the old faun's face. They remained a few seconds, their wings slowly beating, then drifted from the ancient face to the roof above him, then curled out into the air and disappeared.

"I have seen what you confront," he whispered. "You must be brave, young ones. Brave and strong, for what lies ahead."

A chill went up my back.

*Who is this old faun?*

"Sit with me for a while and gaze into the flames." The old man beckoned, indicating five cushions of moss that suddenly appeared around the campfire.

It looked so inviting, I lifted my bag from my shoulder and took a step forward, preparing to sit. But then I stopped, noticing that no one else had moved to sit down.

"We thank you, Old One, but we must be on our way forward," Renée said as she took my hand and drew me back.

The old faun shrugged and rattled the charms on one of his braids. "Safe travels," he said.

Renée grabbed Chance, who seemed rooted in place, with her other hand. She gave his arm a hard yank, and he shook his head and turned to follow.

I glanced back as we all walked away, and the old faun's firelight was fading. As I watched, the shallow recess where he sat turned dark, and he faded entirely from view. I blinked in surprise, stumbling slightly, and looked back one more time. The banked recess was empty. A few tree roots grew down from the dirt, but that was all.

Renée kept hold of my hand, steadying me as I turned to stumble after her and Chance. Laura and Liesl were already a few paces ahead.

Chance seemed in as much a daze as I felt, seeing the old faun recede into darkness, and then disappear entirely. He didn't say anything, but seemed thankful for Renée's helping hand. She grasped his arm, but then he turned his arm and grabbed her hand and squeezed it, and didn't let go for a long time.

We hiked on.

No one said a word.

*This forest holds so many surprises; some of them give me the willies.*

An hour later, Renée finally spoke.

"That was a close one," she murmured.

Chance grunted in agreement.

I knew what Renée said was true, but it bugged me that I had no details. Still, I felt I was always the one who asked for explanations, and was unfamiliar with the Faerie Realm workings, even though I'd lived at Titania Academy for going on two years now.

*Wellllll, one and a half, but who's counting?*

Chance nodded wordlessly.

"Think he was right?" asked Liesl. "When he said we must be brave and strong? Sounds like dangerous times are ahead."

"We already know that," Chance said angrily. He seemed cross with himself.

I didn't know what was going on, but I loved Chance, so I strode ahead and walked beside him, and took his hand.

He squeezed it.

"Holly," said Renée, coming up on my other side. "The others are probably aware, but I want to tell you, never, ever accept an invitation to sit with a wild Faerie, unless you have a few days to spare."

I blinked.

"What do you mean?" I asked.

Renée glanced at Laura and Liesl. "You two know this, right?"

"Of course," said Liesl.

"Yes," Laura said. "All Elfen know this." She turned to

me, "Holly, it's not the sitting and the fire, it's the invitation. If you want to stop and join a wild Faerie by their fire, you ask. If you ask, then things are on your own terms, and they can't impose a magical travelers spell on you."

"What spell is that?" I was curious.

"They enchant the question, and if you accept and sit with them, even though it may seem to you that you only spend an hour with them, days will have passed," said Liesl."

*Oh, OH WOW.*

And I'd almost sat down at the old faun's invitation.

A cold feeling of fear touched my heart, then left.

"It's not malicious magic, but it is mischievous magic, which can be nearly as bad," said Renée.

*Noted.*

I nodded. "Thanks for the heads up," I said. "Now let's get as far as we can hiking today." I turned to Chance. "How much longer do you think we have to go?"

"It's not a matter of how far we have to go," said Chance, "As much as how long we have to travel. The forest knows where we are going. It has to decide to let us through."

I shook my head. "Then why not just camp and wait?"

Renée chuckled. "That would be the worst newbie mistake you could make."

"That's a good way to spend a month in one spot," said Liesl.

"You have to show intent," said Laura. "You have to travel and try to get where you're going, and in the traveling, you are asking to be let through."

I nodded, understanding, then quickened my pace.

We hiked into the afternoon, walking miles and miles through the ever-changing, ever-the-same, magical ancient forest.

At one point, I thought I saw something through the trees, about a mile away. I stopped in my tracks, stunned. A large grey shape was lumbering along, so far away I could barely see it.

The others stopped and stared in the same direction.

"Come on, Holly," Liesl said softly, pulling me forward. "We have to keep going."

"But..." I glanced one more time at the grey shape moving through the trees. We turned and kept hiking, not speaking, just plodding along, trying to make the journey move along.

An hour later I whispered to Liesl. "That looked like a dinosaur."

She didn't answer at first, but then leaned and whispered back, "I think it was a brachiosaurus."

*This forest is amazing.*

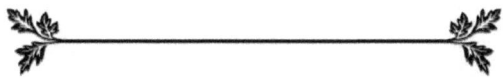

Chapter Twenty
# Blessing

We hiked on, and the sun dropped lower toward the horizon, sending long rays of gold sideways down into the trees.

The angle made the air look like it was filled with golden specks.

"Dust motes and brambles," I murmured. "Turned to gold."

"Beautiful, isn't it?" Chance said at my side. He looked down the forest path. "Let's keep going, I think we can hike for at least another hour before it falls dark.

I nodded, glancing once more at the gold flecks suspended in the rays of the sun.

We walked for about another ten minutes, then, a loud crashing reached our ears.

*What the heck is that?*

A scream came from up ahead. Then another. It was clear some forest creature was in trouble.

"Come on," I called, running ahead.

I raced around the corner and listened for the sounds of struggle. I didn't have long to wait. More screaming bleats came from off to my left, and I leaped into the underbrush, jumping over fallen logs, hurrying to a clearing about twenty feet off the main trail.

A deer was struggling against a cloud of...

"Wild sprites." said Liesl, running up next to me.

The deer was a white stag, its five-point antlers thick with small blue sprites, which were attacking it. The stag was covered in small wounds that dripped with blood.

The wild sprites were tiny, each about two inches tall. Each was armed with a small spear about the same length. They were stabbing the white stag repeatedly.

There were hundreds of the little things. Perhaps thousands. The air was thick with them.

They came from a large stump, crawling out like army ants, and taking to the air on tiny red wings.

Without thinking, I dropped my bag and lifted my hands, closing my eyes and summoning my Elemental

Power.

I could feel my hair lift with a magical breeze. My hands grew hot.

"Holly, no!" Chance cried, pulling at my shoulder.

*What?*

"I have to," I yelled over my shoulder. "They're killing him."

"Be careful, don't set the trees on fire," said Liesl on my other side.

I nodded and concentrated; I wanted to be very careful. Liesl was right: The trick was to contain the power in the clearing.

What had I learned about sprites last year? Oh, yeah. *They hate the cold.*

I summoned an image of heat. A blistering day, the sun beating down on me so hot I was sweating.

My hands surged with Elemental Power.

I opened my eyes and saw my fingers glowed an icy blue.

*Concentrate.*

The white stag cried out as the wild sprites ramped up their attack, perhaps sensing impending disaster.

A freezing blue light shot out from my hands and spread into the clearing. I directed it in a wide spray, to reach every corner where a wild sprite might be hiding.

The wild sprites attacking the white stag suddenly

froze in midair, and dropped to the ground.

I turned and pointed the magical stream at the stump from which they were still emerging.

I imagined a high-pitched squeal of surprise as the icy cold hit the hive.

The march of wild sprites out of the stump slowed, then stopped. I walked toward the old stump, blue-white icy blizzard flowing out of my hands, and stopped a few feet away.

I wanted the cold to reach way down into the hive, and freeze their whole colony.

I spent a few minutes directing the cold at the stump, then sprayed it around the clearing one more time, catching a few errant zingers, dropping them to the ground the instant the blue beam touched them.

I lowered my hands to my sides.

The freezing had not reached the trees or affected them in any way I could see.

I felt a pat on my shoulder, and glanced back. Chance grinned at me.

I nudged one of the wild sprites on the ground. It was frozen.

The stag stood in the middle of the clearing, looking tired and bloody. A few white crystals of ice hung from his antlers, remnants of the icy stream that'd frozen his attackers.

I stared at the creature.

"We should help him. He needs medical attention," I heard Renée whisper next to me.

I nodded, taking a deep breath. I took a step closer to the magnificent white stag, slowly extending my now-warm hand, palm facing up.

"Here, boy. Here, now. Are you okay?" I whispered.

Liesl and Laura came forward, holding flowers in their hands, reaching out.

I stopped and let them come forward, and they both slowly reached forward with the flowers.

The stag came a step closer and leaned out to sniff the flowers, then he made a low honk of pain, and took another step toward us.

Liesl and Laura reached out and hung their flowers on his antlers, hooking the flower stems around the mossy antler lengths.

The flowers seemed to calm the stag, and it stepped even closer.

"Lead him over here. The ground is clear of dead frozen wild sprite bodies, Chance murmured.

I glanced over, and saw him beckoning from the edge of the clearing. He was right: The soft forest floor was padded with leaves, and it was away from the stump and the area where the stag had been attacked.

We laid the poor thing down onto the ground, and

gently washed his wounds clean.

"These wild sprites are venomous," murmured Renée. "We had them in our back field a few summers back. They killed one of our cows."

I shook my head.

"How can these creatures, who basically act like angry yellow jackets, be related to Professor Ó Baoghill?" I asked aloud.

"Too many strains of sprite, not enough names for each sub species, I guess," said Liesl. "These are not the same as the headmistress. These wild sprites are extremely primitive and aggressive toward most everything."

"We need disinfectant," said Laura. "These stabs and bites are going to get infected."

The white stag had laid his head on the ground, his eyes half-closed in pain.

"We need disinfectant, and pain relief," I said.

Renée fumbled in her bag, and fished out a small pouch. "Got this from the healer the night before we left. Might as well use it now." She opened the pouch and withdrew a large tube of ointment, and a small vial of liquid. "I suppose it's safe to use on a deer," she said, almost to herself. "He looks bad; he's suffering." She pulled the stopper from the vial, and Chance lifted the stag's head as Renée put her hand into the deer's mouth and poured the medicine down his throat.

The white stag swallowed, without fighting us. He laid his head back down, and I smoothed his cheek, petting him gently. "I think he knows we're helping him," I murmured.

"He definitely does," said Chance, smiling.

We decided to camp nearby for the night. We didn't want to stay in the frozen-dead wild sprite and stump hive clearing, so together we helped the stag to his feet, and walked about fifty feet to another clearing, far back from the path.

Chance and Liesl built the fire, Renée and Laura put up the tent, and I sat with our patient, stroking his neck softly, and humming a lullaby to him.

He slept with his head lying in my lap.

Night fell.

Renée switched places with me when I had to stretch, and the white stag didn't even wake when Renée slipped under his head.

"Change of laps, dear one," Renée whispered, kissing the stag's nose.

We ate dinner and spoke in low tones, while the white stag slept on.

"It's almost like he's drugged," said Liesl.

"He's not drugged, but with the tonic Renée gave him, he's in a deep sleep while he heals," said Chance. "His body is battling the toxin from the wild sprites' barbed spears. He's winning, but it's a hard fight."

"He's larger than any normal stag," I said, looking the obviously magical creature over. "He's strong. I think he'll be okay in the end."

"What should we do tonight?" Laura asked.

"Leave him here, and we go to sleep in the tent," said Renée. "He's used to sleeping outside. We'll put an extra couple of logs on the fire so it keeps him warm through the night."

*Makes sense.*

I gathered fresh grass with Liesl and left a huge pile of it next to the white stag, in case he woke up and felt hungry, although I felt like a little kid doing it. But it felt good, too.

I grinned at Liesl as we made another trip to collect more sweet grass. She smiled and nodded. It felt good to do *something*.

Finally, it grew late and was time to sleep.

"We need to be well rested," said Chance. "I think we came about twenty-five miles today. I bet we can make that much tomorrow as well." He stretched and yawned.

We each entered the canvas tent and settled into our blankets, and I was soon fast asleep.

The next morning, I was awoken by snuffling noises. My eyes popped open at the same time as Liesl's, and we stared at each other sleepily, and then came fully awake at the same time.

Our eyes went wide, and we sat up, and I pulled on my shoes as Liesl pulled on her boots.

We left the tent and walked to where the white stag lay.

He was awake and munching on the grass we'd left him, which made me feel marvelous.

"I'll fetch him some water," said Liesl.

I knelt next to our patient and petted his head between his antlers.

"Shoo, shoo. There, there, li'l guy," I murmured in a soothing voice. "You're getting better, I know, I can see," I examined his wounds while I spoke and petted him.

The holes where he'd been pierced with the sprite's spears were dried and sealed over. There didn't seem to be any redness or swelling around each one. I was pleased.

The white stag finished eating the sweet grass, and

Liesl came back with a bowl of water, which the stag drank.

"I'll go get some more," Liesl hopped up to return to the nearby stream.

The stag looked at me with bright, clear, intelligent eyes.

"You're going to be all right, sweetheart," I murmured.

Liesl made three trips to bring the stag water, and the noble animal drank his fill.

He finished, and seemed to swell as he took a deep breath and got to his feet.

We stood back and watched.

The stag's majestic antlers reached up ten feet, and the rising sun caught them in rays of sunshine that made golden beams as they shot through the horns and to the ground beside us.

Renée and Chance emerged from the tent.

"Oh, wow, he's feeling better," said Renée.

Laura was the last to emerge from the tent, and she came forward toward the stag, and put her hand out. He nuzzled the palm of her hand gently.

"Deer and The Elfen have an affinity to each other," Laura murmured.

"This one is quite magical," said Chance. "Can you feel it?"

I could. Deeply. Power radiated from the white stag as

if it was pulsing.

We reluctantly broke camp, packing everything away so we could continue our quest.

The white stag stood there, watching us as we worked.

His wounds looked nearly healed, and I was amazed at how fast he had recovered.

I hugged the white stag impulsively, wish he would follow us on our adventure, and he nuzzled my neck, tickling me. I giggled and stood back.

We gathered at the edge of the clearing.

"The sun has been up for several hours, Holly," whispered Chance. "We have to go."

"I know," I said reluctantly.

The white stag suddenly stomped his foreleg and dipped his antlered head. A gold light glowed around his horns, as though he were gathering sunshine and concentrating it.

He stepped forward slowly. We stood still.

*What is he going to do?*

The white stag was obviously full of magic. He came and nodded his great head up and down several times.

I extended my hand to him, palm facing up.

He took a step closer and nuzzled my palm, and some of the golden light from his antlers seemed to flow through his head and into me.

I felt a warmth, and gasped in delight.

The others came forward then, and the stag nuzzled each of their hands in turn.

In his way, the white stag was blessing each of us, giving us good luck on our quest, because we had helped him.

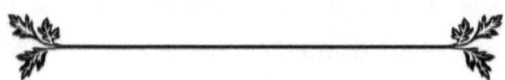

## Chapter Twenty-One
# The Wild Fae

We walked fast and far for the first half of our third day in the forest, and the trees just went on and on and on.

"There is no end to this forest," Liesl said quietly to me as we walked. I giggled, and she laughed back, and soon we were in a fit of laughter and could barely walk.

Renée doubled back from ten feet ahead of us and grabbed each of our hands; she pulled us forward, and we laughed as we went.

We'd been hiking through the forest for such a long time I felt punch-drunk, although I'd drunk no mead.

"Come on," said Renée. "Just come on."

The trail now led us across a ridge, with much of the forest below us shrouded in mist, even though it was midday.

We marched on.

We came to a stream running right across the path, and stopped to replenish our water bags and drink our fill. Ferns grew over the banks of the watercourse, and butterflies and dragonflies flitted over the surface, taking sips of the sparkling liquid.

"Let's get to the end of this rise," Chance pointed. "The path dips back down about a mile from here: I can see it."

I nodded, stepping close to him.

He looked down into my eyes and smiled.

I lifted myself on tiptoes and kissed him, feeling bold.

He put his arms around me, pulling me close.

He deepened the kiss, and I felt the warmth of his breath on my face.

It excited me.

I pushed my lips against his, it felt good to be bold.

"Holly?"

I blinked and opened my eyes.

I had sat on the stream's edge with Liesl and Laura; we'd taken our shoes and socks off, and we'd put our feet into the cold water. It felt invigorating.

I must have lain back and dozed off, because I started

dreaming.

Renée's face hovered over mine, looking concerned. "Hey, you okay?" she said.

"Of course I'm okay," I said, pulling my shoes and socks back on. "Why wouldn't I be okay?"

Renée nodded. "Good." And she went to nudge Liesl awake.

Liesl mumbled in her sleep. "Oh, Jack..." and my eyes went wide with the realization that I'd probably been mumbling in my sleep the same way.

Renée gently kicked at Liesl's leg. "Wake up. It's time to go."

Laura was already pulling her shoes on when I got to my feet. She glanced at me, her cheeks red.

"Some stream, huh?" Renée said. "Put you three right to sleep."

Chance had hiked down the ridge a bit, to scout, and was just walking back. I saw him as he approached, and he looked tired but happy.

"Hey, I saw a hill door from the end of the ridge!" he cried as he came running up, acting strangely. "Hurry, get your things." He grabbed his bag and helped us shoulder our packs.

We walked along the ridge.

"What's a hill door?" I asked.

"You'll see," said Liesl. "Just be careful."

*Be careful?*

"I've been careful this whole trip," I mumbled.

"I meant even more careful than usual, Holly," Liesl laughed.

We hurried along the top of the ridge, following the path. Chance led us down the edge at the end, and into another small valley in the huge forest.

"Hold hands. The slope is tricky here," Chance instructed.

We got to the bottom safely, running down the slanted pathway the last ten feet.

Chance led us around and about thirty feet farther, and up against another hill was...

A door. In the side of the hill.

*I guess this is what he meant by a hill door.*

The door was made of a thick wood, and it was very old.

We stood there staring at the door, and I wondered why Chance had been so excited.

The others seem to be expecting something, and we weren't disappointed: Within a few minutes, the door began to slowly creak open.

A young woman appeared out of the door. She was normal sized, in fact, she could have been a student at Titania Academy. Except she had wings. I wondered why she didn't keep them hidden in a glamour, then remembered we were in a magical forest, and the Fae Folk did not glamour themselves in this forest.

Without the wings she looked like she could be an upperclassman at the Academy.

She was dressed in a plain-looking smock, the color of dirt. Her wings were translucent, the color of water. Her hair was brown, and her eyes were light, and she looked at us as if we had startled her.

"Fàilte don chnoc agam," she said. "Am bu mhath leat a thighinn a-steach?"

I blinked in surprise when the words she spoke were translated in the air a moment later. It was like an echo. Very clearly, I heard: "Welcome to my hill. Would you like to come in?"

I glanced at Chance and the others.

*Had they heard the same thing?*

Liesl and Renée were smiling and nodding. Chance had a worried look on his face, but grinned and nodded as well.

Laura glanced at me and shrugged.

"Did you hear that?" I mouthed to Laura.

She shrugged again and shook her head.

I walked to Laura and whispered in her ear, "The faerie said, 'Welcome to my hill. Would you like to come inside?' You didn't hear the translation?" I pulled my head back and looked at Laura's face.

She looked pale, and shook her head again, then whispered, "No."

I glanced back at the faerie who'd come out of the door in the hill.

Chance was walking forward to talk to her. Liesl and Renée were right behind him.

I turned back to Laura. "You want to stay outside?"

She nodded. "I don't trust that door," she mouthed silently.

"Okay, I'll stay out here with you. We can sit here," I said, sitting on the grass.

I watched Chance and the others.

*I thought we were in a hurry?*

I wondered if I should stop them from going in. I wasn't sure. Chance ought to know what he was doing. Renée too. They were older, after all. Older and wiser? At this point, I wasn't sure.

The door closed behind them and Laura and I sat and waited.

A few minutes later, I couldn't stand it anymore.

I got up and turned to Laura. "Listen, you stay here. I'll be right out. Ten minutes, tops. Okay?"

"No, Holly, don't go in there. It doesn't feel right," Laura said.

"I promise I'll be back in five minutes. Only five minutes," I said.

"I don't feel good about this at all," Laura said.

"Two minutes," I said. "That's it. Look," I said, reaching for the door handle. "I'll leave the door open so you can see me the whole time. I'll just go in a few feet, okay?"

Laura looked scared and didn't say a word as I pulled open the door.

Liesl, Renée, and Chance had just gone in a few minutes ago, and I was hoping to see them just inside, but there was no one.

The door creaked open, and I pulled it wide, and grabbed a big rock, rolling it into place to hold the door open.

The inside path was dirt, and there were candles held in wall sconces about every ten feet.

I glanced back at Laura and gave her a thumbs up, smiling and nodding. Laura looked back at me, a frightened look on her face. She shook her head and her meaning was clear: *Don't go in there, Holly.*

I don't know why I ignored her. Chance and Liesl and Renée had gone in.

*I'll just take a short peek. A few steps in, tops. That's it. Laura is worried about nothing; I'll be in and out in a jiffy.*

I took a step, then another, my foot finally touching the inside of the hill's path.

The candles flared as my foot hit the inside dirt.

*Weird.*

I heard Laura gasp softly.

I paused, glancing back. She was still there, watching me, her knees up to her shoulders as she sat on the grass, and her arms wrapped around her legs. Her chin rested on her knees, and she didn't take her eyes off me.

I took a second step inside, my body moving beyond the boundary of the door. Both my feet were within the tunnel now.

I looked around. The tunnel was plain, just dirt and the candles, nothing more. I couldn't see where the tunnel led. It was tall enough that I could easily stand upright in it.

I took another step.

As soon as my foot touch and my weight shifted onto it, I heard a loud bang, and the outside door slammed shut.

"HEY!" I yelled. I turned back to the door and tried to open it. I turned the doorknob and banged on the wooden surface. It would not budge.

And I could not hear Laura on the other side. Something told me she was probably upset, maybe banging on the door from the outside, maybe even calling out my name.

But all I heard was silence. Utter and complete silence.

*Where did the stone go? Who rolled it away and shut the door? What is going on?*

I turned back to the tunnel into the hill. I was getting angry, and I wanted some answers. This hill and this forest were playing tricks on us, and I for one was tired of it all.

I stomped down the dirt tunnel, hoping the thing wouldn't fall in on me.

"Chance?" I called. "Liesl? Renée? Where'd you go?"

I took a deep breath, and kept walking. I must've gone fifty feet.

"The dang hill isn't even this big," I mumbled to myself. "How is it that Chance and Renée and Liesl were duped into walking in anyway?" Then my step slowed as I realized that *I* had been fooled into walking in.

*Oh, brother.*

I began running. I trotted down the dirt tunnel for what must have been an additional hundred feet. To the end. But it just ended in a dirt wall.

"This isn't funny," I called.

I turned back to run the way I'd come. I sprinted this time, and ran the hundred and fifty feet or more pretty fast. I ran until I came... to the other end, which was... a dirt wall.

*Where is the door?*

I had had it. I was *mad.*

My hands balled into fists as I whirled around.

"HEY! LET ME OUT RIGHT THIS INSTANT!" I screamed at the top of my lungs. I fell silent and listened, and I swear I heard a faint giggling.

*Someone is trolling me.*

"Fine," I said, sitting down in the dirt. "I'm not playing your stupid games." I crossed my arms and sat stubbornly, and waited.

A few minutes later, the faerie woman reappeared, walking down from the long end of the tunnel. I got to my feet.

"Finally," I mumbled grumpily.

"Come," she said, and crooked her finger at me, before turning and walking away.

I followed her, although I'd have much rather gone back out the door to the outside.

We walked about ten feet to another corridor branching off from the main tunnel.

*This definitely wasn't there before.*

We entered a room with a banquet set at a long table. A dozen kinds of food, each cooked to perfection, were laid out on the most exquisite silver platters and bowls I had ever seen.

I stared at the food, at roast turkey with all the trimmings, baked honey ham, desserts, pie, strudels, green-bean bacon casserole, even french fries and ice cream, somehow. It all smelled so delicious.

I was enchanted. Everything else was forgotten. My anger at being trapped melted out of me as the faerie lady led me to a comfortable looking chair, pulled it out from the table, and bade me sit.

I lowered myself in the seat, and it was pushed in as I sat. The plate placed before me was gold, with a peach and silver trim. Everything I looked at on the table, every delicious dish, every morsel, every delectable fragrant delight, suddenly appeared in a smaller portion on my plate.

My heart beat quicker.

I won't lie: I was, at that moment, sick to death of the re-re-reheated stew we'd been eating since we left Titania Academy.

Even the mushrooms Laura had gathered and skewered on thin sticks to roast over the campfire, had seemed delicious at the time. But now, the memory of them seemed gross and tasting of dirt.

I reached for a chicken wing, roasted to perfection.

Before my fingers could touch the delicacy, a voice rang out from across the room.

"HOLLY: NO!"

Renée raced around from the other side of the room, where a door was now visible, and my friends coming through it. Renée raced up to me, knocked my hand away from the chicken wing, and grabbed the back of my chair, dragging it backward.

My heels splayed out, my legs extended, I saw the table draw away from me as I was pulled backward.

Chance and Liesl ran up to me.

"You didn't eat anything, did you?" Chance panted. "DID YOU?!"

"N...no. I didn't get a chance," I stared longingly at the food on the table I could see beyond my friends.

Chance stepped in front of my face, blocking my vision.

Liesl and Renée stood on either side of him.

"DON'T TOUCH THE FOOD," Chance said in a loud voice.

Renée knelt next to me, where I was still seated in my chair. "Holly, this is a Faerie Mound. This food is enchanted. If you touch any of it, if you eat any of it, you'll be happy and spend the night dancing and partying in the Faerie Mound with the Aos Sí, and you'll fall asleep at the end of the evening, and when you finally wake up and go out the door; a hundred years will have passed," she said in an intense voice.

*WHAT?*

Renée looked up at Chance and Liesl. "She doesn't know. She has no idea. Oh, *why* did we leave her?"

"You said it earlier, Renée," said Chance grimly. "They

enchanted us, just for a few minutes."

"Holly," Liesl said, bringing her face two inches from my nose. "That food is death. Don't even look at it."

I shook my head, as if waking from a dream. Now I was remembering. The warning had been in the first-semester classes. "Do not eat the Faerie food inside the Faerie Mound."

*I remember now.*

Suddenly, I felt angry. I had almost been doomed, lost inside a Faerie Hill for a hundred years.

I got up roughly and stomped about.

*This is not their fault: They were enchanted, too.*

I felt angry at myself, for all the mistakes I had made, for what I had almost allowed to happen. I glanced at Renée.

"Thank you for catching me just in time." I looked over and saw the faerie woman. She was Sídhe. The Aos Sí. Faeries who lived in the hillsides across the land.

She stared back at me and giggled, then stuck her tongue out at us and skipped from the room.

Still mad, I sighed and turned to my friends. "Let's go."

They nodded.

I turned to the room at large as we walked out. "AND YOU'D BETTER LET US OUT THE DOOR, BUBS. THE JIG IS UP!"

Chapter Twenty-Two

# The Magic Hill

The Aos Sí did not appreciate being yelled at, apparently. We stormed out through the banquet hall door and into the dirt tunnel, and we spent the next half-hour running from one end to the other, searching for the door.

It was gone.

There was no door, not anymore.

We sat to rest, munching on a few crackers from our packs. I was sad, because I knew the food just twenty feet away, in the banquet hall around the corner, would taste so much better.

"Where did you guys disappear to?" I asked. "Because

I swear, I was in the tunnel just a few minutes after you, and you were all gone."

"Oh, Chance showed us the gem cavern," said Liesl. "Didn't you, Chance?" She looked over at him.

He nodded. "Every Faerie Mound had one, or, at least, that's what they say," Chance said.

"Okay, what's a gem cavern?" I asked.

"Oh, Holly. It was *intense*," Renée whispered.

"Show me?" I asked.

I shoved the rest of a cracker in my mouth, coughing from the dryness, and stood up.

"Okay," said Chance. "Follow me, and DON'T touch any food. I mean it."

I rolled my eyes. "I know, I know."

We walked back into the banquet room, and I turned my eyes from the massive table laden with food. Chance led us around it, and it was hard because, although I averted my eyes, nothing could stop the smells from drifting into my nose.

*Oh, God.*

I stopped without realizing it. Liesl reached back and grabbed my sleeve and pulled me along.

"Fine, fine," I said grumpily. "I SAID I'M FINE."

Liesl did not let go, not until we were through the other door and down a dark tunnel.

"Watch your step," Chance whispered.

It was a short walk down, then through another door into...

*Oh My God.*

The gem cavern wasn't that big: It was maybe the size of two of our classrooms put together. But the walls, made of rough rock, were studded with huge deposits of every kind of gem you could imagine.

There were diamonds, rubies, sapphires in every color, emeralds, tanzanite, citrine, and every gem imaginable. Huge hunks of them. MASSIVE CHUNKS.

I stared.

In the middle was a pool of water, and from this water came light rays that hit the gems embedded in the walls, send colorful rays in every direction.

"Holly, look in the water," said Liesl.

I walked over and peered into the small pool, and gasped. It was full of pearls, of every size and shade. Big, gorgeous pearls, small pearls, medium sized pearls, and every size in between. Black pearls, creamy white pearls, brown pearls, pink pearls, blue and green and silver pearls.

I found myself leaning over the water, almost tipping over, so I backed up a few steps.

I stood there, not touching anything, just letting my eyes drink it all in.

The gems were not only embedded in the cave walls,

they were loose and strewn around the edges of the floor, like so much debris tossed aside without a second thought.

I stepped closer and saw not only gems but what looked like polished petrified wood on the edges of the floor, just lying there.

I shook my head.

"Wow," I said.

"Told ya," Liesl whispered. "Amazing, isn't it?"

I shook my head, then turned to Chance. "Is this real?" I asked.

He nodded. "The Aes Sídhe love to collect pretty things, kind of like crows," he said. "And they live a very long time." He pointed to the gems with his chin. "This is their horde."

I looked at all the sparkling colors.

"It's beautiful," I murmured, walking away.

Chance came and put his hand on my arm. "You okay?" he asked in a quiet voice.

I nodded, glancing again at all the gems. "If I'd had even one of those, when I was growing up, my Aunt Clare and I could have never gone hungry. Never had to sleep rough." I shrugged. "And these Sídhe just leave them here, lying on the ground, discarded like yesterday's trash. It's just weird. I'm fine. I really am," I said, falling silent.

Chance wrapped his arms around me and stood there, holding me.

A minute later, I heard Liesl gasp, and I turned to look.

The Faerie lady was walking into the room, hesitant. She walked up to Chance and me as we stood there, arms wrapped around each other.

"I... we heard your story," she said softly in a strange foreign accent. "We feel for you keenly." She turned to indicate the room. "Take one, each of you. Take one gem, one piece each, and you may leave with it."

Now it was my turn to gasp.

Chance turned to the woman. "Are you sure? They're ours to keep, outside?"

The Sídhe woman nodded.

"And not cursed or anything?" he asked.

She nodded again. "And... and take one for your friend outside, the Elfen girl."

Laura!

I had left her sitting in the grass, almost in tears for fear of what would happen to me if I entered the door in the hill.

I had propped the door open so she could see me as I took a few steps in, but that hadn't mattered: The door had slammed shut, and Laura was probably frantic, still waiting outside.

*The door had slammed shut.*

This Sídhe faerie was probably the one who shut it. I had seen no one else here. Just her.

I looked at her, and my eyes narrowed.

She blushed and dropped her eyes in embarrassment, and I swear, it was as though she could read my mind.

My breath puffed out in a rough sigh.

She moved around the room, waving her hand at the walls, the floor, the pool of water, the edges, everything. "Take one, take one, each of you."

She put her nose up and closed her eyes, then bent and cupped a large emerald in her hands. It was of the deepest green.

She brought it to me, and handed it to me, "For your friend," she said softly.

I put out my hands and she placed the emerald in the palms of my hand. The thing was the size of an ostrich egg.

I raised my eyebrows.

*Laura would probably like this.*

I looked back up into the Sídhe faerie's face, and she beamed at me, a bright happy smile that seemed to light the room. Then she moved to the pool's edge and sat on the rocks and waited.

Chance and Liesl and Renée and I turned to the gems and treasures of the room and began to search for the jewel we would each pick.

We took a long time deciding.

Chance chose a deep-blue sapphire, as large as his fist. Its facets were exquisite, and the inside was clear and glinting and perfect.

Renée searched and decided on a large black pearl, almost a smokey silver in the bright light, and it was large: the size of a chicken's egg. It was smooth and round and perfect.

Liesl selected a large yellow diamond. It was the size of a large quail egg, and it glinted with a clear golden hue when she held it up to the light. It had been cut in large facets, and was clear in the middle, and I thought it was just about the most beautiful gem I had ever seen.

I searched and searched and searched, for the longest time of all. For almost an hour, I think.

I finally settled on a deep-red ruby the size of my fist. It was perfect. It almost glowed when I brought it up to my face.

"Good gems, all," the Sídhe faerie said as we placed our selection in our bags.

She rose to her feet, and I saw she had picked up a gem in her hand that I hadn't seen before. She approached me with it.

"Everyone in the forest has heard about your quest by now," she said in a soft voice. "I have a special request for you." She pointed at me.

*Me? I'm nothing special.*

But I was curious.

"Yes? What's your request?" I asked.

"Take him to the king?" she said, and handed me the gem she held. I accepted the purple-and-brown sparkling gemstone and stared at it. It was the size of a small child's football, and it was heavy. It was composed of a material I hadn't seen before, and the more I stared at its depths, the more intrigued I was.

"Sure, I'll take it to him," I said. I opened my bag and putting the gem inside, next to the ruby.

"Tell the king to take good care of him," said the Sídhe faerie. "Now come, I will lead you out." And she turned and walked out of the room.

She led us out of the cavern, down the dark tunnel, and out into the banquet hall.

The table that had been laden heavy with exquisite food was now empty.

*Proof that it had been enchanted.*

As we walked past, I couldn't even smell the food I had seen before. It was as if it had never been there at all.

The Sídhe lady led us into the dirt tunnel and down to the end, where the door had reappeared.

It opened as we approached, and I could see Laura there, still sitting on the grass, dried tears on her face.

She jumped up as the door opened, and I ran past everyone and out the door and tackled her.

"Oomph," she said, as I fell on top of her.

"Laura!" I exclaimed. Then, in a humbler voice: "I'm sorry."

She hugged me tightly. "I'm just happy to see you guys, so happy!" she said, wiping new tears from her eyes and grinning from ear to ear.

We were so happy to be reunited that we didn't look back at the door in the hill or the Sídhe faerie, or anything. Several minutes had passed before I heard Renée exclaim, "Oh, it's gone," in a sad voice

I turned and saw that the door had disappeared. The Sídhe faerie woman was gone, and the hillside looked like every other hillside in the forest: overgrown, with trees and roots and bushes and leaves, and it looked like no door had every been there before.

We stared for a minute, then realized the faerie woman had been magical and that since the door had disappeared, she probably didn't want to be bothered again.

So we gathered up all our stuff and walked on.

"Oh, I almost forgot," I said. "Here, the Aos Sí faerie said to give you this," and I handed Laura the deep-green emerald the size of an ostrich egg. It was even more beautiful out in the natural light.

Laura took it and went pale.

"You okay?" I asked, concerned.

She nodded, dazed. "It's just that, this... this emerald. It looks like the emerald from an old Elfen fable I heard as a young child. It looks exactly like it." She raised her eyes to meet mine. "There're books talking about this emerald, in the library at home. It's pictured exactly the same." She looked back down at the huge gem. "Father and Mother aren't going to believe this," she muttered.

I remembered how Laura's house had been partially destroyed in the bombing when she had fled, and I vowed to help her family rebuild, and find the book she was talking about, and make sure her home library was built again.

*Lucy deserves to grow up with the same book Laura grew up with.*

As we hiked the rest of the day, Laura carried the giant emerald, and stared at it nearly the entire time.

Chapter Twenty-Three
# The Rumble Hill

We hiked out of the forest and onto another wide moor, and we saw wetlands off in the distance.

"Does this mean we should get to Álfheimr soon?" Liesl asked.

"Soon," Chance said. "I hope."

"You don't know?" I asked in a quiet voice.

"Again," said Chance, "The path to Álfheimr is magical, and only Gaia can let us through. We follow the path, and hope to be let through." He shrugged. "Hope for the best. Hope to be found worthy."

*Oh, dear.*

We hiked up a low hill. The forest was visible in the

distance ahead of us.

"So, if the path leads down again," I said. "Will we be re-entering the forest tomorrow?"

"Quite probably," said Chance, looking at the horizon. "Although I think we should camp out here tonight."

The sky was clear, and the sun was setting: It seemed a beautiful afternoon.

"We have several hours of daylight left," Liesl said. "You want to hike farther?"

"Sure," Chance said, "Let's go."

We hiked across the moors, the grass riding the gentle slopes, lush and green.

A few hours later, we stood on the last hillside looking down on the forest again.

"How does the path go, Chance?" asked Renée.

He stopped and murmured the spell, and the path fluoresced for a few seconds, the edges bright and sparkling in the dying light. It led down the slope of the hill we were on, across a short valley, and back into the woods.

I sighed.

I was getting a little sick of the forest, but I'd never tell my companions. I was feeling jaded and tired, weary from our long expedition. And I had a feeling we'd just begun the journey, even though it felt like it had been years.

*Eons.*

Laura came over and patted my shoulder, as if to say, "I'm tired too, my friend," then turned to Chance and asked, "SO where shall we camp for the night?"

The sun had been dipping lower and lower, down to the horizon as we'd been standing there. The sky glowed orange and pink, and would soon turn to purple and then indigo.

"How 'bout down there," Chance pointed.

The bottom of the slope had a stream running alongside it. A perfect spot to camp.

Chance and Renée led the way down the hill.

"Let's make camp right here, though," said Renée, still a dozen feet from the bottom. "We don't want to be that close to the stream. It's probably soggy and damp in the middle of the night."

I looked over at the stream. Several dragonflies buzzed over the water, which glinted with light from the sunset.

So, we made camp. The sloping hill had a bit of a flat spot right there, and Laura and I set up camp in this flat bit, while Chance and Renée went for firewood.

Liesl gathered stones from the stream and arranged them in a circle in preparation for the campfire.

"Ugh," I said. "The food we saw inside the faerie hill looked so good, and I'm so sick of reheated stew. Blah."

"I brought a rabbit I shot," said Laura, "from two days ago. The bag of holding has kept it in stasis, and it's as fresh as the hour I drained it of blood," she laughed.

I stared at her.

She nodded.

"You have fresh meat?" I asked in a quiet voice.

"Enough for us all. It's a huge rabbit," she said.

"You... you shot it?" I asked. "With a gun?"

"No, silly. With a bow." She grinned and brought a slim longbow out of her bag of holding. "I've got my sword in here, too."

I blinked.

"You're the best, the absolute best," I murmured.

"Oh, I don't know about that," she said shyly. "You brought me a giant emerald, after all."

I grinned.

Chance and Renée were soon back with wood, and, upon hearing about Laura's rabbit, Chance erected a primitive tripod, and soon had the rabbit hanging over the fire, roasting.

Laura wasn't lying: The thing was over five pounds. We would dine like kings tonight.

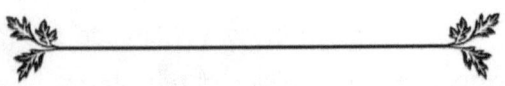

Several hours later, we all sat back by the crackling fire, our bellies full of rabbit, watching the stars winking into view.

Upon sunset, the sky had filled with a cloudy mist, blown in by an errant wind. It had stayed for a while, and was just now blowing away to the east.

"On to the mainland," I murmured, waving my hand. "Go away, clouds. We want to see the stars.

Liesl giggled.

Renée cleared her throat. "I would like to salute our huntress, who, without making a huge fuss about it, shot and bagged a giant rabbit, and fed us all tonight." she lifted her cup of water to Laura, who bowed her head.

"To Laura!"

"Here, here!"

"Fabulous hunter, wonderful friend!"

"Elfen huntress!"

Laura chuckled.

We sat back, feeling contented.

"I think today was weird and scary and wonderful," Liesl said.

"That's a good description of the day," Chance said.

"Since we were all enchanted to enter the faerie hill, and I think the Elfen are immune to those enchantments," I began."

"I *know* we are," said Laura. "Ya'll, that was beyond

creepy. You guys just smiled and walked into the dirt."
She shook her head.

I grinned. "As I was saying, I think, since Fae Folk
seem so easily tricked."

Chance nodded his head.

"... even I was tricked, eventually," I said.

"Ha!" Laura said.

"...I think because of this strange anomaly, that Laura
should have veto power, should we encounter any more
doors in hillsides," I finished.

"I second the motion," said Chance.

"I third the motion," chuckled Liesl.

"Sustained!" Renée said, laughing. She turned to
Laura. "You shall be the Protector of the Quest with
regards to Doors in Hillsides. Do you accept this regent
honor?"

Laura smiled and bowed her head. "I do, most
seriously."

"Then it's settled," said Chance. "Laura is the
Protector!"

"YAY!"

"HURRAH!"

"Thank God!"

"YEssssSSSSS!"

I think we were all punch drunk from the dangers and
amazements we had endured. We soon crawled into the

tent and curled up in our blankets and were all fast asleep.

I slept soundly, solidly, and deeply. For the first few hours.

Sometime in the middle of the night, Liesl shook me awake.

I opened one eye.

"Li, why?" I muttered.

She shrugged.

I yawned.

I was about to turn over and go back to sleep when Liesl patted my shoulder again.

I ignored her.

She grabbed my shoulder and gave it a jiggle.

I sat up, mildly grouchy. "Okay WHY? What? And why NOW?" I exclaimed.

"I heard something," Liesl said.

"But..., and why didn't you, um... you know, Chance is right there, he's pretty strong, you could wake him," I gestured over at where Chance was asleep in his blanket.

"I did," said Liesl.

"She did," said Chance from the tent-flap door.

I blinked, trying to wake up more. I looked over at Chance's blanket. It was flat.

"Oh," I said. "Fineeeeeee." I began to pull on my shoes.

"I walked the perimeter of the camp," Chance said to

Liesl. "I heard it, too. There's definitely something nearby."

I stood up. "What?" I rubbed my eyes.

"Liesl heard a rumbling," said Chance. "I heard it, too."

"A rumble?" I yawned. "What time is it?"

"It's about an hour before dawn," said Chance.

"What's going on? said Renée sleepily.

Suddenly, a deep rumbling sound, not very quiet, streamed through the tent.

I whirled around. "WHAT is that?"

Laura sat up in her blankets.

*Well, hell. Now we're all awake.*

I walked out of the tent and out into the cold morning air. The stars were still visible, and far on the eastern horizon, the sky was slightly less than pitch black.

I walked around near the fire, trying to listen for any noise.

I heard nothing.

"Where were you when you first heard this sound?" I asked Liesl.

"Inside the tent," she replied.

*Inside the tent. The nearly soundproof tent.*

*That's a big sound.*

I walked back inside the tent. Nothing.

I threw wood and dried grasses onto the banked fire, then stirred it gently to light it again. Laura had been teaching me woodland survival, and it was actually pretty neat.

Ten minutes later, we all gathered around the fire, chewing on cold flatbread while listening for the sound to come again.

"We're on a Scottish moor, next to a magical forest full of Faeriekin," I said. "I'm just saying, it might have been one of them. Should we really be that alarmed?"

"Might have been a herd of unicorns," said Laura. "They make a lot of noise."

Chance shook his head. "This is something big." He looked around, concerned.

The sky was lighter now, and the effect like twilight in reverse. The approaching dawn seemed to call forth all sorts of magical creatures. I had learned about this phenomenon during my first year at the Academy: If these creatures were around, they would most likely make an appearance now, when the light was barely there.

I glanced around from my spot beside the campfire, my hands wrapped around a mug of hot cocoa I was indulging in.

Everything was quiet and still: almost as if the moors were holding their breath, waiting for something.

A strong sense of expectation filled me.

Chance and Liesl *had* heard this sound, and so had I,

although only the one time.

Laura and Renée hadn't yet heard it, but they watched the landscape and searched for the source with the rest of us, trusting that there *was* something out there.

Something that might pose a threat to us.

We waited.

Another ten minutes passed.

The sky was pink now, and the birds were starting to wake up. Several especially loud squawkers were making a massive racket, flying back and forth over the side of the hill, loud as heck.

I glanced overhead at them.

They flew from our fire, back over the hill, and I could hear their loud calls recede and then get loud again as they returned.

Chance murmured a magical word, and suddenly, his hawk familiar appeared on his arm. He whispered to her, and the hawk stretched her wings one by one, then leapt into the sky, flying away.

"She's checking things out from above," said Chance. "Those birds are being so loud I'm thinking they know something we don't."

"Mmmm," I said. "Good idea." I sipped on my cocoa while we waited.

The morning mist was gathered around the slopes of the moors, and pooled near us thickly. Our fire kept it away from us, but it gathered near, touching the edges of the tent and shrouding everything in a ghostly fog.

It dampened the noises of the morning. The stillness was almost a noise in itself.

The noise of morning.

Chance stood. His hawk still hadn't returned. "Well, since we woke so early, I'm going to pack so we can get an early start. Who's with me?"

I sipped the last dregs of my cocoa and stood up. The chocolaty drink had energized me, and thanks to Liesl, I was wide awake at dawn. I washed out my cup and stuck it back in my pack, then began to help pack the blankets and tent.

The others pitched in, and we were ready to go in less than ten minutes.

I took a deep breath and glanced around.

Chance was standing off to the side, scanning the sky. I followed his gaze and saw his hawk familiar circling, then slowly dropping to land on Chance's outstretched arm.

The hawk put his head close to Chance's while they conferred.

"Oh my God," I heard Chance mumbled. He glanced up at all of us. "Well, at least they're ready," I heard him say to the hawk. He threw the familiar back into the sky, and she pumped her wings hard to gain altitude more quickly.

"Okay, we're all packed," he said hurriedly. "Let's go. Come on."

We walked down to the path, about forty-five feet or so from the campfire, which we had covered in dirt. Chance murmured the spell, and the path appeared, and most of us had both feet on it, except me. I was behind Liesl and had one foot on and one foot off.

"Holly," Chance said tightly. "Get on the path."

I blinked at him and shrugged, adjusting my stance, so that both feet were firmly on the path.

Chance nodded and then looked back at the spot where we'd camped.

I gasped.

From our vantage point back on the path, far back from the hill, we could plainly see that the hill we had camped on was no hill.

It was a sleeping giant.

Most of it was covered with grass and moss, and a few small trees were growing out of its back, far on the lee side, but it was definitely a giant.

As we watched, our jaws dropped open in astonishment, and we finally heard the rumble again. The giant's head was down by the stream, and although the massive creature didn't move, the reeds at the side of the stream, which we could now see were very close to its mouth, trembled slightly.

"It's snoring, isn't it?" Liesl asked in a small voice.

Chance nodded.

"What did your hawk tell you?" I asked. I had noticed that his familiar hadn't rushed, hadn't seemed alarmed, and hadn't been worried at all when reporting back to her master.

Chance grinned. "She said she scouted for a few miles and saw nothing out of the ordinary, and that the area was free of danger, probably because of the giant sleeping there." He chuckled to himself.

I shook my head slowly and turned to Liesl. "It was a giant." I swatted her. "Nothing more. Didn't you know?"

She ducked and giggled. "No, I grew up in the south of Germany, in a thick forest. Giants mostly nest on the moors, and in colder climes. Stop that!" She swatted me back, and we chased each other for a minute, laughing.

"Come on, you guys, we need to get going," said Renée. "Lots of ground to cover today."

Chapter Twenty-Four
# The Old Man

We hiked down the path, which followed the stream into the forest. Although it was less than ten miles from the forest we'd first crossed, this wood was darker and older.

The trees were taller, at least two hundred feet high, and their foliage spread wider at the top, so that the forest below was less overgrown, and darker.

Here it was clear that the Old Way had been cleared for travelers: The path was no longer invisible, but paved with old, old stones. Thousands of years old.

Each stone that made up the pathway was more than a foot wide, and three were set side-by-side, running up and down the walkway.

The stones were dark and worn, as if feet had walked down them thousands of times.

The path rose a few inches off the forest floor, which was mostly clear of smaller plants and bushes. The branches of the trees started their spread fifteen or twenty feet up, and these lower branches were mostly clear of leaves. They were dark and foreboding, holding many secrets in them, and crows were perched in these lower branches, as well as robins and blackbirds.

There were, in fact, an oddly large number of birds perched in the trees.

They watched us as we passed.

The path we walked curled back and forth around the larger, dark trees, but headed in a straight line forward, more or less.

The forest was full of birdsong at first, as the moor had been, but as we walked deeper into the wood, the birds fell silent.

Still watching us.

Waiting.

I shivered.

"Liesl," I whispered. The walkway was rather more narrow than the path we'd been following in the other forest, so we'd subconsciously been walking in a line, spread out.

It made me nervous.

I felt unprotected.

"What," Liesl said, coming up to walk next to me.

I took her hand, saying nothing.

She nodded. She was feeling it, too.

We walked for hours through this dark wood, not seeing anything but those creepy birds, staring down at us.

After a while, I realized that the birds would probably have to poop. If we were underneath them when this happened, it would drop down on our heads; thankfully, none had yet.

I began to giggle as I walked. I put my hand against my mouth and tried to stop, but the more I giggled, the worse it got.

At one point, Laura stopped and glanced back at me curiously, then kept walking forward.

The forest was spooky enough that it made us nervous, and I don't think any of us wanted to fall behind and lose sight of the others.

We walked close together.

At midday, after we'd been walking a good six hours, Chance stopped, and we took a much-appreciated break.

*God, I needed to rest.*

We stepped off the pathway into a nearby glade where glowing mushrooms grew under the trees.

The stream, which had wandered in and out of view, curled around a bend nearby. We topped off our water bottles, attended to our toilet one by one, and generally rested.

I munched on a muffin I had fished out of Cook's bag, and watched the birds as they gathered over the path.

"Why are they only over the stone path?" I asked no one in particular.

Chance glanced upward at the dark shapes and shrugged. "I'm just happy there are no spiders or rats," he said. "This is the type of wood where you'd see those things, at least in my particular nightmares."

"You had bad dreams last night?" I asked.

He nodded.

"I'm sorry," I said.

He shrugged. "It is what it is. Unspoken fears of the unknown, of what lies ahead. Not important to the quest."

"See, that's a good attitude to have," Renée said, smiling. "Instead of getting freaked out, you just shrug off a bad dream. I know lots of people, adult people, who would take it as an omen."

Chance made a rude sound. "The future is not written in stone. Anything can happen. I know what creatures to expect on our quest, although the hill giant was a bit of a surprise."

I grinned.

*A surprise to us all.*

"Well," Laura said, looking around. "This forest reminds me of the Meggido Shade Woodland on the far northern edge of the Elfen lands. There are giant spiders there, for sure. But that's not what would hurt you." She stopped and waited.

I took the bait.

"What would hunt you in that forest?" I asked in a quiet voice.

She turned to me, her eyes wide. "That forest is haunted by specters. Elfen use it for paintball." She burst into laughter.

*Paintball?*

I shoved Laura playfully, and she fell over sideways, still laughing.

"Come on, you guys, let's get going," said Chance, standing up and shouldering his bag.

We stepped back on the pathway and continued our hike.

It went on and on and on. Moody birds watching us from the trees, not much sunlight making its way down to the forest floor, spooky lighting.

The whole bit.

After this many hours, I was getting bored. There was no break in the sameness of the landscape.

Monotony.

*Ugh.*

I fell back to the end of the line, and, scooping up a few acorns, began tossing them onto Liesl's bag as it bounced on her back.

At the first one, she jumped. After the next few, she glanced back and caught me.

Liesl was just as bored as I was, so she picked up some acorns herself, and we both began tossing them onto Laura's bag.

Laura, feeling the first acorn hit, whirled around, pulling her sword from the invisible scabbard at her side, and landed in a crouch, her eyes darting from side to side.

"Something's there," she said.

The others stopped.

"Something hit my bag," said Laura.

Liesl and I dropped our hands to our sides and let the few acorns there fall to the ground.

Laura looked sheepish and sheathed her sword, standing up straight.

"I guess we're all on edge," Renée said, sighing.

Chance looked at the treetops.

"It's hard to tell, but I think it's late afternoon. We just need to go a few miles further, then we can stop."

"You're pushing your team," I heard Renée whisper to him. "They're getting tired."

"We're not tired," I piped up. "We're bored."

Liesl giggled.

"I think," said Chance, "that maybe Holly and Liesl should come up to the front. You two lead for a while. I'm tired." He waved his hand at us, beckoning us forward.

Liesl and I glanced at each other and shrugged.

*Sure, we can do that.*

So that is how Liesl and I ended up at the front of the group, leading Laura, Renée, and Chance.

"Let's run for a bit," said Liesl, glancing back at the others.

*Why not?*

Liesl took off running, as fast as she could.

I sighed and took off after her. I heard the others running as well.

We ran for nearly a mile before stopping.

As I trotted up to Liesl, she was stopped, bent over, her hands on her knees, breathing hard.

"You okay?" I asked.

"Yeah," Liesl answered. "That was awesome!"

I chuckled.

"Good way to break up the monotony.

Laura and Renée and Chance ran up to us. Laura stopped by grabbing my waist, laughing.

I whirled and smiled.

"WOO!" Laura said. "I feel better!"

We all did.

Happier, we continued hiking through the dark, monotonous woods for another hour, until the light coming through the trees began to lessen.

"Let's get off the path and go camp by the woods, okay?" Liesl suggested.

"Not a bad idea," I said.

We both glanced back and gestured the others to follow us.

It was a bit of a hike through the dim forest, I guess the path had veered away from the stream a bit. We had a ten-minute walk to get to it.

When we finally heard the water trickle, I stopped Liesl with my hand and pointed.

"What's that?" I asked.

A small man, about three feet high, looking old as the hills, sat next to the stream. He had a campfire going, and a fish on a stick held out over the flame. A long pipe dangled from his mouth, and every twenty seconds or so he would take a drag from it; a moment later, a small puff of white smoke would flow out of his nostrils.

He was on the far side of the stream.

The waterway was about a dozen feet wide here, and a small steppingstone path was set in the water: Wide black stones rose a few inches above the water's surface, about eighteen inches apart.

We gathered about twenty feet from the water's edge and just watched him for a minute.

He was dressed in green and brown clothes, and wore a tall pointed hat, and his beard was long. Very long. I couldn't see where it ended. The white beard grew from his chin and flowed down his tunic, and to the ground, and along the stream, and it disappeared down into the wood.

That beard had to be a hundred feet long.

Maybe more.

The old man saw us and raised a hand in greeting, then went back to cooking his fish.

He seemed like the most interesting character we would ever meet, and I couldn't take my eyes off him.

Suddenly, Chance came forward. "Sir," he called. "May we share your fire?"

The old man nodded and gestured at the campfire, mumbling, "Help yourself. Glad to have the company."

Chance grinned at me, shouldered his pack, and began to skip from stone to stone, and cross the small river.

*Well, I'm not going to be left behind.*

Without another thought, I jumped after him, and hopped over the water, stone by stone.

The others soon followed, and we were all approached the old man's fire.

He smiled at us, his mouth turning up at the corners around the pipe, and nodded again, indicating stumps that were already gathered near the campfire.

We dragged them forward to the fire, and sat down.

Chance pulled a bar of chocolate from his bag and handed it to the old man, who took it with a broad smile.

"Thank ye, son," the old man's high voice crackled. "Tha's mighty delicious, I've heard."

Chance grinned.

Renée leaned and handed the old man a small leather-bound book of poems she took from her bag.

The old man bowed his head, thanking her.

"Thank you for sharing your fire with us," said Chance. "We were just thinking of setting up our tent and camping for the night when we saw you sitting here."

Laura rose and took Renée to the stream to catch more fish. The water was jumping with them, they were so plentiful.

The old man puffed on his pipe and nodded contentedly.

Ten minutes later, Laura and Renée returned with a huge amount of fish.

"There were so many we just dipped our basket in, and they swam right in," Renée laughed.

"I cleaned them, and put the guts and scales back in

the water," said Laura. "The other fish gobbled them up."

"Ewww," I murmured.

Liesl laughed.

Chance had been gathering more firewood and as many long sticks as he could find, and he walked up, his arms full.

Through this all, the old man watched and smiled and nodded.

Ten minutes later, we all had our long sticks with fish at the end, extended over the fire in the same manner as the old man.

Fish cook fast, and I wondered at the old man still holding his out. Then I noticed he didn't have his fish out far enough over the fire: His arms weren't long enough.

I handed my stick to Chance to hold, and went to help the old man. Kneeling next to him, I turned to him and held out my hand. "May I?" I asked.

He nodded and handed me his stick.

I took it and leaned and held the fish over the fire, so it began to cook faster.

Liesl and Renée handed out bread, and we filled cups of water, and all of us had a merry old time.

I loved how sharing food put everyone in a better mood.

The old man loosened up, too.

He withdrew a bottle from under his coat and

uncorked it. After he took a sip, he handed it to me and indicated I should pass it around. He smacked his lips, and I saw a dark drop on his mouth.

Sniffing the bottle, I smelled blackberries. I took a taste, and a wonderful flavor flooded my mouth.

*Blackberry wine.*

I only had a sip, then passed it around.

We soon were telling him of our adventures: about sleeping on top of a giant, fighting red wild sprites off a magical white stag (this impressed him greatly), and getting trapped in the faerie hill.

His eyes went wide at the last.

"Inside the hill?" he asked.

We nodded.

"Over yonder a bit," he pointed back the way we'd come.

"Yep," Liesl answered, nibbling on a bit of fish.

The old man's eyebrows shot so high I thought they'd disappear forever under his cap.

"Well, that is a story," he murmured. "That is indeed a story."

The campfire had died down, and Chance threw few more logs onto it.

The old man brought forward a pouch of fragrant tobacco, and offered it to us. We shook our heads politely no. He shrugged and opened the pouch, withdrawing a pinch of the dark-brown flakes and stuffing them in the bowl of his long pipe, which had gone out.

I finally had to ask the old man, for it had been burning at the back of my mind since we'd sat down. "Sir, your beard, it is so very long. How did it get this long?"

The old man chuckled and sat back, relighting his pipe. "Well, lass, I am a very old man, a very, very old man," he began. "And where I set, I set for a long, long while. I've been set here at this fire for a long time, and before that, I was visiting the moors. That was for years, if I remember correctly. Which sometimes, I admit, I don't. But I know I have been here, in these lands, for a very, very, very long time.

"You see, I am the oldest halfling in the world. The very oldest. I lived with my brethren for most of my life, but about a thousand years ago, I became weary of the youngsters. Just a little bit. They cavorted and danced and they were so active. They wanted me to cavort, but I just want to set a spell in one spot, and smoke a pipe full." He nodded, his head bobbing slowly up and down.

"And so I came here, to this land, at the invitation of my mother. These forests, these moors, they are better suited to an old halfling like myself. You know of the halflings?" He looked up at us.

273

Laura nodded vigorously. Liesl and I joined in.

"I live beside a village of halflings, Sir, my house is in the Elfen lands. I live there with my brother and mother and father. And my uncle, too," said Laura.

The old man nodded sagely. "And do they still do much trading?"

"Oh, my goodness, yes," said Laura. "In fact, the halfling caravan through the Elfen Academy commons on a weekly basis. At least, they used to, before the current..." she fell silent.

The old man nodded. "I have heard of the current danger," he said quietly.

Wanting to change the unpleasantness to which the conversation turned, I took a deep breath and looked around. "Where do you make your home, Sir?" I asked.

The old man shrugged and gestured behind where he sat, with his pipe.

I glanced back and saw a small mound. It looked like a natural part of the forest. I wondered if he slept beside the mound, or if the mound hid a small cave, and after studying it for a minute, decided it must be a combination of the two.

"Eons ago," the old man said, "when I was a young man, I got into a lot of trouble with the people who lived near me. This was the Elfen and also some of the Fae Folk," he puffed thoughtfully on his pipe. "This was long before the Chaos War, when the lands weren't yet split, you understand." He chuckled. "I had a sordid youth, a very sordid youth."

"What do you mean, Sir?" asked Chance. "Were you in trouble with the authorities?"

The old man laughed out loud at this. "You could say that. Yes, you could indeed say that. You see, when I was a much younger man, I was very bored, and I decided to use what gifts I had to grant wishes. But I wanted to have some fun with it, and I was very crafty, you see. So I would make bargains. I would grant wishes, and use my talents, and trick people. Oh, so many people I tricked. After a while, I began to feel bad about it, see?" He rocked back on his stump chair, looking up at the sky and the dying light, blinking fast.

I saw he was blinking back tears.

I patted the old man's shoulder.

*How bad could it be? We all have a past. Heck, I stole apples and bread so many times I lost track.*

The old man was shaking his head.

Chance tossed another log onto the fire.

The night wore on.

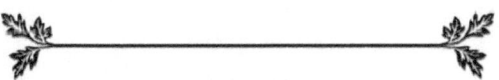

Chapter Twenty-Five
# Not Just an Old Man

The old man was chuckling now, his eyes half-closed. Tears dropped onto his long, white beard.

Chance handed the elder a handkerchief out of his bag.

The old halfling took it with a "thank you" and dabbed at his eyes, before handing it back.

"Well, I am glad that I ended those sordid ways, yes, I am glad they ended," he said. He looked up at me. "Young lady, do you know what finally stopped my mischief?"

I shook my head. I didn't know.

"My mother," the old man said simply. "She loved me so much that she came and took me away, and settled my spirit. She brought me back home, away from the far-off lands I had been causing mischief in, and settled me in one of the older halfling villages, and I lived there, for a very, very, very long time. They revered me, and it further settled my spirit. And that's when I began to grow my beard."

*Oh.*

"Do you know it is as long as this river?" the old man asked. "I have been here for so long, it had grown and grown and grown.

The fire was dying down.

Liesl was curled up next to the stump she'd been sitting on.

Chance picked her up and led her to the tent, which he'd help Laura set up an hour earlier.

Renée yawned.

Laura seemed rapt, listening to the old halfling.

"I am very old now, and I don't move much," the old man said. "And I guess I will be setting here on my stump for years to come."

"Aren't you lonely?" I asked, unable to stop myself.

He shrugged. "The animals come visit me, then bring me food and drink. Who do you think brought me this wine?" he held up the bottle of blackberry wine, wiggling it.

I was astonished, because he had been handing it

around the fire for several hours now, and we'd all been sipping from the bottle. The old man had been sipping from the wine most of all. And the bottle was still full.

"And did the animals bring you your fish, too?" Chance asked, returning from settling Liesl into her blanket.

The old man nodded. "They did, young man. They certainly did."

"But," I said, looking around, "We haven't seen any animals, other than the birds. Are they hiding?"

"I think they are, young lady," the old man said. He glanced around all of us. "It does seem very abandoned here, right now."

"The other forest was teeming with life," I said. "They weren't as afraid of us."

The old man nodded, puffing his pipe, and said nothing.

One thing that I thought was odd: Chance had not made any introductions to the old man, not at all. He hadn't told the halfling who we were.

I looked at Chance, and noticed, for the first time, that his eyes were merry, yet guarded.

"Young lady," the old man said to Laura, "You say your house is near a halfling village?"

Laura nodded, smiling.

"And you are obviously Elfen, correct?" he asked.

"I am," said Laura.

The old man turned to me. "And you, young lady, are you Elfen as well?" he asked.

"I am one-quarter Elfen," I said. My mother was half-Elfen. She died." I looked down at my feet briefly.

"Oh, dear. Oh, I am sorry," the old halfling said gently.

I nodded. I had developed a knot in my throat I couldn't talk around.

"And the rest of you, you are all Fae Folk, correct?" the old man asked.

"Yes, that's right," said Renée.

Aspen and Tundra were asleep at my feet, and they had begun to snore gently.

"Not unlike the hill giants, eh?" I asked Chance, grinning.

He chuckled.

"Oh, have you met the hill giants?" asked the old man.

"Not exactly," Chance said. "We did not realize it, but we actually made camp and slept the night on one, or against him, or something."

The old halfling chuckled and puffed his pipe. "Ah yes, this is not uncommon. They only wake every century or so. This is how they get the grass growing over them."

*That makes sense.*

"Sir," said Laura, "if I may ask?"

The old man nodded.

"You mentioned things that led me to believe that you, sir, are of a very old age?"

He nodded.

"And you are a halfling, Sir?" she asked.

He nodded again.

"Well, I was wondering," Laura asked. "Have you ever heard of Thornton the Elder? We were told stories of him when I was very, very young."

The old man smiled, and tears came down onto his beard. "Yes," he said in a rough voice, "I have heard of him, child."

"Do you, have you heard what ever became of him?" Laura asked. "We were told tales of him, tales of how he was so old he was ageless, how he was the oldest halfling in the world."

The old man nodded, wiping his eyes. "Thornton traveled far and finally went home to rest," he said, his voice getting clearer. "I held him myself, as he fell into the final sleep." The old man looked up at Laura. "Thornton was my grandson."

Laura gasped and nearly fell off her stump. "Your... your gr... grandson?!"

The old man nodded, this time quite deeply.

"But..." Laura gasped again. "That would... that would make you..." she fell silent, her jaw dropped open.

"You may say it, young lady," the old man said. "You

may say it aloud. Go on ahead. It's okay."

Laura remained silent, her jaw working to find the words that would not come.

"What is it, Laura?" whispered Chance. "Who is this old man?"

"He..." Laura swallowed and began to cry softly.

"Oh, my dear. Don't cry," the old man said softly. He reached out and patted Laura's hand, and this seemed to greatly calm her.

She was able to collect her thoughts.

After a while, she could speak.

Staring at the old man, she told us what she'd been unable to say earlier.

"Stories about Thornton are revered among Elfen children. His adventures and his great deeds, they're amazing and used to teach Elfen children not only about right and wrong, but about bravery and courage." She took a deep breath. "Thornton's grandfather is mentioned only briefly. At the beginning of most Thornton's stories, they tell of Thornton's grandfather and how he was the bravest halfling of them all, of how Thornton learned everything that safeguarded him during his adventures, at his grandfather's knee. Of how Thornton's grandfather was the very first halfling born."

She sat back, staring at the old man.

*The first halfling?!*

The old man nodded. "I will admit to being very old. Very, very old."

"Sir, if you are indeed Thornton's grandfather, and the very first halfling in the world, that would mean... um..." Chance stammered.

The old halfling nodded. "Yes."

Chance shook his head. "You do indeed have a sordid past, I guess. But so interesting." He thought for a minute, staring at the old man. "I'm good friends with your brother," he murmured softly.

Renée yawned. "Well, I'm not sure at all what is going on, but we seem to have met a famous person mentioned in books, eh?"

The old man chuckled and shook his head. "I'm just an old man, sitting in front of a fire, cooking his dinner," he said, although dinner was now in his stomach.

The shadows were growing deeper.

The old man yawned, and then yawned again, and I began to feel guilty.

*Old people need their sleep.*

"Perhaps we should all retire for the night," said Chance softly, still staring at the old man.

"Yes," the old halfling agreed.

"Will we see you in the morning, Sir?" Chance asked.

"Oh, don't need to call me 'sir', no indeed, no need for such formality. It's lonely being this old, I am just glad for the company," he chuckled. "And yes, I will be here in the morning."

We all went into the tent, leaving the old man by the fire.

I glanced back one last time.

When we were in the tent, lying in our blankets, I asked softly, "So we're just going to leave him out there?"

"He knows what he's doing, Holly," Chance murmured, drifting off to sleep.

Laura looked at me, her eyebrows still raised in surprise. "I can't believe it; I just can't believe it..."

She soon fell asleep.

It was very late.

I could hear the fire crackling.

I drifted off to sleep.

A short while later, I started awake, opening my eyes and glancing around. I wasn't sure what had woken me.

*Perhaps a bad dream...*

It bothered me that we had just left the old man out by the fire, alone.

Aspen raised her head beside me. Her sister slept on, snoring softly.

I thought for a minute, then ruffled in my bag and brought out my second blanket, and crawled out of the tent with it. Aspen followed me, padding soundlessly beside me.

Several hours had passed.

The old man was gone from his stump.

The fire had died down to nearly nothing.

It was in the dead of night.

I glanced around. I saw the old halfling huddled next to the mound of dried leaves and flotsam. He lay there, still in his clothes, his back to the mound, his hat pulled down low over his eyes.

I went and spread my blanket over the him, covering his body, tucking the blanket in under his shoulders.

So he'd be warm.

It was a cold night.

As I walked back to the tent, I saw several sets of glowing eyes watching me. Aspen glanced at them, then glanced at me. She didn't make a sound, but I could read her thoughts in her eyes.

*Deer.*

We went back to our blankets in the tent, and both of us fell back to sleep in minutes.

In the morning, Chance and Liesl were up first, and the rest of us shortly afterward.

As I emerged out of the tent, I saw the old man was awake and back at his stump, sitting contentedly, his long pipe back in his mouth.

A tendril of sweet-scented smoke drifted lazily up from the bowl, and as he inhaled, the contents briefly glowed red.

Chance waved and yawned at the old man.

I stirred the banked fire, adding more wood, and soon had the flames flickering high. They cut through the morning fog and warmed the old man; I could tell because he loosened his arms, which had been curled around his coat.

Laura came to sit beside him, just wanting to be close to him, it appeared.

Renée, Liesl, and I got busy heating up stew and breaking out flatbread, and cleaning up the space in preparation to break camp.

Laura brought the old man a bowl of stew and a large piece of fragrant flatbread, with berries baked into it. "I made this bread myself, at school last week, try it? Tell me how you like it."

"Thank you, my dear," the old man said, taking the food and beginning to wolf down the stew. "Very kind of you, very kind."

We were packed and ready to go in less than twenty minutes. We all sat quietly by the fire, and I handed the old man a mug of hot cocoa, which he sipped gratefully.

"We really must be going, Sir," Chance said softly. "We are on a quest, you see. My king has sent us to rescue The Oak King, not sure if you're aware, Sir..."

The old man nodded. "I am aware, young man. I understand, and I thank you, all of you, for being so brave. Of course, we will help as much as we can. The spirits of the forest, all of us, we will help."

Chance nodded, his cheeks pink in the morning cold. He sighed and stood up. It was clear he didn't want to leave, but the quest was of utmost importance.

We all got up.

The old man stood and handed me back my cup, and my blanket, folded neatly. He looked into my eyes a long time. "I will not forget your kindness, Holly."

*I had not told him my name. None of us had.*

"How... how do you... how do you know my name?" I asked in a quiet voice.

He laid his finger on the side of his nose. "We communicate without words, we Old Ones." He patted my arm and put his head close to mine. "Rumpelstiltskin knows more than people think," he said.

I started in shock, staring at him. "You're..."

He nodded. "I am known by many names; that is just

one of them, dear one." He sat back down on his stump, and gazed into the fire.

We walked away, and used the steppingstones to cross over the creek again.

Before we were out of sight, we turned back to look and saw him still sitting there.

"If he is the first halfling," Chance murmured, "then his mother is the queen, and he himself is one of the kings of the earth."

I stared, my gaze reaching through the mist, which was curling thicker than ever over the water of the stream. As I looked, I thought I saw the view of the old man sitting on a stump before a small fire, flicker. In its place I saw a great king, sitting grandly on a wood-carved throne. He held a royal staff, and had a golden crown on his head, and many deer had come to gather to him.

I blinked my eyes again and just saw the old halfling.

I took a deep breath and turned, and we hiked back up to the path and continued on our journey.

## Chapter Twenty-Six

# Black as Night, Cold as Ice

We traveled along the stone path, which led out of the forest some hours later. We emerged into the sunshine again, and each of us raised our faces to the light, weary of the darkness of the forest.

We weren't quite on the moor, but we had left the thick forest. We were now in a light forest of silver birch trees, and I could tell this wood was much younger.

"It's like a different island entirely," said Liesl.

I turned to Chance. "Are we seriously still on the Isle of Skye?" I didn't think that was possible.

"We are, sort of," said Chance. "The Isle of Skye in modern times is only fifty miles long. In ancient times it was much larger, and since we are in the Faerie lands, and we have been in Faerie lands since we stepped foot on Skye, it's longer than fifty miles. At least five times that long."

I blinked.

"So, while we came through ancient faerie forests, in modern times, those forests..." I trailed off.

"In modern times, they are mostly open moors, a few trees, and several villages. Tourists, paved roads, trolleys, that sort of thing," Chance explained.

It was confusing and made my head spin. I was glad to be with Chance and Renée, who seemed to be extremely familiar with this area in ancient times.

"I can't believe we shared a meal with Thornton's grandfather," said Liesl, coming up to walk with me.

I nodded. "It's incredible," I said. I would always think of the old halfling as Rumpelstiltskin, the mischievous character of legend.

*Or perhaps as one of Titania's children, and therefore, brother to The Holly and Oak Kings. Or, actually, I would remember him as a kind old man who was happy to share his fire and his companionship with us. Yes, that's how I knew I would remember him.*

We walked on.

We came upon a mass of berry bushes and spent a half-hour picking berries, carefully placing them into our wooden bowls from our bags.

I stuffed the overripe ones into my mouth, reasoning that they'd just get mushed and wet and untidy if I tried to store them.

My mouth was ringed with dark juice by the time we moved on.

"Okay, let's go," Chance called. "We can clean up on the way."

Liesl and I licked our fingers as we walked.

"I love berries," said Liesl. "I always forget how much, until I taste them again, and them I'm all like, Oooooooh: berries!"

"Especially wild berries," I said between licking my fingers.

Liesl nodded.

The birch forest we hiked through was full of small birds that twittered and sang as if they were mad.

"Must be mating season," I said, looking around.

Liesl snorted. I grinned at her.

"Speaking of mating season," she said, "How's it going with you and our fearless leader?"

I barked out a laugh. "Which one?" I pointed my chin at the front of our straggly group, where Renée and Chance led, talking together as they hiked.

Liesl laughed. "Chance, silly."

I skipped along a few steps. "It's going okay, I guess. I

wish this war wasn't making everything more difficult. I'd rather be back at school and kissing him on the front lawn."

"Tell me about it," murmured Liesl. "I'm not even sure where Jack is right now."

"What do you mean? He's at the Academy, with the other kids, in class," I said. "Right?"

Liesl got serious. "I hope so, but I'm not sure. I spoke with the headmistress a few days before we left, and she mentioned that the Academic Council was playing it day by day. The Faction wasn't active anywhere near the school, she said, but that could change at any moment."

"You mean, they're worried The Faction will start bombing near the Academy grounds again?" I whispered. "But Father put up that barrier; they can't get near the castle again."

"First of all, they *can* get close to it. The barrier extends only fifty miles out," said Liesl. "Second of all, and this is important: Remember Jessica? She got in, and that was after the barrier was erected. So you don't know. None of us knows." She looked worried.

My stomach started churning. I knew I couldn't really do anything to protect Titania Academy directly, but it felt as though my presence there *had* helped to keep it safe.

*That's silly, Holly.*

I worried as I hiked. I didn't know what was going on right now at my school.

Liesl put her arm over my shoulder as we hiked. "Hey, I'm sorry, I didn't mean to worry you. I'm sure the Academy is fine, and those kids are going to class and carrying on just peachy. Jack's probably playing soccer on the front lawn. The professors can keep it safe, with the help of the barrier. Just because Jessica got in, that doesn't mean a thing. The barrier blocks out explosives, not people."

I nodded, breathing easier.

*That's right. That's right. I need to calm down.*

I looked up and saw Renée and Chance were getting farther ahead. I was falling behind.

"Come on, Li, let's run," I said, grabbing her sleeve as I took off running to catch up.

Liesl laughed and ran after me, and caught up, and we both jogged up to the others.

"Hi!" I said, patting Laura on the back as I started walking again. "Good berries, huh?"

Laura glanced at me and laughed. "Your cheeks are smeared with juice!"

I wiped my face on my sleeve.

Chance suddenly stopped, putting his arm out.

We'd been too loud.

We were hiking up a rise in the birch forest, and

Chance preferred we stay hushed, to blend in better.

"You want to scare away every single thing within a mile?" he whispered.

"No," I mumbled.

"Okay, then. Let's walk quickly and quietly." He nodded and smiled and started hiking again.

I look over at Liesl and smiled.

We would be quiet.

After another hour of hiking, the birch forest got thicker. We'd seen wildlife all over the place, and now, with the trees growing closer together, the squirrels got ridiculously numerous.

We stayed together now, hiking in a close-knit group. We'd stopped at a little stream, where I was able to wash my face and hands, and I felt immediately better for it.

Chance and Renée led us over another rise and down into a small valley.

The path here was just dirt, but it had been kept up, and it was free of weeds and stone.

The valley sloped gently, and the birch trees got much thicker, the further we went.

Soon, it was harder to see ahead. The path wound back and forth through the trees. We could only see about eight or ten feet ahead at any time.

After a half-hour of this, Chance suddenly stopped. He held up a finger for quiet, and we stood there, still and noiseless, waiting.

He turned and motioned for us to remain where we were, while he went on ahead.

*This means he senses danger. Seriously, that's the only thing this could mean. Danger.*

Renée, Laura, Liesl, and I remained still, not even talking, as Chance carefully and quietly creeped ahead.

He disappeared around some trees and was gone for quite a while.

At least, it seemed quite a while. It was probably only ten minutes.

We waited.

Chance suddenly reappeared and, holding his finger to his lips, motioned for us to come forward.

He led us forward on the path about thirty feet, then turned off the trail, and we followed him deeper into the wood.

It grew noticeably colder as we moved through the trees.

Chance stopped, turning and again putting his finger to his lips for quiet. He mouthed silently the words, *no sudden movements*, and we all nodded in understanding.

He crept around a half-dozen more trees and stopped. We followed and stopped with him

We looked.

I put my hand over my mouth, because I almost exploded in surprise.

Chance had found a small glade completely ringed by trees.

Sunlight streamed through the tops of the trees, sliding sideways, slanting into the glade in ribbons of gold.

It was cold, really cold. Frost covered the ground inside of the glade.

In the glade was a family of miniature black unicorns. The two adults were probably as tall as Chance was, the colts were maybe three feet high.

The adults lay on the soft leaves that filled the glade, and the babies stood near them.

The colts' ears were swiveling a mile a minute as they sensed us.

The mare and stallion seemed less concerned.

They were beautiful.

Their coats were all black as coal, shiny black, and each of their cloven hooves looked as if they were made of obsidian.

Long manes and tails fell many feet from the adults, while the colts, who were very likely twins born that spring, sported manes that were a few inches long and stood straight up into the air, giving the babies a comical look. The colts' tails were foot-long bottlebrushes that kept swishing back and forth, although there were no flies nearby to shoo away. *What sass.*

We stood watching them; we didn't move. We didn't budge one inch. We were afraid of breaking the magic spell that had to have been cast for such a miracle to appear before us.

I tried not to breath. Slowly, my chest rose, in and out, in and out, as calm as I could make it. My heart, though, thundered in my chest, and I feared the family of miniature unicorns would hear it and become spooked.

After a long while I realized the gorgeous creatures could not hear my thudding heartbeat, and that I wouldn't spook them away, not with my heartbeat.

I tried not to blink. I didn't want to miss one second of them.

We stood there for hours.

After the first hour, Laura slowly lowered herself to the ground, and sat, her back against a tree, watching the fabled creatures.

The rest of us eventually joined her.

We said not a word.

I knew these were far different from the raggedy unicorns we had seen pulling the wagon in the Elfen lands, even different from the unicorns we had seen the first day, pulling the carriage Lord Fancy-Pants had taken us in.

*Don't speak ill of the dead, Holly.*

I closed my eyes, silently agreeing with my conscience. Especially in the enchanted land of Faerie, it was important to adhere to the old customs.

*I wonder if that one is true?*

I made a mental note to ask Professor Farryn about it when I got back.

I realized with a start that I had a positive feeling, and I had all along, about this quest. There was no question: I would return triumphant.

Maybe it was because my father, The Holly King, had sent us, deliberately. I trusted that he would not set us to a task we had no hope of completing.

Maybe it was because we were with Chance and Renée. Chance was The King's Liege, and I realized I had known this all along. He'd been given extra magic in that position, and in the position of Finder for Titania Academy, even more magic.

And Renée, upperclassman. Fourth Year. Straight-A student. Teacher's Pet. Teacher's aide, come to think of it. I'd been aware that Renée had been instructing me in various forms of magic all throughout this journey. I could tell. It was obvious.

*Hey, class lessons must continue.*

I stared at the family of pitch-black unicorns as they dozed in the glade. The colts had lain down next to their parents, and all four had closed their eyes.

The sun began to set.

The light in the glade began to wink out, quicker than the forest behind us.

I glanced back and saw the rest of the birch forest was growing dimmer, but not nearly as fast as this private little glade.

This nest of miniature black unicorns.

We waited.

I knew something would happen; I just didn't know what.

I shivered as the temperature dropped even further. The frosty air of the glade became an icy chill, and I turned my collar up, pulling my coat's hood over my head.

Liesl and the others did the same.

It was cold and dark.

We could barely make out the unicorns.

Suddenly, Chance got to his feet, and we followed his lead.

The adult unicorns got to their feet, as well, and then the colts, too. The obsidian-colored horns spiraling forth from each smooth equine forehead were lifted toward the sky by all four unicorns.

The glade was now nearly pitch black, black as night.

The air was as cold as ice.

If I turned my head away from the glade into the slightly brighter forest, the moonlight illuminated my breath, and I could see the steamy air coming from my lungs.

The unicorns kept their horns pointed as high as they could, straight up into the air.

They made no move to leave the glade, and if they had, we would've melted out of sight, out of their way, because it was very clear these magical creatures were on a mission.

We watched as the moon rose, ascending above the tree trunks and high into the night sky.

Slowly, the moon's light cascaded down into the small glade, and as it did, each unicorn's horn sought it out.

The first horn tip to be touched by moonlight was the largest unicorn's. The stallion.

The moment the moonlight touched it, the unicorn vanished in a flash of black light, soundless, as if in a vacuum.

Next to be transported was the mare, the colt's

mother. Her obsidian-colored horn reached high; the moonlight touched it, and she was gone in the same kind of noiseless burst that had taken her mate.

The colts remained.

They were restless.

They knew what to do, though.

Still and quiet, the raised their little heads high, lifting their unicorn horns to the moonlight.

They were obviously twins, and their heights were the same. The moonlight touched their horns simultaneously.

With silent *pops!* they both disappeared.

The clearing was empty.

With the miniature unicorn family now departed, the cold also fled. Warmth slowly entered the glade, tentative at first, then more steadily.

We withdrew.

The glade was like a chapel.

Chapter Twenty-Seven
# Álfheimr

$W$e walked on about a mile, down the moonlit path, and made camp in the forest under the friendly birch trees.

We were quiet, each of us still feeling awed at what we had observed.

The tent went up, firewood was gathered, the stone fire ring was arranged, and after less than an hour, we were all gathered around the fire, warming ourselves and eating rabbit again.

Laura had gone hunting as we searched for a camping spot.

"I have to clear my head; it's full of magical miniature black unicorns," she had said.

She'd returned with two massive jackrabbits, tied and hanging from her shoulder.

"I couldn't have gotten a third if I had wanted to," she said. "They're so heavy."

We were happy but subdued.

Roasted rabbit, skewered and cooked over the fire, filled our bellies, and we were content.

As we sat there, waiting to get sleepy, I asked what I'd been wanting to ask for hours.

"Does everyone know what the story is with those unicorns we saw but me?" I asked, feeling out of the loop, once again.

Liesl, Renée and Chance all looked at each other. Laura glanced at them and then turned to me. "I don't know about the fables of the Fae Folk lands, Holly, but I know we've got real unicorns in the Elfen lands, and although none of them look like the ones we just saw, we have our own legends about their kind. It's said the tiniest unicorns carry away bad dreams, and allow the restless to sleep. They are supposed to come in the night, to bedrooms and caves, and tents and coves and anywhere a person falls asleep. They give aid to the troubled. They stand by the sleeper, and dip their horns and suck away all the nightmares." She finished and sat back, glancing once again at the others. It was clear she was curious to find out if the Fae Folk myths and legends were different than what she'd grown up learning.

Chance cleared his throat and smiled. Liesl and Renée gave each other a knowing look.

"Well?" I asked.

Renée nodded at Chance and said, "You're the storyteller."

Chance grimaced and put his head to the side, then said, "We have much the same legends concerning the miniature unicorns: They come to take away bad dreams. But the myth goes a bit further." He thought for a minute, then continued. "See, these unicorns were pitch black. And their presence made the glade icy cold. In the myths and legends of the Fae Folk, this means that they had been taking away bad dreams for a long time. They were filled with them. They were black with them. They were icy cold with them.

"Nightmares are physical things. When the dream unicorns soak them up, it slowly fills them to the brim. They grow from snowy white, to grey, and slowly to black. Filled up, you see. In the legends of the Fae Folk, those unicorns were full to the brim." Chance shook his head. "I only hope they can release the nightmares somewhere. Get rid of them. I don't know what will happen if they can't."

Liesl tentatively raised her hand. In her softly accented voice, she said, "I'm from Germany, and we have similar legends about the miniature unicorns. But we go a bit further. In our Old World legends, the unicorns soak up the nightmares, yes. They turn from white to black with them. And when they are pitch black, completely filled up and icy cold with the terrible dreams, they go to the heavens and release all the blackness, which they've changed from nightmares to just inky cold blackness. They catch the moonbeams and are transported into the night sky, high, high up, and the night sky, the stars and the moon, drains the cold and black away, so the unicorns can return to the Faerie Lands warm and white and bright again, ready to visit more dreamers and soak up the nightmares."

Liesl sat back, satisfied.

I stared with love at my best friend.

She was perfect.

We slept so well through the night in the birch forest that, for the first time in a long time, I didn't wake up until dawn.

My eyes came open and settled on the inside of the tent ceiling, and I felt more refreshed and rested than I had in a very long time.

*I wonder if the miniature unicorns visited us in the night and soaked away any bad dreams we might have had.*

I felt so good, I believed it to be true.

I lay there in my blanket, turned on my side, and felt contented.

Everyone else was still asleep, but I could see by the faint light against the tent walls that the sun had risen at least an hour ago.

Aspen and Tundra lay against me, their white fluffy coats keeping me toasty warm.

Liesl and Chance each lay against one of the wolves; they had taken to sleeping against them to stay warm, and my darling familiars had been happy to oblige.

*Happy for the fun and company.*

I grinned.

I withdrew from my bag a small book I had brought, and lay there quietly reading in the morning light.

The adventure I read had me riveted to the page, and I didn't realize at first that Liesl and Renée had woken up.

I was vaguely aware that Aspen and Tundra were awake, though.

It was a very good book, about an angel and a demon and the end of the world, and a little boy everyone was trying to find. And my favorite part was about how the lady in the book kept consulting her ancestor's book on predictions and prophecies of good omens.

I finally noticed everyone was awake and moving about when I heard Liesl's soft gasp of surprise. I looked up when she ran to get Chance and Renée, and they all stumbled out of the tent.

*I guess I have to stop reading.*

I carefully placed a leaf in the book to hold my place, closed it slowly, held it to my face for a moment, promising I would return to reading it as soon as I could, then returned it to my bag and sat up.

Aspen and Tundra were alert and facing the tent flap door while I pulled on my shoes and stood up.

I pulled on my coat and stepped outside and into a dream.

We had fallen asleep in the middle of a birch forest, and we woke up in a dream.

Aspen and Tundra poked their heads out and brushed past me, walking a few steps forward, then whining, and coming back to sit on either side of my legs.

The landscape I looked out on was bleak.

The sunlight was fitful.

The trees were gone.

The land and air were... well, *dim* was the only way I could think to describe it. It was as if we had been transported to an alien planet where the sun was half the size it was on Earth. Half the size and red, from the looks of it. I shaded my eyes and peered up at the scrawny star and felt worry.

Liesl, Laura, and Renée were all moving about the campfire, trying to get it going again.

Chance came walking up, a grim smile on his face.

"What... what happened?" I asked.

He took a deep breath. "The ferryman brings those who are deemed worthy, across the dreamboat while you sleep, and you wake up here, Holly" he grimaced. "Welcome to Álfheimr."

Chapter Twenty-Eight
# Faerie Haunt

A bloodcurdling scream filled the air; it seemed to come from nowhere and everywhere. It moved over the land from the right, across the ground, and ended in the land to the left.

A chill went up my spine, and I shivered uncontrollably.

"Everyone gather around. Stay very close, and listen," Chance said in a fervent whisper.

We all sat next to the fire, huddled around its fitful flames.

"Álfheimr is a very dangerous place," said Chance. "Humans think it is a place of light and beauty. It is not.

Not anymore. Álfheimr is the land of chaos, now. It's where the dark chaos was defeated, and where it has been awakened by The Faction, and the land has been laid waste by the dark chaos."

He turned to Laura. "The Elfen have known this land has been cursed, have you not?"

She slowly nodded her head. "We learn of the great war, the dark chaos which was finally defeated, but not before the two Faerie people were split into two lands," Laura said in a small voice.

Chance nodded. "Álfheimr lies between the Elfen and Fae Folk lands. You and Holly and Liesl were trying to travel home from the Elfen Lands last fall, but you never even made it to the border. That's actually a good thing: The border between the two lands is a miles-deep gorge no creature can cross." Chance put his head up and looked around as another scream sounded across the bleak landscape. "This land," he continued in a whisper, "is haunted by the Faeries who died in the great war. It is inhabited only by the Fae creatures who thrive on negative emotions, on fear, cruelty, and devastation. This part of our journey, while the shortest in terms of distance, is also by far the most dangerous."

My heart was beating a mile a minute as Chance spoke. I felt cold and terrified. And my hair was frizzing up something awful.

"Now," Chance said. "Listen very carefully to me." He looked at each of us in turn, his eyes boring into each of ours with an intensity borne of desperation. "The enemy in this land is fear. Fear will freeze you. Fear will reduce you to a frightened rabbit. Fear will leave you curled into a fetal position and crying. Fear is the enemy." He paused to let his words sink in.

"Here in Álfheimr, only the strongest survive. So the best way for us to get through this and rescue The Oak King is to get angry at the things that will surely, before long, attack us. If you find yourself getting angry at one of us, that is another Faerie haunting your head. Stay together; stick close. Be angry at the land, at the monsters. Because this land is full of them."

He closed his eyes briefly.

"The Holly King gave me one piece of advice to help guide us through this time: Get in and out as fast as we can. We don't want to fall asleep here if we can help it. We don't want to rest; we don't want to let down our guard.

"Álfheimr used to be a lush green paradise before the dark chaos took it over. The Faerie forces may have defeated that chaos, but the lush green beauty never returned, not in thousands of years. What does this tell you?"

"It tells me that the darkness still lives," I said in a

quiet voice. "That's how The Faction revived it. It never died."

Renée nodded. "That's it, exactly, Holly. You've hit the nail on the head."

We got to our feet.

"All familiars should be out and running beside us, to help, if they can," said Chance.

I glanced down at Tundra and Aspen, my white wolf familiars.

I brought out my magic staff, and I drew out my magic stick from my bag, and slipped it into my waistband.

Liesl had her own magical staff, and Snowbear, her snowy ermine familiar, sat across her shoulders, her head low, chattering softly.

Chance's hawk was on his shoulder, her sharp eyes scanning the landscape.

Renée's rabbit Jade sat at her feet, up on hind paws, sniffing the air for danger.

Laura's new familiar was perched on her shoulder, the parrot's bright plumage a beautiful visual in the bleak landscape.

Chance took a deep breath and nodded. "Let's pack up and get moving. I don't think we have far to go, but we need to be ready for anything.

All of us worked rapidly to pack the tent and our bags, and throw dirt on the fire. We were ready in ten minutes.

I coughed a few times as I worked, and I heard Liesl and Renée cough as well. Chance came and handed us our bandanas, telling us to tie them around our faces, that they would help a little.

"The air is as sick as the ground," he said, then went to pick up the tent and put it into the large bag we had to carry it. He walked behind us and began struggling with it.

I tied the bandana he'd given me around my face, knotting it at the back of my neck. I looked worriedly down at Aspen and Tundra, and wondered if I should tie cloths around their faces, too.

"They're magical," said Liesl. "They should be unaffected, cleansed of any ill effect as soon as they transport back to their realms."

"We're magical, too," I retorted, "And we need to wear the bandanas."

Liesl shrugged. "We don't transport to alternate realms, though. They do. In fact, we should be sending them back every night."

"I have been, for a few hours," I smiled.

She nodded.

The land was mostly barren of plant life. I couldn't believe it had once been lush and green.

Here and there, a few scrubby plants struggled to

survive. They grew a few inches into the poisoned air, their color was dull and greyish brown.

The ground was dirt and rock, and the dirt seemed diseased. I bent to look at it. There was trash and sticky residue spread out over the ground, and black animal hair, and it looked filthy.

"Don't touch it with your bare skin, if you can help it," said Renée.

I nodded and glanced at Aspen and Tundra.

"Come here, girls," I murmured. I lifted their paws to check the skin there. It seemed unaffected, but I didn't know how long that would last.

*This place blows.*

I brushed my hands off as I rose to my feet.

"Now," said Chance, studying a map he held in his hands, "We need to proceed forward, and follow the path, just as before. Only watch out for tricks. The creatures here won't just be living and meeting us. They'll be actively trying to trip us up, to hurt us."

I looked out on the land. I couldn't see anything there, and since there wasn't any real vegetation to speak of, certainly none more than a few inches high, I wondered if we weren't actually alone.

"Are there any creatures around at all?" I asked, voicing my thoughts. "I see nothing, absolutely nothing. No life, no movement."

Chance glanced at me, an indecipherable look on his face. "Wait for it. You'll see."

A chill traveled up my spine as I stared into his face.

He had been distant since we'd started this quest, and I'd assumed it was because we weren't ever really alone. Chance was a private person, I figured. But his attitude was starting to freak me out.

Chance did a double take and came up to me.

"Hey," he said softly. He took my hand and brought it up to his cheek. "We'll get through this."

I ducked my head, embarrassed he'd been able to read my thoughts just by looking at my face. "I know," I said, bringing my head back up and looking in his eyes. They looked distant, like stranger's eyes. I was suddenly filled with such a worried feeling my breath quickened.

He pulled me into a brief embrace.

I put my hands around his waist and shivered.

Something doesn't feel right.

I looked up and screamed.

"Holly! Holly!" Chance shook me gently.

I backed away from him. "I... I saw something on your back!"

"What?" Chance turned his head and tried to look behind him.

Renée turned him around, and jumped.

A giant spider, about the size of a beach ball, was

emerging out of a hole in Chance's T-shirt, and slowly climbing up Chance's back.

I screamed again, filled with horror.

Chance bent double, a gargling sound coming out of his mouth.

"WHAT IS THAT?" Renée screamed.

Chance's form was crumpled on the ground, deflated. The large spider climbing out was swelling and scratching at the ground, and it had grown to three feet tall.

"AIIEEE!" Liesl screamed.

"MOVE BACK!" I lifted my hands, summoning a vision of a snowstorm to my mind. Fire flared in my palms.

"But... but that's Chance!" cried Laura.

"That's not Chance," said Renée. "Chance is behind us."

"Make sure," I said, not wanting to take my eyes off the spider.

The Chance suit it had been wearing was now a puddle dissolving into the ground.

I shuddered, thinking how the monster had been embracing me.

*Now's not the time to get grossed out, Holly. Remember what Chance said: get angry, not frightened.*

I closed my eyes briefly and felt anger growing in me.

The fire growing in my hands flared.

The spider rose on its hind legs, and a piercing cry filled the air.

Suddenly, it jumped at me.

"Burn it, Holly!" Renée's cries came to my ears just as I let loose with my Elemental Power and caught the thing midair with a ball of flame.

It caught and fell to the ground a foot in front of me.

I backed up and kept the flame shooting from my hands on it, steadily.

I took several steps back as the thing burned, and it writhed and screamed as it died.

I flamed it until it was a pile of ashes.

Renée and Liesl stepped close to peer at it, wrinkling their noses.

Laura stayed back, holding her mouth, clearly trying not to vomit.

I finally quieted the fire coming from my hands, took a deep breath, and dropped my arms to the side.

"Jesus Christ," said Chance behind me.

I whirled in surprise. "You gave me a heart attack." I put my hand on my chest.

Renée pulled us together, bodily, she grabbed Liesl's and Laura's sleeves and yanked them close.

"Listen," she said. "We need to be on our guard. Holly just now thought that was Chance. It wasn't."

"Duh," I said cheekily.

"Any of us, at any time, can be tricked," said Renée. "Any of us. Be careful. Nobody leave. Everybody stay close. Watch each other. Be careful. And from now on, no touching if you can help it."

"I already know," said Chance.

"That wasn't him," I said, "That was the monster."

"Yeah, yeah, just be careful, okay?" Renée said, tense as a bowstring.

We were all tense and, on our guard, and I was sure we would remain this stressed until we got home.

*This place is a nightmare.*

Chapter Twenty-Nine
# The Trow

We began walking in a tight group, and although we stayed together, we didn't touch each other. It was hard, but we were very motivated.

Giant spiders crawling out a copy of your boyfriend will do that.

After less than an hour, we were all panting.

I felt like I was dying of thirst.

*What is going on?*

"It's the air," said Chance. "And the sunlight and the gravity."

*The gravity?*

At this point, we were walking slower, but Chance

explained as he walked; he didn't stop.

"The sun here is severely blocked, both by the toxic atmosphere and by the dark chaos magic in this realm. The sunlight drains you, instead of filling you. And the gravity is at least fifty percent stronger than normal. Can't you feel it?"

I realized I could. My steps were harder to take, my arms and legs felt heavier, and it was getting worse.

*What happens when we can't even move?*

"Chance," asked Laura, "You said we're in a different realm?"

He nodded as he walked. "Just as our familiars have their own realm, this dark chaos has taken hold of this place and made it its own. This realm has been ripped from our reality. There is no way to walk to this place, or walk away from it. We were brought here by the ferryman, and that is the only way we can return."

His voice was quiet at the end, and I had to strain to hear it. He sounded sad and dejected, and his tone of voice scared me more than his words.

None of us said anything. We were all afraid.

I suddenly remembered.

"Fear is the enemy," I said in a loud voice. It took most of my energy to say it, but as my words filled the air, I felt lighter.

I felt my energy returning to me.

"FEAR IS THE ENEMY," I called out. My voice echoed over the land. I stood straighter and walked better, and my steps were easier.

"FEAR IS THE ENEMY!" Liesl cried out, and then looked at me and grinned. "It helps, it really helps," she said.

I jumped up my fist in the air. "FEAR IS THE ENEMY!" I called out in an exuberant voice.

Laura and Renée grinned, but looked tired.

"She's got the right idea," said Chance.

"Let's run!" I said.

"I can't. I just don't have the energy, Holly," Chance said in a weak voice.

I grabbed his hands.

"We're not supposed to touch," he protested.

I didn't let go.

"FEAR IS THE ENEMY!" I called out, and pulled Chance into a run.

He stumbled.

"Say it with me, Chance," I said.

"Fear is the enemy," he said. "Fear is the enemy!" He stood up straighter.

We all jumped up and called out, "FEAR IS THE ENEMY!" and it gave us energy.

We probably looked like a bunch of crazies, but we didn't care.

We jumped again, "FEAR IS THE ENEMY!" and started running together.

"Don't leave anyone behind!" I called out.

We ran. We yelled to the air, "FEAR IS THE ENEMY! FEAR IS THE ENEMY! FEAR IS THE..."

Ghhrrrooooaaaaannnnnn...

The sound was loud and low and reverberated through the land so long the very soil we were standing on trembled.

"Uh oh..." I murmured.

A crack appeared in the ground next to us, and a giant head popped up, dirt and rocks falling off of it as it rose.

"Run!" I cried, unnecessarily. We were already running.

At least we had the presence of mind to stay together. We ran directly away from the big grey lump rising out of the ground.

The thing lifted itself out of the crevice and sat there, scratching its head.

"That's a trow, I think," said Laura as she ran. "Read about them in mythology class last term."

We ran at least a couple hundred yards away before we felt comfortable stopping.

The thing wasn't coming after us, thank goodness. It was just sitting there on the dirt, looking around.

We all crouched together behind a slight rise in the

ground, and watched it from what seemed like a far distance, but what was probably ten steps for the giant.

"You called it a trow, Laura?" I asked.

She nodded. "Sometimes called a troll," she said.

"Ah," I replied. "I wonder if we woke it?"

"I think that's a certainty," said Renée. "But I think what we were doing was important. I'm feeling a lot better just because of our yelling."

"But let's just be less noisy from now on," said Chance. "I don't know what else is around here that we might wake up."

"Agreed," Liesl chuckled.

We watched the thing as it sat and moved around a little, scratching itself and then lying back down in the crevice.

It fell back asleep and started snoring.

We moved on.

"Chance, can you illuminate the path?" Laura asked.

He muttered his spell, and the way glowed for a few seconds, as if the dirt and rocks were mildly, fleetingly fluorescent.

Chance gestured. "The way to The Oak King."

We began to walk again, leaving the snoring trow behind us and off to the left.

"Did Father teach you that spell?" I asked, curious.

"It's actually not a spell, it's a charm," said Chance,

grinning. "And yes, he taught it to me, after a fashion." He reached into his bag and brought out a small pipe. It was intricately carved with vines and leaves out of medium-brown wood. It was slightly discolored on the mouthpiece.

"This is The Oak King's pipe," said Chance. "The Holly King enchanted it, so it would lead us to him. It's actually tracking to the owner of the DNA on the mouthpiece, here, see?" He slowly turned the pipe; the discoloration was around the bowl as well. "The trace is always there. I just illuminate it for a few seconds with the spell I utter." He put the pipe back into his bag.

"Wow, that is actually really cool," I said, smiling. "I can't wait until we get to him." I looked out on the landscape. It was barren and desolate, and I could see absolutely no sign of anything that could be hiding a magical king.

I sighed.

"Don't worry, Hols, we'll get there," said Liesl, putting an arm around my shoulders. "We're probably really close." She glanced at Chance.

He shrugged. "Closer than we were before."

"What if it takes days to find the king?" Laura asked. "You said we shouldn't fall asleep here in Álfheimr, but what if it takes a long, long time?"

"Then we sleep with a watch," said Chance. "A

lookout. We take turns."

"That's going to be rough, but I shudder at what could happen if we don't take precautions," Laura said, looking around.

This place was harsh.

We hiked for a few more hours, quietly cheering each other up, trying hard to combat the depressing place we found ourselves in.

"I can't even imagine, The Oak King here, probably all alone," said Renée.

"He may very well be in a coma when we find him," Chance said.

"How are we going to get him out of here?" I remembered my previous attempt at rescuing The Oak King, with the help of just a handful of halflings. It had not gone well.

"I have a plan," said Chance.

"Care to let us in on it?" Renée asked.

Chance looked thoughtful. "Soon," he said enigmatically.

327

Chapter Thirty

# Dangerous Times

The red sun that illuminated the land so fitfully, giving everything a kind of half-light, was setting.

*Oh, no.*

We kept hiking as it dipped closer to the horizon.

I wondered what Chance was up to, but I didn't want to ask. I was afraid he really didn't have a plan, just overflowing dogged determination.

The sun finally disappeared. We had been hiking all day, with no sign of ending, no sign of any trees or water, or any place we might camp that looked better than any other place.

It was all like the surface of the moon.

Chance finally stopped after tripping two times.

"I guess we need to stop for the night. It's not safe hiking in the dark," he said grimly. "Let's set up the tent, but I think it might attract unwanted attention if we made a fire."

"But a fire might ward off any dangerous critters," said Laura.

Chance shrugged. "Okay, you may be right."

We set up camp, and built the fire. There were no stones to ring it, but we made do. We had to use my elemental magic and make the fire from scrub brush.

Renée gathered more scrub brush, making a small pile so the fire would last until morning.

The flame was fitful, a far cry from any other campfire we'd made. It flickered and nearly died several times, despite the magic we were using to keep it going.

"Let's use it for the lookout," Liesl said. "I'm too tired to stay up anyway. I'm going to bed."

"I'll take first watch," I said.

Chance came and hugged me. "I'll take second watch."

Everyone went into the tent, I sat down next to the tiny campfire, and wondered what would happen in the next four hours.

The first three hours, everything was quiet. No sounds whatsoever. Not even a hooting owl, which would have been nice, but I could understand why there were no owls.

Heck, the only living things we'd seen were a demon spider wearing a Chance suit, and a giant trow.

A small, scabbed-looking moon rose into the night sky, looking embarrassed, as if it wished it didn't have to show itself.

I spent the time drawing an elaborate spiral design in the dirt.

After a long time, I heard a howl, far off.

I raised my head sharply as I knelt there; the stick I'd been using to draw in the dirt went still in my hand.

I studied the dark horizon, and held my breath for a minute.

Aspen and Tundra, who'd stayed by my side as I kept watch, got to their feet, and both looked out in the same direction.

But after ten minutes I relaxed, because the sound had been far off, and it hadn't come again. Plus, I felt secure because neither of my wolf familiars had started growling.

They always growled when a threat came close.

I went back to my drawing.

Hey, it was something to do.

Ten more minutes passed.

Aspen lay down on her belly beside me, her eyes still watching the horizon, her ears alert and pointed forward to catch any sound.

Tundra stayed standing beside her sister.

I drew another spiral in the dirt.

My drawing was getting bigger, and encompassed a wide arc around the campfire.

I was engrossed in the art, studying the ground and what to do next, when Tundra began growling, a low, almost inaudible sound deep in her throat at first.

My head went up.

Aspen got to her feet.

Oh, great.

I heard a sound behind us and jumped.

"Hey," said Chance, yawning as he crawled out the tent flap. "How's everything been?"

"Not good," I said softly, looking back out at the horizon.

Tundra continued to growl.

Chance stood and came to us. "What do they see?" He murmured.

"Not sure," I said. "But something is out there. We heard a howl, about a half an hour back."

"Nothing after that?" he asked.

"Nope. It was quiet since then," I said. "But they started growling a few minutes ago. They sense something."

Chance stood there, watching the horizon for a few

minutes. "I think I'll send my hawk out to scout," he said softly.

"Do you think it's safe?" I asked.

"Don't know. But we are in a bad realm right now, and we can't afford to get eaten by a rogue trow, or anything else that might be out there." He called to his hawk, who appeared on his arm.

"Go look, see what there is to see," Chance murmured to his familiar. "Stay high, stay hidden in the sky."

The hawk squawked softly, touched her nose to her master's cheek, and launched herself into the air.

She flew higher and higher, her wings beating hard to gain altitude in the cold night air. Then she was gone, a speck in the distance.

We waited.

I threw the last of the sticks we'd gathered onto the campfire and flamed it again with my elemental power.

Aspen and Tundra slowly relaxed and lay down, but still kept their attention on the far horizon.

Half an hour later, Chance's hawk had still not returned, so we settled in by the fire and relaxed a little.

"Not sure if the danger is passed," Chance said. "Do you want to try and get some sleep?"

"I don't think I'd be able to close my eyes," I said, glancing around us. "But I guess I will lie down. We probably have a full day of hiking ahead of us. I'll leave a wolf out here with you."

"Thanks a million," said Chance, settling down and warming his hands on the flickering, fitful fire.

I whispered to Tundra, and took Aspen inside the tent with me.

Lying down in my blanket in the tent, I tried to rest. I put one hand on Aspen's fur, and closed my eyes.

I was so tired.

At one point, I thought I was still awake, lying there with my eyes closed, my hand still on Aspen's fur. I thought I heard a strange sound coming from inside the tent, followed by Liesl grumbling about something in her sleep, but I might have been dreaming.

Later on — it might have been a few minutes or several hours; it was hard to tell — I felt cold. I snuggled up to Aspen's long furry length, and burrowed my shoulder under her.

Aspen's low growling woke me up. Before my eyes were even open, I could feel the hair on the back of my neck rising.

*Something's not right.*

My eyes popped open.

The tent was gone.

I sat up, looking around wildly.

The small, red, barely-there sun was just beginning to rise.

Liesl, Laura, and Renée lay huddled together, shivering in their sleep. Aspen lay next to me, staring at the campfire, a low growl in her throat.

Chance and Tundra were gone.

*What the heck?*

I looked around wildly.

*Where is the tent?!*

I patted Liesl beside me.

She opened her eyes. "Wha...?"

"Wake up, Li," I whispered, although I had no idea why I was whispering. There was no one there, no reason to whisper.

Liesl sat up, rubbed her eyes, and looked around. "Huh? Where's the tent?"

"Good question," I stood up. "Where's Chance and Tundra?"

Renée and Laura woke up.

"WHAT THE...?!"

"HEY!"

Glancing around at where we'd slept, kicking aside our blankets, I thought something looked off.

"Someone's been in my bag," Liesl mumbled, opening her sack and rummaging inside.

I grabbed my own bag to looked inside.

The giant ruby was still there, and the large brown gem for the king. But, wait...

"The food is gone," Renée said, looking up. "They didn't touch anything else but the food, and it's gone."

I rummaged through my bag, dumping half the contents onto the ground. She was right. Our food was gone. Even Cook's biscuit bag was gone.

I sat back down, looking through my sack. I looked through it three times, just in case my eyes were deceiving me.

Liesl got up and began wandering around the camp.

What was left of it.

Snowbear sat on her shoulder as she walked around, kicking at rocks and scrub brush.

Renée began swearing.

Laura just shook her head and mumbled, "My uncle gave me that tent four years ago..."

"WHERE IS CHANCE?" I said in a loud voice. "WHERE IS TUNDRA?" I had had it with this place. I couldn't care less about Álfheimr, about The Faction, about any stupid dark chaos dude, I didn't care. "I DON'T CARE ANYMORE," I yelled to the morning sky.

My boyfriend is gone.

My familiar is gone.

My tent is gone.

My food is gone.

*What the heck am I supposed to do now?*

Wait.

Aspen had been following me, staying glued to my side as I paced and ranted.

I stopped now and looked down at her thoughtfully.

The others were grumbling and walking around, too upset to talk.

We were all really upset.

But I realized I could solve one problem.

Staring at Aspen, I whispered the spell to call my familiars to me.

Aspen looked up at me.

Tundra popped into existence on my other side.

I kneeled down.

"Where have you been?" I whispered to her. She head-butted me and licked my cheek, then stared into my eyes.

I nodded.

"Grab your stuff. We're heading out to find Chance," I called out.

I turned and grabbed my blanket, stuffing it into my bag.

The others hurried around, and were ready to go in just a few minutes.

I bent to Tundra again, looked into her eyes, silently communicating with her. Nodding, I rose and pointed. "Go!"

The wolf turned and began trotting, and I ran after her, Aspen at my side. The others followed us.

We traveled an hour before we saw him, crumpled on the ground in a ball.

"Chance!" I ran up to him and kneeled. "Chance, hey. CHANCE!"

I was rewarded with a groan.

Renée and Laura ran up, followed closely by Liesl.

"Chance, are you hurt?"

I ran my hands over his back and legs, but could see no injury. I gently tipped him over on his side. He fell over slowly, his arms and legs staying curled together.

"Here," said Renée, pulling Chance's arms away from where they were wrapped around his legs.

I rubbed his arms. His eyes were tightly closed.

"Chance, wake up," Renée murmured. She grabbed his ankles and gently pulled them out to lie flat. "CHANCE."

Chance mumbled again, his eyes still tightly closed.

"He's asleep," Laura said. "Is he in a light coma?"

"I don't see any injuries. Is he hurt?" Liesl asked.

Renée began slapping at Chance's face. "We don't have time for this," she said.

"What? Hey, gentle!" I protested.

Renée briefly pointed off to the hill next to us. I looked up and saw another trow lying there. Standing up, I saw that the remnants of our tent were next to it. Shredded.

I swore under my breath.

The thing was too close for comfort.

I grabbed Chance's arm and pulled. "Chance," I whispered. "Wake the heck up. NOW."

We heard a groan come from the trow.

It raised its head, and a brown wrapping fell off its mouth.

The paper bag my bread had been in. *Holy...*

"That thing..." Liesl sputtered.

"Yeah," I said softly. "It stole and ate our food. It stole our tent." I looked down at Chance. "It drugged our boy. I think that's enough for one day." I grabbed hold of Chance's wrist, and Renée grabbed the other, and we pulled Chance off.

After about a dozen feet, Tundra grabbed one pants leg with her teeth, and Aspen grabbed the other, and we were able to go faster.

Liesl and Laura directed us.

We got over a slope, then over a second slope, then stopped to rest.

I heard a cry from overhead, and Chance's hawk flew down and perched on her master.

"We need to wake him up," Liesl whispered. She kicked at Chance's leg in frustration.

I fished out my water canteen, unscrewed the top, and dribbled a few drops on Chance's face.

His hawk pecks his cheek, then grabbed his lip with

her beak.

"OWWW," said Chance, finally coming to.

"Get up, Chance," Renée kicked at his foot. "NOW."

Chance blinked his eyes and sat up. "Where are we?" he said.

"Never mind that," I said. "We need you to stand. NOW."

Chance got to his feet, yawning. His hawk hopped up to stand on his shoulder.

He was still wearing his jacket, which was good, because the hawk's talons looked sharp as she gripped her master.

He looked around, still very groggy. "What happened?"

"I'll tell you on the way," I said. "I'm taking charge of this expedition." I looked at Laura and Liesl. "Grab his arms, don't let him fall down." I leaned my face within an inch or two of my boyfriend's. "Chance, march. NOW."

I turned to Renée, "Can you fluoresce the path?" I asked.

She nodded and murmured the magic, waving her hand. The trail appeared off to our right.

*Well, thank goodness it's not leading toward the trow.*

"Come on," I said over my shoulder, and I began to hike at a rapid pace.

Aspen and Tundra trotted on either side of me. I was

trusting them to alert me of any danger. We were out of food. We had no tent. We had to finish this quest fast. Today, if possible.

Chapter Thirty-One
# Spriggans

We hiked for two or three hours, and we were going fast. At times, I was almost at a run. I wanted to get to the end as fast as I could, and I was tired of all the delays.

I stomped along, fuming, for quite a long time.

After a while, Liesl ran up beside me. "This trail we're following — Renée says she has no idea how far it goes, Holly."

"Yeah, so?" I said crossly.

"Well, what if we're following it for the whole day and night falls?" Liesl asked. "We have no tent. What're we going to do?"

"I don't know!" I said in an angry voice. "We just have

to get to where we're going before then."

"But what if we don't?"

I scowled and shook my head, hastening my pace.

Liesl backed off, and I didn't blame her. No one likes to talk to a friend who's steaming mad.

I didn't even know why I was so angry.

I just was.

The thing about being angry that I knew was that it made you oblivious to nearly everything around you. So every few minutes I glanced out at the land, scanning every direction, before continuing my stomp. I was also relying heavily on my wolf familiars to alert me of any danger.

At one point I glanced back and saw Chance and Renée whispering as they hurried after me.

*I don't care, I really don't care. As long as they follow me, they can talk and whisper and gossip as much as they want.*

In truth, I knew my friends wouldn't gossip about me behind my back.

They're probably talking about how we LOST OUR TENT and ALL OUR FOOD.

I was fuming in part because, whatever had happened to Chance to get him to the point where we'd find him passed out near the trow who'd silently trashed the camp he was supposed to be guarding, he needed to do better. And I was going to do better, now that I had taken over leadership of our expedition.

I vowed not to fall asleep, for one. I mean, I'd taken first watch and managed not to fall asleep. How hard was it?

SHEESH.

By the fourth hour of my angry stomping hike down the trail, which I kept asking Renée to fluoresce, I was tired.

I needed a rest.

Turns out the faster you hike, the shorter it lasts.

"Hold up," I said, putting my hand up. "Let's rest for a minute."

The others sighed with relief as I stopped and turned around.

I gasped.

Renée and Laura were behind me.

Chance was twenty feet back.

Liesl was behind him about ten feet.

I stared at them as they walked up to us and dropped to the ground to sit.

They looked sweaty and spent.

I felt horrible.

I was not taking good care of my team.

I glanced at Renée as she shared her water with the others.

"Hey," I said. "I'm sorry I was going so fast. We can

slow down."

"I understand you're angry," said Renée, not looking at me.

"Well, I guess I just want this quest to be over, before we lose anything more," I said."

"Holly," said Chance, coming up to me. "I think I was drugged, by the trow."

"Well, that's obvious," I said. "Doesn't take a genius to figure that one out."

Chance looked hurt.

Renée threw down the scarf she was holding and stood up. "And it 'doesn't take a genius' to figure out that you're just being angry to hide how scared you are, Holly."

My face blanched white. I could actually feel the blood drain out. I felt cold, as if someone had poured ice water over my head.

Renée stood there looking down at me, and I stared up at her, my jawed dropped open.

And then I started to cry.

I was horrified. Leaders aren't supposed to cry.

Renée bent down and patted my shoulder. "It's okay to be scared," she whispered.

I couldn't speak, the tears and shivers were coming so fast.

Liesl walked up. "Has she finally stopped being a

jerk?" she asked Renée, who waved her down.

"Yes," Renée said. "And she's sorry," she said, looking at me. "Aren't you?"

I nodded, blubbering.

Laura and Chance came up to Liesl and Renée and sat down. They watched me silently, waiting for me to stop crying.

"We're all scared, Holly," Chance whispered.

"B... but a... at least you weren't mean to your boyfriend," I sobbed.

Chance grinned.

"Holly, just calm down," said Liesl softly. "Everything's going to work out," she said.

I nodded and tried to wipe my face. Renée handed me a small towel.

"This is why your father sent all of us," said Laura. "We can take care of each other. If one of us falters, the others can pick up the slack."

"L... like m... me taking over leadership?" I asked.

"No," Renée said sardonically, "Like Laura and Liesl helping Chance with meds, when you just wanted to take off and hike."

"Meds?" I asked, looking at Chance.

He nodded. "They gave me a tonic. I was drugged. I could barely stay awake."

"Oh, Chance," I said, fresh tears coming down. "I'm

sorry."

He shook his head. "Don't worry about it. I understand. You had a reaction of anger to your internalized fear. This is why it's good we're a group: They were able to pick up the slack and help me."

"Yeah, but I shouldn't have made the slack in the first place," I said. I got up. "I'm sorry, everyone. I'll work on being better. Chance, you should lead."

"I'm in no fit state to lead," he said. "Renée, can you do the honors?"

Renée rolled her eyes and laughed. "Of course. Let's get going, everyone. That is," she glanced at me, "if you're ready?"

I nodded, wiping my eyes one last time.

Renée fluoresced the path and started hiking. We all followed her.

Liesl came up to me and put her arm around my neck. "Hey, you okay now?"

I nodded and smiled.

We hiked for the rest of the afternoon.

The small, red sun was shining fitfully from nearly directly overhead when we heard the first scream.

Aspen and Tundra swung around and began growling, the hackles along their backs rising.

I jumped a foot.

"What was THAT?" I twirled around, trying to see

what had made the noise.

I never had a chance.

The horde ambushed us, coming out of nowhere. The ferocious little creatures were about two feet tall, and sported big, elephantine ears that flopped as they ran. And skin as green as leaves, which made me briefly wonder if they had once been indigenous to a forest environment.

There had to be at least fifty of the things, although I didn't stop to count. They screamed as they attacked, a loud shriek that was chilling as much it was shocking.

Aspen and Tundra jumped repeatedly at creature after creature, biting, snarling, knocking over and tearing throats out right and left: doing everything a wolf does to kill.

I withdrew my magical staff from where it hung, invisibly, at my waist, and flicked my wrist to extend it from a two-and-a-half-foot baton to its full length of eight feet.

I swung it in a great arc, catching several of the things as they came at me.

Liesl brought out her staff and fought the little green creatures as she stood beside me.

I lost sight of Laura and Renée, but I saw Chance as he blew a dozen of the critters back with a spell.

I swung again and knocked half a dozen more away.

My magical staff caught them on the sides of their heads, and dropped them. They lay still at my feet.

Soon Liesl and I had to move back to fight them effectively, because the bodies started piling up.

"HEE-YAH!" I cried, mimicking an old movie Aunt Clare and I had once snuck in to see at a drive-in. "HIIII-YIA!" I screamed, swinging my staff a second time.

Several green bodies flew to the side, landing and not moving.

Thank goodness the creatures weren't that tough, or we would've been in a heap of trouble.

The things were easy enough to subdue: Just hit them hard on the head and they dropped. That wasn't the issue. The issue was in their numbers. At first, I'd thought there were about fifty of them, but I now realized there were at least twice that many.

"Back to back," I screamed, and Liesl and I faced away from each other, our magical staffs twirling in the air, batting little green creatures off to the right and left.

We were fighting well, but there were too many of them. We couldn't keep up

Liesl and I had multiple bites on our bodies from the creatures' teeth. I glanced over at Chance and saw him nearly overrun with the things.

We weren't going to make it, not with hand-to-hand combat. Not even with the magical staffs.

I suddenly stopped swinging my staff and brought it up parallel to my body. In that time, which was just one or two seconds, the things swarmed in and started to climb my legs and torso. I felt a dozen stinging bites as they attacked.

I closed my eyes and lifted my staff, bringing it down with a strong thump: *BOOM!*

The shock wave knocked the little critters backward a good fifteen feet, and, best of all, seemed to disorient them for a few seconds.

They began jumping back to their feet, clutching their heads, and looking around wildly to see what they could reach.

I only had a few seconds, and I used them: I brought my hands out, palms down. I surged my elemental power. My hands began to glow with red heat.

"HOLLY!" Chance yelled at the top of his lungs. "FREEZE THEM!"

In an instant I switched the cold in my mind to hot: the hottest summer day on the planet. The lakes dried up, and the sun beating down and my skin getting crisped red, blistering, painful.

I dropped my hands to the ground, yelling fiercely at the same time: "YAHHH!"

A white crystalline frost spread out from me like a shockwave, and the ground was frozen for miles around within seconds.

Our shoes protected us, but the little green creatures, ears flopping, teeth snapping, claws reaching, were instantly frozen.

Each little critter was glaciated, like they were caught in time.

Limbs frozen in mid-movement, faces frozen in mid-snarl, arms and legs frozen in mid-grab and mid-leap.

I took a deep breath.

*Lordy.*

I looked around.

Liesl walked up to me and patted me on the back. "Have I told you lately that I love it when you do that?" she asked, smiling through the blood on her face.

Laura, Renée and Chance hobbled up to us. They were much worse off than we were.

Chance dragged his leg behind him, and I saw the worst bites were near his knee. His arms were bloody, and his lip was bitten and torn, bleeding profusely.

Renée's jacket was shredded, as were both the arms of her blouse. Blood was soaking through in more than a dozen places.

Laura looked wild. Her legs and arms were covered with bites; there were a few bites on her face, too, and one bad bite had actually torn a corner of her scalp away from her head. It flopped down over her ear as she walked.

"Did I get them all?" I asked.

We all swung around in a mild panic, looking to see if any more were coming. But the land was quiet.

Frozen two-foot-tall bodies of the little gremlins stood silent as far as the eye could see.

A wind gusted suddenly, and a dozen of the things fell to the ground and shattered into a million ice cubes. Probably two million. The frozen bodies splintered.

I blinked.

*Nice!*

Chance fell to the ground, unable to stand on his injured leg anymore.

"Help me get him to his feet, Li?" Renée asked.

We decided to get as far away from the things as we could.

Liesl tied her sock around her staff, and Chance was able to use it as a crutch, with Renée's and Liesl's help.

I held my staff as I walked, in case we encountered any more of the things.

Laura walked beside Chance, ready to help if needed.

We walked a couple of miles this way, and by the time we'd escaped the carnage, walking had become hobbling.

"When we stop, I have a few healing unguents I can use," Renée said.

Chance groaned.

"Give them out now. I don't think things are going to get much better," I said.

Renée nodded, and we all stopped.

She knelt and searched her bag.

"I know I had them..." she said. "Hold on." She stretched and put her whole arm in the ten-inch bag of holding, up to her shoulder. It was such a strange sight, something I would never get used to.

It took at least ten minutes for her to find them, and she had to empty out almost the entire bag of stuff. There was a pile of her things around her when she finally exclaimed, "AHA!"

Chance was sitting next to her, and she moved to apply it to his wounds first. Then she passed the tube around, and we all used it.

I helped apply the cream to Liesl's scalp wound, which looked horrible but actually seemed to begin healing fast as I applied the cream, sticking the flap of scalp back into place.

"There," I smiled at my roommate.

"Thank you," she said gratefully.

"Put a dab on your tongue, and swallow it," Laura said. "It'll taste awful but it works from the inside out, too. Trust me."

I shrugged and did as she said.

"OH BLECHHH!" I gagged, but swallowed the bit of paste. It tasted incredibly bitter.

We sat and waited a few minutes, and Chance was the first to stand.

"I feel much better," he announced with a smile.

I grinned and got to my feet and went over to him.

"I'm glad," I said, kissing the tip of his nose. "Also: you need a bath," I chuckled.

"We all do. We're covered in dirt and blood and sweat, and it's soooo gross," said Liesl softly. She smoothed her scalp over, where it had been torn. I saw it had healed enough to stop bleeding.

*This is good. Very good.*

"So, freeze them, eh?" I asked Chance.

He nodded. "I am familiar with this particular warped fae. Fire would not have stopped them."

I shivered, glad he'd told me just in time.

I looked around. "Are we going on, then? I asked.

"Let's go another mile, just to be sure," said Laura.

I nodded. Those little green creatures were deadly.

Scanning the horizon as we walked, I wished more than ever for some kind of big tree or shack or cabin or something. Anything we could get up or inside of, in case they came back.

"What were they? Does anybody know?" I asked. I turned to Chance. "You said they were 'warped fae'?"

He nodded.

"I think they were corrupted spriggans," said Laura. "They're normally blue, solitary, and shy as anything."

I shook my head. This Álfheimr took any kind of Faerie Kin and warped them into something monstrous.

For the first time, I faced the fact that we were going to need a ton of luck to even get out of this land alive, let alone get home.

I gulped down my fear and scouted out a good place to stop for the night, but there was nothing.

We walked on.

And on.

*I wish we'd get there.*

Then I chuckled. I sounded just like a little kid on a long car ride.

Then I thought of cars.

*Boy, what I wouldn't do for a fully gassed-up car.*

I grinned as I walked.

*We could be there in an hour. Two, tops.*

I sighed as I walked, fantasizing about various motor vehicles.

We walked on through the barren landscape, through miles and miles of Nothing.

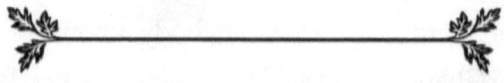

Chapter Thirty-Two
# Alt Fae

Hours later, the sun was setting and our goal was nowhere in sight.

*Don't be afraid. Don't be afraid.*

"We'll stop here for the night," said Renée, dropping her bag on the ground. It was very dim, and the flat; the barren ground showed no hint of anything getting easier.

"We'd better ration our water; we don't know how long we have to go," said Laura. "I wish there was some kind of wild game around; I could go hunting and bag us some dinner."

Renée scanned the horizon. "That would be nice," she said softly.

We made camp with what little we had.

Liesl and I gathered up bits of dead brush and sticks, and Laura fashioned it all into a fire.

"It's not much," I said apologetically.

"It's better than nothing," Laura said, grinning.

"Okay, since we lost our tent, let's just arrange our blankets around the fire," said Chance. "We can cuddle up to our familiars for warmth." He glanced at Aspen and Tundra. "Some more than others," he winked.

I had a thought. "Hey, it didn't go so well last night, with just one person on watch at a time. I think we should take watch in twos. What do you think?"

"I think that's a great idea, Holly, and just what I was thinking, too," said Renée, putting her arm around me. "Other than staying up all night, I think it's the best we can do."

"Short of tunneling into the ground to shelter," Liesl laughed.

We relaxed around the fire for a few minutes, and were soon lying in our blankets.

Renée and I volunteered to stay up for the first watch.

The others were quickly asleep.

It was a quiet four hours.

"How much longer do you think we have to travel?" I asked softly, so I didn't disturb my sleeping friends.

"No way to tell," murmured Renée. "But I don't think

it was like the first half of the quest: when we had to go through the forest until we were found worthy."

I shook my head. "Being sent by The Holly King should have been enough to get us through, immediately."

"I don't think it was a matter of who sent us," said Renée. "I learned in class last year about this kind of passage. The magical being letting the travelers through looks to see if they've experienced enough to understand what they have ahead of them. Or something like that."

"Hmmm," I said. "Okay, well, that makes sense. Still," I shook my head.

Renée nodded. "It gets trying, I know." She looked around. "What's scarier is this place, this haunted, chaotic, cursed land. It's almost like it's trying very hard to stop us from getting to The Oak King."

I stared at her. "Is the land sentient?" I asked. "Is there some magical being watching us? Throwing all this stuff at us?" A chill ran down my back at the thought.

"No, I don't think so," said Renée. "It's just the land itself. It's a very dangerous place. When you get to your third-year spring semester classes, you'll learn all about Álfheimr. About what happened here and why the land became so corrupted."

We fell silent and spent the next few hours keeping watch and patrolling the camp area.

Around two in the morning, Liesl and Laura took second watch. Liesl's familiar, Snowbear, curled around her neck, and Laura's parrot sat on her shoulder, leaning against her ear.

"The familiars will probably notice danger first," Renée said. "So be aware." She handed Liesl the rest of the brush she had gathered. It wasn't very much. "Try to keep it going," she said, then went to lie down on her blanket.

I yawned. "It's been a quiet night, you two. But last night the craziness happened in the second half, so look out. Walk the perimeter every half-hour."

Laura and Liesl both nodded, serious looks on their faces.

Renée and I lay down in our blankets, and I was so exhausted from the day I was soon fast asleep.

I was awakened by a loud shriek from Chance. After everything we'd been through, my eyes popped open, and I immediately sat up, my magical staff in my hands.

Tundra and Aspen were unconscious, next to me, and I briefly wondered that they didn't leap up, awake and alert, at the sound of the shriek.

I turned my head toward the scream, then screamed myself.

In a second, my eyes took everything in:

The sight of Liesl and Laura, unconscious next to the cold, dark firepit, which looked like it had been out for a while.

The sight of Renée, face down and motionless, next to Chance.

The sight of a coal-black humanoid figure crouching over Chance as he shrieked again.

"HEY!" I leapt to my feet, staff in hand. I took a step toward the creature, brandishing my magical staff. "GET OFF OF HIM!"

The thing looked like it was about six or seven feet tall when upright. Its skin was the color of the void itself. Its head was bald, and its hands and feet ended in long, sharp claws. A ridge of spiked fins ran down its back.

When I challenged it, it turned its head to look at me, and I gasped involuntarily at its blood-red eyes and the sharp three-inch fangs extending from its mouth.

They dripped blood as the thing hissed at me.

Chance's blood.

It crouched over Chance's prone form, holding my

boyfriend down with muscled arms.

Chance's neck looked like the thing had just started to feed off him.

He screamed again and opened his eyes.

"OH HOLY SHIT JESUS GET IT OFF ME GET IT OFFFFFF MEEEEE!" Chance screamed.

I leapt forward and swung my staff, and the thing was caught off balance; it was knocked off Chance's body and to the ground.

It jumped up and toward me in a challenge, screaming out in fury at being interrupted in its meal.

I swung my magical staff again, and it reared up and caught the large staff with its clawed hand.

*Uh oh.*

It wrenched the staff from my hands, tearing it away and flinging it far into the night. I saw it turning in the air as it flew, and made a quick mental note to retrieve it after this fight.

We faced each other: the black-as-tar creature with the blood-red eyes, and me, the small platinum-headed student with no weapon.

I saw Chance roll away from the thing, and bump into Renée's prone form on the ground.

Laura and Liesl were still motionless as well, and I briefly wondered what had knocked them out.

The creature screamed out a challenge, spitting blood

out of its mouth.

I backed up, scrambling for something I could use to fight the thing. My foot kicked out and hit my bag, and I glanced back and grabbed it in an instant. When I turned forward again, the thing had advanced, and was now twice as close as it had been a moment ago. It was less than ten feet away from me.

I swung my bag in an arc, screaming at it.

It reared back and retreated a few feet.

Keeping my eyes on the thing, I screamed at it while I reached into my bag for something, ANYTHING I could use.

"Keep away from me, you foul beast! Get back! Bloodsucking stain! YOU STAY BACK!" I screamed at it, keeping its attention and hoping it didn't jump on me while I searched my bag.

My fingers closed on a cup.

*Nope.*

My hand moved on to fumble past a book and grab onto a fork.

*Nope, not that.*

I reached deeper into my bag of holding, putting my arm in up to my shoulder.

The creature screamed a challenge, advancing a step.

"BACK! STAY BACK!" I yelled.

My fingers touched something hard and slim in the

bag.

*MY STICK!*

I pulled it out and pointed it at the creature.

*I don't know any spells yet. That's in next year's class. What do I do? What do I DO?!*

The stick glowed, and the tip let loose a lightning bolt the struck the creature in its forehead.

It screamed in pain and leapt back ten feet. I advanced on it.

"Not so tough now, are you? EH?!" I stepped closer and mentally urged my stick to zap the monster again. It obliged, and another bolt of lightning leapt out from the tip to hit the creature on its chest, flinging it backward a few dozen feet.

It swiftly got to its feet, crouched as it bared its teeth, screamed at me one more time, and turned and fled across the barren wasteland, traveling fast.

I watched it go, and then scanned the landscape for any more of them. I walked around the camp perimeter, grasping my stick tightly.

"I'm never letting you go, stick," I murmured at it. I kept walking around the camp perimeter, widening my circular path, until I came upon what I was searching for.

My magical staff.

"AHA," I said softly, picking it up and wiping it off. It has slime on it where I guessed the thing had touched it.

I trotted back to camp, worried about the others.

They were just starting to come to when I jogged up.

"Uhhnnn...."

"Hfff... uhh..."

"Wha... ?"

"Oh, God," said Chance, sitting up and touching his neck. "I think I'm okay."

I stood in the camp, scanning to make sure it was clear of any other dangers, then crouched and petted Aspen and Tundra. They were still unconscious, and I was worried.

Liesl, Laura, and Renée were sitting up slowly.

*Wake up, wolfies.*

I took out the last of my water and dribbled a few drops into each of my wolf familiar's mouths, then patted their shoulders and blew into their faces.

"Wake up. Aspen, Tundra. Wake up, puppies," I whispered.

Tundra slowly blinked. I rubbed her neck and head, praising her. Then Aspen woke up, and I sat between them, rubbing their backs. They were still very groggy.

"Hey," Renée stood and walked over. "What happened?"

"Chance screamed and woke me up, and I saw some... thing, on him, trying to suck his blood or something. You all were out, and my wolves were out, like you'd all been drugged," I said in a small voice.

Renée and Liesl looked around the camp and saw the signs of battle.

Laura checked out Chance. "It seems to have torn the skin but missed your jugular," she murmured, examining his neck. "You're very lucky. Another half-inch, and we'd be planning your funeral."

"Holly got the thing off me. It woke me up when it bit my neck," he said.

I described the creature to the others, and told them how the fight went.

"Sounds like some kind of altered faerie or something," said Renée. "Definitely something vampiric in nature. It was able to send out a psychic slumber spell. But it didn't affect you, Holly."

"Thank goodness," Chance said dryly.

I didn't say anything, just sat there between my two wolves, who were now fully awake.

I felt lucky. If this had happened yesterday, I knew I would have been more shaken, but I was becoming immune to being surprised at the different nightmare forms we were encountering in this chaotic realm.

*Álfheimr, land of nightmares.*

I had my magical staff and stick next to me, and I decided then and there to keep them out and at the ready for the rest of the time we were in this cursed land.

Chapter Thirty-Three
# Knockers

We gathered up our meager belongings and broke camp, glad to have survived another night.

*Barely.*

"The psychic slumber spell knocked out the familiars worst of all," said Renée. "I had the hardest time waking Jade up." She glanced down at the large rabbit hopping next to her as she walked. "She's still groggy."

I nodded. "Aspen and Tundra took a long time to come out of it, while you guys seemed to wake up as the creature left the area." I put my hands out and buried them in wolf fur on either side of me. As we hiked, Tundra stumbled a step, then regained her footing. "Still groggy, my pups?" I asked them. They both looked at me, their tongues lolling out of their mouths.

I could almost read their minds: *Don't call us "pups."*

I grinned.

Chance's hawk rode on his arm, her wings half outstretched as he stepped. Chance nudged the large bird up higher, and she nestled against Chance's head as he hiked.

"I wonder why the animals were more affected?" asked Liesl, rubbing her snowy ermine familiar's neck as he rode on her shoulders.

"Don't know, but I think when we get back, EVERYONE'S going to need to get checked out by Mrs. O'Bambury," said Liesl.

"Oh, definitely," said Renée.

We walked on.

The fluoresced path soon led us into some hills, and found ourselves ascending. We stopped for a rest at the top of a rise.

I had an idea, and decided to try to get us water out of the air using my elemental power.

"Rig up some bowls or buckets," I said.

The others did, and soon we had a half-dozen containers set in a row.

"Okay, back up," I said, extending my arms.

I closed my eyes and imagined being in a parched

desert.

*I don't need much imagination to feel this.*

Dry. Hot. Blowing wind. Clear sky with no raincloud in sight. So thirsty...

I felt a breeze on my cheek, then I felt a drop on my face. I opened my eyes, and the sky, which had been clear and dimly lit by the weakened sun's fitful illumination, opened up.

Dark clouds roiled overhead and the rain fell thickly, drenching everything for miles.

*So much for backing up, this rain is extending for miles.*

Our containers were filled within minutes.

*At least we won't die for lack of water.*

The ground grew dark with the rainwater, and, being normally parched and dry, the water didn't sink in very fast, and rivulets began gathering into streams. I glanced down the hill and saw a flash flood barreling past.

We loaded up all the water containers, water bags, and canteens. Having water in abundance put me in an especially good mood.

What we couldn't fit into our bags we drank.

Chance splashed water all over his neck, washing off the grisly evidence of the black alt-fae's attack. Laura applied ointment and a bandage, and he looked good as new.

We started hiking again.

"I've heard you can go a week without eating, if necessary," Renée mused. "But I hope we don't have to. The water will definitely help, though." She smiled at me gratefully.

We walked down the hill and across the still-barren but now-damp landscape. The flash flood had washed away much of the topsoil across a wide swath of ground. The newly wet streambed was a good foot deep into the ground, and we climbed down it, walking a short way across, then climbed back out of it.

"I wonder what the creatures that live here will make of the water," said Laura.

"I'll bet they'll be curious," Liesl said. "They might even like it."

"All living things on earth need water to survive," said Renée. "Whether a little or a lot, they all need it. So this should keep them occupied for at least a day, I hope."

"Pffttt, yeah," I said. "Hopefully keep them from bothering us."

We had not been able to go a whole night without some kind of attack, and I was not looking forward to spending another night in Álfheimr.

It was still before midday, though.

*Maybe today will be The Day.*

We hiked through the valley, up another hill, and down into a second valley.

*This is different.*

The ground in this second valley was full of rocks and what looked like pieces of metal. Rusted and darkened scraps of metal.

*Or are they?*

The dark scraps almost looked like alien flowers, stuck upright between the rocks, which were every size, from pebble to boulder.

"Chance: What do you make of this?" Liesl asked.

"Well, since it's a different ground covering, I hope it means we're getting close," Chance said wryly. "I did not expect the journey through Álfheimr to be this long."

Renée turned to him, "You didn't?"

"No, I did not," he replied. "I figured once we crossed into Álfheimr, we'd be nearly there. Remember: It was a magical glyph that got us here. The Ferryman transported us, I assumed we would be deposited into Álfheimr close to The Oak King's position."

"It's been more than a week," Liesl said. "Possibly two weeks: I've lost count of the days."

"I hope the others are faring okay," I said. "I hope The Faction hasn't done too much damage since we've been gone. This war is so bogus."

I kicked out at a large scrap-metal flower. It twanged forward a few inches, then twanged back to where it had been.

*Huh. I guess it's stuck in the ground.*

I kicked at another, and this one toppled over and set on the rough rocky surface. I kicked it again and it tumbled a few feet.

I stopped to rub my toe through my shoe.

*That was harder than it looked.*

I grabbed the piece of scrap-metal that I'd kicked. It *was* heavy, as though it was made of steel. I stood upright and examined it.

Liesl and Laura came over to look at it. Chance and Renée kept walking.

"Weird," I said.

I raised my head suddenly. The land around us seemed to be holding its breath, although if you'd asked me how I knew, I wouldn't have been able to explain it.

I just knew.

I threw the piece of metal back down, and it rolled a few feet and came to rest against another piece with a *clang.*

The piece of scrap metal it had hit flipped over, and I could see shiny gold on the underside.

"Huh," I said softly, stepping over and reaching for this second piece. A smaller piece lay next to it, this one looked like it was pure gold, so I grabbed it, too.

The larger piece was smaller than the first one I'd picked up, but definitely heavier. Part of it looked like it had been layered with raw gold: very yellow, speckled with impurities, but gold nevertheless. The second piece was the size of my hand and made up of heavy gold. I slipped it into my bag, and looked at the first piece again.

I turned it over in my hand and jumped back, dropping it in surprise.

Tundra barked sharply.

The other side of the metal scrap had a face on it.

It popped up after I dropped it, and I saw it was actually a little man about two-and-a-half feet tall. He seemed to be made of metallic shapes, but his face was fierce as he jumped up and ran at me.

I screamed and fell backward.

The little scrap-metal man growled fiercely and advanced on me, jumping and hopping as he came.

"Holly!" cried Liesl.

"WHAT IS IT?" exclaimed Laura. "Chance! Renée!" she called out.

I scrambled backward on my hands and feet.

Aspen and Tundra barked and lunged, snapping at the metal man. It didn't seem to do any good. I could hear their teeth snapping on the thing and making a bone-against-metal sound, then sliding right off.

The scrap-metal man was none the worse for wear, and he jumped onto me, climbing from my legs to my torso.

Its finger ended in sharp points that look like metal spikes, and it used these to climb across me, leaving bloody marks as it went.

They didn't seem to hurt me, though. I felt nothing at these spikes pierced my skin.

I fleetingly wondered about it, but the scary creature's grimacing face took all of my attention.

My breath came fast and fierce as the metal gremlin climbed up my torso and buried its clawed metal fingers into my shoulders.

It lifted one hand and sank those fingers into the side of my face.

That's when I finally screamed.

Chance and Renée ran up.

"OH MY GOD!"

"GET IT OFF HER!"

"IS THAT A CAVE KNOCKER?"

Chance tried to kick the thing off, but it hung onto me, its metal claws deep in my flesh.

I screamed again.

"If it's a knocker, she took something off the ground. What was it? WHERE IS IT?" Renée cried.

"I... I don't know, I think she put a piece of metal in her bag," Liesl yelled.

"WELL GET IT OUT AND THROW IT BACK!" Renée cried.

My breath was coming a mile a minute.

The thing's angry face was nose-to-nose with mine. Its eyes bore into mine. It began to stab me over and over with its sharp metal fingers.

Laura and Liesl fumbled with my bag. I was partially lying on it, and they had to push me to the side to get at it.

"Sorry, Holly!" said Laura.

Liesl stuck her hand into my bag and withdrew it with the gild piece of scrap metal.

As soon as it was out in the open, the creature's eyes were riveted on it. It growled even louder.

Aspen and Tundra were still trying to bite it, with no effect.

"THROW IT!" yelled Chance.

Liesl flipped the gold piece of scrap metal, and it flew in an arc; the little gremlin on top of me jumped after it.

"COME ON!" Renée and Chance grabbed me and pulled me to my feet.

Blood dripped from dozens of little wounds all over me.

The thing had grabbed the scrap of gold Liesl had tossed away, and was sniffing it.

Then it looked back at me and began to come after me again.

"RUN!" Renée screamed.

We ran. We ran like the devil himself was after us, because now, other little scrap metal creatures had begun flipping up.

"Run run run run run!" Renée called out, unnecessarily.

"Go back," I commanded to my wolf familiars as I ran. They ran alongside me, and glanced at me as I talked. "Go back! Delay them. Help us escape!"

Tundra and Aspen whirled around and ran back, and I raced forward.

Liesl stumbled and went down, and I grabbed her arm to help her up.

Laura grabbed Liesl's other arm, and together we got her back on her feet and began running again.

We ran until we got to the hills again and ran, puffing, up the side of a hill.

The scrap metal and rocks were left behind, and we got to the top of the hill, which was barren earth.

We turned around to look.

I needed to know if the things were coming after us.

I needn't have worried; my fierce wolf familiars had done their job.

The metal creatures were settling back down: Just a few were still walking around on their little legs.

Aspen and Tundra ran back to me, having delayed the scrap metal men long enough for them to forget about us, it seemed. Their tongues lolled out of the sides of their mouths as they ran up the hill and to my side again. They jumped and pranced playfully; they were happy with themselves.

"Good job, Tundra! Good job, Aspen!" I patted their backs, praising them. Each of them licked my hand.

We watched as metal creatures settled back into the earth and went still, then we walked a few dozen yards along the top of the hill before finally stopping to tend to our wounds.

Liesl's knees were bloody where she'd fallen. Her hands were scraped up as well.

I was the worst off, though: The little monster had dug its metal nails into me with abandon. Each wound dripped blood.

I stared.

The blood coming out of the wounds looked nearly black, like oil. It dripped slowly from my face and dribbled down my arms and legs, practically oozing out.

*That can't be good.*

I watched as a drop of black blood hit the ground. It steamed the ground for a few seconds and then sank into the earth. In a minute, a flower was growing up out of the little hole the blood drop had made: a flower with black petals.

"Oh, how pretty," I murmured, feeling slightly

delirious. My head felt so woozy I wondered if I was going to faint then and there.

I stared at the black flower as it grew.

*Wait.*

As the flower grew, the petals hardened into metal. It got so top heavy it fell over, but still continued to grow.

It grew into a... *OH NO!*

A creature was uncurling from the metal flower!

More drops fell from my wounds onto the ground.

"HOLLY!" screamed Renée. "Lie down!" She pulled my arm, and I dropped to the ground.

Renée began dabbing at all the bleeding wounds. "They're turning her skin black: It must be poison!" she said.

"Oh, ya think?" said Liesl, tears running down her face.

Chance grabbed the metal creature and twirled and flung it down the hill. Then did the same with the three others that were unfolding from the metal flowers.

"Quick! Where's the ointment!" Liesl cried.

Laura hurriedly shoved it into my roommate's outstretched hand.

Liesl and Renée began furiously dabbing my wounds, while Laura and Chance used towels dampened with water to wipe the dripping blood away.

Only a few more metal gremlins grew out of the dirt

as they were ministering to me. Chance flung each one out into the air and down the hill.

Aspen and Tundra stood sentinel at the edge of the hill and growled down at the metal creatures, keeping themselves between us and the metal gremlins.

Eventually, all my wounds were doctored and sealed over.

"I think the salve will fix the poison," said Renée, "The blackness is fading from around each puncture."

*Thank goodness.*

"Stick out your tongue, Hols," said Liesl.

I complied. She smeared a bit of paste on my tongue, and I swallowed, grimacing.

Renée handed me a canteen. "Drink," she said.

I swallowed a half-dozen mouthfuls, one by one, while lying there, looking at the grey sky.

Tundra came and rested her chin on my forehead, and I smiled.

I rested there for a few minutes, then felt energized and got to my feet.

I looked around.

"Okay, let's go," I said.

Chapter Thirty-Four
# The Search

After we had hiked for two more hours, we spotted something in the distance.

"Is that...?" Laura said, sighting it first. "IS THAT A BUILDING?!"

We all squinted as we walked.

"Sure looks like... something," Renée said.

"Something... square," Liesl said.

"Hmmm," Chance murmured.

"You know what I think?" I said. "I think that looks like a hut. Some kind of a cabin."

I began to trot. I was still sore from my morning monster attack, but the longer I trotted, and the closer I got to the hut, the more energized I felt. I started to run faster.

"Race you!" called Liesl as she passed me.

I grinned and surged and began to sprint.

Chance and Laura ran alongside me.

Renée ran after us.

It was maybe twenty minutes before we got to the little cabin.

Liesl arrived first. I ran to a stop and stood next to her. The others soon joined us.

We stood about ten feet away from the structure: the only obviously manmade thing we had come across in all of Álfheimr.

Chance muttered his spell to fluoresce the path.

It ran right up to the cabin's door, which was facing us. There was one dark window.

"Hello?" Chance called out.

Renée and Laura both picked up rocks to throw at the walls.

They checked the rocks carefully before throwing.

"Don't want to awaken any more hidden creatures," said Renée.

They threw their rocks at the wooden sides of the hut. Each thrown rock made a loud BANG! when it hit the wood, then fell to the ground.

We listened and heard nothing.

"I don't think there's anyone inside," Liesl said.

I shrugged.

*Maybe go up and knock?*

I took a deep breath and walked up to the door.

I wanted this quest to be over with perhaps more than anyone else. I felt like I'd experienced more anguish and fear than the others. Certainly no one else had cried about our situation.

*Welllll, that I know of.*

I raised my fist to the wooden door and knocked.

There was no answer.

With a glance back at my friends, and a shrug, I put my hand on the knob and turned it. The door creaked open as I pushed it wide.

The interior of the cabin was empty, and the wooden floor was covered in dirt and dust. A small wooden table and a lone chair stood in the corner beside a small stone fireplace; its blackened interior offering evidence that someone had lived here, however briefly.

And there was one thing more.

A trap door set into the floor. The wooden flat had a metal loop on one end.

I turned back to the others. "This might be it," I said excitedly.

We entered the wooden hut, and closed the door behind us.

I bent and hooked my finger on the metal loop, and pulled.

It swung up and open with ease.

I balanced it on the opposite floor and looked inside.

The trap door covered a small hole in the bare ground.

"It looks like a huge gopher made it," I said.

"We've got half a day of daylight," said Chance. "Let's investigate."

*Well, obviously. Pffttt. Like I was going to wait for morning.*

I peered into the hole.

It was about two feet in diameter, and dark. No light shone at the bottom. It might have been ten feet, it might have been two hundred feet. There was no way to know.

"Here, let me," Renée said. She grabbed a towel from her bag, and tied it in a knot and held it out. "Light it, Holly."

I nodded and extended two fingers, closed my eyes and called up my elemental power. A flame appeared at the end of my finger. I flicked it onto the towel knot, and it caught.

We all leaned over around the trap door hole as I Renée dropped it.

It fell a long way before landing.

"That's about a hundred feet," Chance murmured.

I stared at the flame on the floor down in the hole. It looked like a pinpoint of light.

Chance was fumbling in his bag. He withdrew a rope. "Thought we might need this," he said. He glanced around, then tied one end of the rope to the table. It was small, but sturdy. And it was nailed to the floor's wooden planks.

*Why would anyone nail a table to the floor?*

I wasn't sure, but I was glad they had, because it gave us an anchor.

"Who wants to go first?" Chance said, looking from face to face. "I'm just kidding, I'll go first."

Chance wound the rope around one ankle and began to slide down into the hole.

One by one, we descended into the hole in the ground.

It was not a little unnerving, but at least the hole widened after a dozen feet and, as I dropped to the ground beside the others, I realized we were in a cavern.

I looked around as Renée slithered down the rope, the last of us to join the group.

*Underground.*

"Where is that light coming from?" Liesl whispered.

"Why are you whispering?" asked Laura.

"I dunno, I just am," said Liesl.

"Well, okay then. The light is coming from that way," she said, pointing.

Chance reached into his bag and withdrew a large flashlight.

I blinked.

"And when were you going to let us know you had a flashlight?" I asked.

He grinned. "I was instructed to save the batteries."

I shrugged.

"Come on," Chance said, leading the way. He muttered the reveal spell, and the path fluoresced in a wide blue light.

It looked stronger than before. Brighter.

*I bet we're getting close.*

The cavern was large, reaching up maybe seventy five or eighty feet high. It was three times that wide.

The lit path led us to the side wall, where there was a cave opening into a tunnel large enough to stand up in.

It led through the earth farther than we could see. Much farther.

"Will this never end?" Liesl asked.

"No," Renée said solemnly. "This tunnel goes on forever. We'll never get out, and they'll never find our bones, not in a million years."

"Oh," Liesl laughed and playfully shoved Renée's arm. Renée grinned.

We walked slowly down the long tunnel, Chance out front waving the flashlight beam back and forth. The tunnel was completely barren, and reminded me of the surface of Álfheimr above us.

It took us over an hour to make our way to the end of the tunnel; the last few hundred feet, the walls changed from packed earth to rock.

"Granite," muttered Laura, running her hands over the rough surface. "This tunnel has been blasted with explosives; whoever created it blew straight through solid rock."

I actually felt better knowing were passing through rock: A tunnel through stone seemed sturdier than an earthen tunnel. Growing up in the human world, I'd heard about plenty of cave-ins. Packed earth made me nervous.

We stopped at the end of the tunnel.

Except it wasn't the end.

"It's a door," Liesl said.

We all gathered at a small, ancient-looking wooden door set into the rock face. Chance fluoresced the path, and it was still there: We were right on top of it. And at this point, it glowed so brightly it hurt the eyes.

Chance gripped the door's ancient handle and pulled. It slowly scraped open, and we looked inside.

Wires and tubes extended from a large box of machinery and curled all over the dirt floor. Some old rags lay in the corner.

The machine was thrumming with power, and we could see different fluids running through the transparent tubes that wound around the room.

"What is this?" Chance said, almost to himself. He bent to examine the machine, shaking his head.

"What are all these tubes and wires?" I asked. "This almost looks like something from the human realm."

"I think it might be," Chance said, standing up. "Search the room."

He got down on all fours and began to examine every little thing on the ground.

Liesl, Laura, and joined him. Renée held the flashlight up high, so it would illuminate as much of the room as possible.

"What are we looking for," I asked.

"Anything," said Chance. "A rock, a stick, a leaf, anything at all."

"Chance, this room is full of debris," Laura murmured. "Do you want us to gather it all up?"

"Yes," Chance said briefly. He reached into his bag of holding and, a minute later, brought out several large burlap sacks.

We stuffed them full of rocks, twigs, leaves, sticks, dirt, anything and everything. It took an hour to gather it all up.

Liesl, Laura, and I tied each of the large sacks up and hoisted them over our shoulders.

"Renée, help me?" said Chance.

The two began trashing the large machine in the corner. They tore up the wires, chopped up the rubber tubes and plastic gizmos. Chance even withdrew two large hammers from his bag, and they set to destroying the machine itself, hitting it repeatedly with both heavy hammers, until it was reduced to a pile of rubble.

Chance regarded the broken pile of metal and gear and trash had once been an expensive piece of machinery.

"I think it's dead, Chance," I whispered to him.

"I want to be sure," he said. He hit it a few more times with the hammer, until several more pieces fell off and dropped to the floor at his feet.

Only then did he seem satisfied.

He turned and surveyed the room. "Did you get everything?"

"I think so," I said, looking around us.

Renée shone the flashlight beam into every corner, under every shadow, and finally, at the pile of metal rubble.

Chance nodded grimly.

"Let's get out of here," he said, walking out the door.

"Chance wait!" I cried, when we were ten feet along the tunnel.

He stopped and looked at me.

"What about The Oak King?" I asked. "Where is he?"

Chance muttered the magic spell to reveal the path. Out in the tunnel it still shone, but it no longer went all the way to the door and into the room. It stopped with us.

"The Oak King is in one of the bags," Chance said briefly. "Now let's get him out of here."

Chapter Thirty-Five
# Back in the Barren Chaos

We were once again on the surface. Standing in the old hut, we considered our options.

"I think we should stay in this shack," Renée said. "It offers protection, more than the tent did. Plus it'll be warmer."

"We can use the table and chairs as fuel and build a fire," Liesl pointed out.

There was the small stone fireplace in the corner, behind the table.

"Yes, this will do, at least for one night," said Chance, looking around. "Although there's not much room to lie down."

"We'll make due," said Renée.

We carried the loaded sacks through the door and out about ten feet, then emptied the sacks out on the dirt, scattering all the junk out.

I looked down at it. It was hard to believe that a piece of this was the old king we sought.

Chance came to stand next to me. "Transfiguration," he said. "Comes in Sixth Year. Very complicated magic."

"Sixth Year?!" I said. "No one here is anywhere near Sixth Year. How are we going to undo a Sixth Year transfiguration spell?"

Chance turned to me and smiled. "None of us is. You don't need a person to undo a spell; you just need a really, really powerful magical conduit."

I blinked.

I almost wanted to ask him what he was on about, but instead I just waited.

*He'll tell me, given enough time.*

"Can you get out your wand, Holly?" said Renée.

*My what? Oh! My stick.*

I pulled the stick from my waistband and handed it to her. She put her hands up.

"No, no no. I don't need it," Renée said. "I just need you to do something with it."

"Okay," I said. "Do what?"

Chance and Renée and I stood around the junk from

the sacks. Liesl and Laura joined us.

"Hold hands," Chance instructed us. "Good. Now, close your eyes and think of magic."

"General magic?" asked Laura.

"Yes," he said. "Think of how it works, how you use it, how the spells you've been taught work, all of that."

"Holly? Toss your stick up and out," Renée said.

I flipped my stick into the air, my eyes still closed.

"Okay, now everyone, open your eyes and watch," said Renée.

I opened my eyes and saw my stick, glowing and spinning lazily in the air. A purple light shone at its narrow end, which circled slowly, then dropped suddenly and came down on a dirty old rag lying under some other stuff. Liesl, Laura and I shrieked as the stick touched the rag and disappeared in an explosion of light. In its place was a naked old man, crumpled into a fetal position. My stick was balanced on his head.

Chance leapt into action. "Okay, let's get him inside, hurry, he looks like he needs medical attention." He grabbed the stick off the old man's face, quickly handed it to me, and then grabbed the old man's shoulders.

We all picked him up in a different spot and carried him into the shack. He was huge. I lifted one of his legs.

We built a fire in the fireplace using the wood from the table and chair, and sat down on the floor surrounding the figure.

The old man was unconscious and visibly shivering. I hadn't realized you could do both at the same time.

The small, fitful red sun was just sinking to the horizon, and a wind was beginning to blow outside. The shack was cold, very cold, and the fire was just beginning to warm the air inside.

Chance gave the flashlight to Renée to hold, and knelt beside the old man as she shone it on him.

The man had a long beard that was mostly grey, but still showed some blond. His body was on its side, and was well muscled. His skin was a golden brown.

Chance fumbled in his bag and withdrew a blanket, and covered the figure.

"Laura," he said over his shoulder. "Do you have the medicinal paste?"

She handed it to him, and he squeezed some of it into a small bowl from his pack, added some water, and stirred it into a weak soup.

I put my arm around the old man and turned him onto his back.

He was filthy, and dried blood covered his face.

"Try to lift his head," Chance whispered.

I lifted, and Liesl helped me, and we got the unconscious figure to a semi-sitting position.

Chance opened the old man's mouth and dripped a bit

of the medicine soup in.

"Tickle his throat to make him swallow," Chance said softly.

"Here's another blanket, Chance," said Laura, handing it forward.

We spread it on the old man.

Chance touched the multiple wounds on the old man. "We need to tend to these," he said. "Laura, Renée, get bandages." He began carefully examining each of the old man's wounds. Each was still fresh, and they bled, draining vital fluids and power from the old king. Laura and Renée worked to bandage them, first smearing medicinal paste on each wound.

Once they had all been bandaged, all we could do was keep him warm and keep giving him the medicinal soup.

Chance kept trying to drip a few drops down his throat.

He finally swallowed a bit. Then a little more.

It took nearly an hour, but finally, he had swallowed all of it. He was still unconscious.

"How are we going to get him out of Álfheimr?" I whispered.

"Let's worry about keeping him alive for now," said Renée.

Chance thought for a minute, then turned to me. "Holly. Your necklace."

I grabbed the charm out from under my shirt and rubbed it vigorously, willing my father to appear. I rubbed the darned thing for a long time, but nothing happened.

"Last time, it just took a few rubs and The Holly King appeared," I said worriedly, still rubbing the charm.

"It probably doesn't work here in Álfheimr," said Liesl in a worried tone.

This was discouraging, but understandable. This place was backwards. Upside down. It was just wrong.

*Cursed.*

I took a deep breath and closed my eyes, forcing myself to calm down. I was the daughter of The Holly King, the niece of The Oak King. The granddaughter of Titania herself. We would get through this. We had to.

I glanced at my necklace.

*We'll just have to think of something else.*

Chance and Liesl began rubbing the old man's arms, to warm him up.

The fire was quickly warming the cabin: It was the largest campfire we'd been able to build since crossing over into this barren land. All we had available to burn was the table and single chair, so we rationed the wood to last the whole night.

As the sun dropped below the horizon, we all huddled in the cabin, cozier than we'd been since starting the quest.

*We have the old man.*

*We are sheltering in an actual building.*

*This is almost over.*

*Soon, we'll be able to get back to Father and the Academy, and hopefully help out with the war.*

I began to exhale. I allowed myself to begin to relax.

*Big mistake.*

Chapter Thirty-Six
# The Wild Hunt

We all settled our blankets around the fireplace. Next to the fire, the old man lay on a bed we'd fashioned from spare blankets, and he looked much improved. Four hours had passed: His color was returning, his fever was nearly gone, and most importantly, he was no longer curled up and writhing in pain.

He now lay, snoring softly, next to the small but hearty fire we'd made out of the pirated wood.

There was only one problem: He was unconscious. This was worrying.

"Not sure what else to do," said Laura. "I've bandaged all his wounds, Chance, you've spread salve and cleaned his mouth, Liesl, you helped warm his feet with alcohol, Renée, you've given him the tonic Mrs. O'Bambury sent for him. That's all we can do right now. All that, and keep him warm."

"And get him home," I said dryly. I looked around at my friends. "Seriously, we all need to get home. It took us weeks to get this far, and we're out of food, thanks to that trow." As if to accentuate my words, my stomach rumbled loudly. I took another sip of water, feeling peaked.

"Let's just take one day at a time," said Chance.

"One hour at a time," whispered Renée.

It was nearing midnight. Liesl and Laura lay on blankets next to me, sound asleep.

Renée was sipping water she had warmed by the fire. "Tasteless tea," she called it.

I had nodded. I was familiar with the very same tea. I'd drunk plenty of it during my time growing up homeless on the streets of New York.

*You do what you have to do.*

I was worried about tomorrow. And the next day. And the next. I wasn't even sure how we'd gotten into Álfheimr. Into this barren land of chaotic darkness.

*How does one bad faerie curse an entire land?*

It was unbelievable. This place was crazy, utterly crazy.

*Unsurvivable.*

Aspen and Tundra snored next to me, warm fluffy familiars I loved.

I stared into the fire, wishing I had a hot cup of cocoa, then felt guilty. We didn't have anything to eat. Nothing.

*Nothing to give the ailing king we've just rescued. Nothing to fill our own bellies. Nothing to stop my stomach growling.*

I still wished I had hot cocoa.

At least we had a fire.

"Holly," whispered Chance. I glanced over at him. "Did you hear that?"

"Hear what?" I murmured.

Had I been so deep in my own thoughts that I'd zoned out?

*Probably.*

I listened to the stillness outside. All I could hear was a gust of wind buffet against the wall of the cabin every now and then.

Thank goodness the little hut had glass in its one

window. It was thick and, although it had started to warp from age, it kept out the wind, which had started to blow earlier.

I turned my head to stare out the window. It was dark and... *wait...*

I sat up straighter. I glanced at Chance and Renée, and they stared back at me in the firelight.

I looked at Aspen and Tundra. If anyone heard anything, it would be the two wolves asleep next to me.

*Sharp ears, sharp senses, the best companions.*

As I watched them, Tundra began to softly snuffle in her sleep.

*Oh, brother.*

*Woooooooshthump*

I heard that.

I got to my feet and went to look out the window; Chance joined me.

"See anything?" Renée wondered from her spot near the fire.

I stared out the window. There was no moon (*of course not*), so there was no light, except from the fireplace behind me. This effectively made me blind to anything outside. It all looked like a dark void.

I moved to the door. Aspen awoke and raised her head, then jumped up and followed me.

Chance stayed at the window and stood there,

looking out.

I stepped outside and walked a dozen feet away from the cabin, Aspen at my side.

It was cold, and I wrapped my arms around myself as I looked around.

Everything looked cold, barren, and desolate.

*Your basic Álfheimr night.*

Aspen's ears pricked, and her stare penetrated the darkness, scanning the landscape.

"See anything, girl?" I whispered.

Suddenly, I heard a faraway call, a whooshing that sounded like it was coming from...

I looked up at the sky.

My jaw dropped in surprise.

I glanced at the cabin window. Chance was still there. Trotting to the window, I motioned for him to join me outside.

He came out, and I pointed.

*Oh my God.*

A streak of... something... arced slowly across the night sky. It was lit up, but I couldn't quite make out what it was.

My heart raced.

*Could it be Father?*

"Is that... is that... Santa?" I asked in a quiet voice.

Chance smothered a grin. "Holly, Santa Claus is just

an Old World religious myth. If you mean, is that your father, The Holly King, no, it is not. He does not ride a sleigh pulled by flying reindeer."

I watched the thing unblinkingly, and stepped forward, as if that would give me a closer view. "Well, then, what is it?" I asked.

Chance studied the object. "Hmmm," he said softly.

I blinked. There was now... something... trailing behind the initial *thing*.

"Is it coming closer?" Chance said, and I heard the slightest hint of hope in his voice. I pulled my eyes away from the sight in the sky and stared at my boyfriend.

*This quest has taken its toll on Chance.*

He had dark circles under his eyes, and his cheeks looked just a little grey.

I laid my hand on his chest as he watched the night sky object.

I reached up on tiptoes and gently kissed his lips.

*Please don't turn into a giant spider. Please don't turn into a giant spider...*

"Oh," he said. "OH!"

I turned to look at the thing in the sky. It was coming closer!

*I think...*

We both stared at it as it approached, slowly turning in a wide arc and descending.

Aspen began to growl.

A chill ran up my spine.

"Uhhh... maybe we should go inside?" I said.

Chance stared up at the approaching... *whateveritwas.*

"Chance?" I murmured.

"Oh my God," Chance whispered. "OH MY GOD."

I stared up at the approaching thing. It looked like some kind of someone was riding a something with a bunch of things following it.

"That's Herne," Chance whispered. "Wake the others."

I glanced at the window. Renée was now looking out. I ran to the side of the hut and tapped on the glass, motioning her to wake the others and come out.

I ran back to Chance.

"Is he going to land?" I asked.

"I hope not. Those are hellhounds trailing him," Chance whispered.

I looked down at Aspen. She had stopped growling and was silently watching the approaching Herne.

Renée came out to join us, trailed by Tundra. Liesl and Laura came out after a minute, rubbing their eyes.

"It's the Wild Hunt," Renée said. "Oh, God. It's Herne." She glanced down at my wolves, looking worried.

"Those hellhounds have been known to chase their

prey to the ends of the earth," Chance said. He glanced at his hawk familiar on his shoulder, whispered to her, and she vanished.

Renée held Jade, her rabbit familiar in her arms, and she bent to whisper in the rabbit's ears. The familiar disappeared.

Liesl did the same with Snowbear.

Laura sent her parrot away.

Aspen and Tundra stood sentinel by my side, their attention on the approaching forms, utterly rapt.

"Should I send my wolves away?" I whispered. "They don't seem frightened."

"I would," said Chance.

"So would I," murmured Renée. "Unless you want to lose them for a fortnight. Or forever."

*But they're magical.*

I sighed. Not wanting to take a chance, I glanced down at my familiars. They looked up at me and whined. I shook my head, and whispered, *"Go."*

They poofed back to their realm.

We watched The Wild Hunt approach.

"The hope is that he doesn't land," said Chance. "But that he helps us."

*But why?*

"I don't understand," I said quietly.

The wind was beginning to pick up, and my hair

whipped back.

"Herne and his hounds are a fearsome, wild group," said Chance. "Not suited for tame company."

"What do you mean?" I whispered.

"He means that Herne is wild, he and his hounds, and what does a wild animal do with their prey?" Renée offered, not taking her eyes off the approaching group.

They came low, within just a couple hundred feet of us. I could see Herne clearly: He rode a wild white stallion with a crazy long mane and tail.

Herne had the head of a stag, but the face of a man, and thank goodness this was barely discernible, because from what I could see, it was a frightening sight.

As I stared up at Herne and fear rushed through me, I fleetingly thought, *he must be lonely.*

This thought was replaced by the realization that this God of The Wild Hunt was utterly untamed. *Chaotic.*

*He must feel at home passing through Álfheimr.*

The hell hounds followed Herne, and their baying filled the night sky. They were huge, massive dogs, very dark, with red eyes. They followed Herne on his stallion like a pack of foxhounds.

Herne raced across above us, and something fell from him and spread out like glitter over the cabin and all of us.

I stared as it fell on me. I watched whatever it was

land on my arm and dissolve like light hitting the ground.

"It's magic," Chance whispered. "He's imbuing us with extra magic."

"I hope this means what I think it means," Renée murmured.

Herne and his hounds raced back up and away, and we watched them until they disappeared.

The night was quiet again.

"What now?" I whispered.

"Now?" said Chance. "We go to sleep."

Chapter Thirty-Seven
# Titania

We woke after the sun had lightened the landscape outside. The fire had died down to just embers, and they crackled and blinked red in the ashes of the fireplace.

The old man slumbered in his blankets, unmoved from the night before.

The hut was quiet and dark, but as I turned my head, I saw dim light coming through the window.

*Dawn has already come.*

What would we find outside? The barren desolation of Álfheimr? That's what one would expect.

*And yet...*

I closed my eyes again, not wanting to get up out of

my warm blankets.

The little shack was quiet and still: The only sound I could hear was the slow, easy breathing of my friends, the faint breathing of Aspen and Tundra, who had returned to lie next to me, and the very faint sound of...

*Birdsong.*

My eyes opened wide. I turned my head back to look at the window. It was still showing pale light and nothing else.

*I imagined it. I was dreaming...*

Another sound came to my ears.

It sounded like... *what is that?* I thought I heard the distinct sound of something hitting the outside wall.

*Shruff... shruff... shruffffffff...*

I sat up.

*That's the sound of a branch full of leaves hitting an outside wall in a breeze.*

"Chance, Liesl, you guys, wake up," I said. I sat up and looked around. A gust of wind blew against the side of the hut, and I heard the branch of leaves brush against the outside wall again.

*Well, I'm not waiting for them.*

I pulled on my shoes and got to my feet, and gingerly picked my way through the tumble of blankets and sleeping teenagers, and walked to the door.

I closed my eyes, whispering a silent wish to myself,

then opened the door...

I was greeted by the sight of the forest.

*But which forest?*

"Hello," a voice said. "Good morning, sleepyhead."

I looked over and saw a large ring of rocks encircling a healthy fire, and the welcomed form of Old Alwined O'Malley, the driver who'd first brought me to Titania Academy and who had rescued me when I was kicked and shoved and hurt the previous spring. It seemed like a million years ago.

"Ned?" I asked.

He grinned.

*Am I dreaming?*

I looked back and saw the old man and my friends, all asleep on the floor of the old abandoned hut we'd found in the middle of Álfheimr. I didn't want to step from the hut's doorway, worried it might disappear.

I cleared my throat. "Ned," I said, "Be right there, okay?"

He raised his tin mug in salute, and nodded.

I turned back inside.

"CHANCE, WAKE UP," I said in a loud voice. *They need to wake up NOW.* "LIESL, LAURA, RENÉE. UP. WAKE. UP. NOW."

I walked over and bent to examine the old man.

*We'll need help moving him.*

The others were beginning to stir.

"Y'all, we're home," I said.

That woke them instantly.

"WHAT?!" exclaimed Renée.

I grinned.

Chance pulled on his shoes and got to his feet. "Holly, are you sure?"

"Pretty darned sure," I said. "Go look for yourself."

We all helped bring The Oak King out of the cabin. I noticed as we crossed the doorway, there was a shimmer of magic. We were actually being magically transported through all of Álfheimr and the forests on the Isle of Skye, straight to the forest surrounding Titania Academy.

Ned stood and helped us bring out the old man, reaching for him as he was passed through the old hut's doorway.

As soon as the last of us had passed through the door, it vanished.

I stared for a moment at the spot where it had been. The forest did not look any different.

*Magic.*

I turned back to the others.

After the old man was settled on the ground by Ned's campfire, the old driver straightened and pulled out a small flute. He put the flute to his lips and played an intricate tone.

There was a brilliant flash of light.

As the light faded, the old woman in rags, whom we had last seen in the forest of the Elfen lands, appeared next to Ned.

She straightened and lifted the hood from her head and looked at us.

Chance dropped to his knee and bowed his head, murmuring, "Your majesty."

Renée glanced at him, then looked back at the old rag woman, and followed him to the ground, taking a knee and bowing her head.

Liesl and Laura both gasped.

I gulped and came forward to her. "Grandmother, please, please help him," and gestured toward the old man lying on the ground.

We parted the path, and the old rag woman came to the old man.

Tears were in her eyes as she gathered him up in her

arms, no longer a frail old woman, but now strong.

She looked up at all of us, now gathered to her side.

"Gather close," she said. "Hold hands."

We joined hands, and I placed a hand on Titania's arm. Chance, on the other side, did the same.

The old rag woman closed her eyes and the forest glowed in a bright light once again. So bright I had to close my own eyes.

When I opened them again, we were in a different forest.

Titania stood up straight, and we could see her true form.

She was tall, as tall as The Holly King. Her face was young and smooth. Her arms were strong, and they held her son easily. The wings on her back were a sparkling, translucent gold and moved slowly back and forth in the fresh air.

Chance turned his head and whispered at his hawk familiar, perched there on his shoulder. The hawk gave one squawk, turned and launched herself into the air, and flew off.

Titania waved her hand, and a massive tree appeared before us. It looked like Jess's tree house only ten times bigger.

"Open the door, Chance," Titania said softly.

We brought the old man inside, and the queen laid

him gently on a soft fluffy bed. He groaned as he lay back.

He was in bad shape. Titania hovered over him. With a wave of her hand, the old man was clean; his superficial scrapes and cuts were healed. But still he lay there, weak as a kitten.

The door opened suddenly, and The Holly King entered, Chance's hawk on his arm. The hawk immediately hopped from the king to Chance's arm and nuzzle her master briefly.

"Mother," he said softly. "How is he?"

The queen bent over her son, The Oak King as he lay on the bed. "I need Jess," she whispered.

Chance whispered to his hawk familiar once more, and opened the door and the hawk flew out. Chance closed the door gently.

The Holly King bent low over his brother and exhaled into his face. Color returned to the sick old man, and the lines on his face, which I hadn't realized were even there, relaxed.

"He's very weak," said The Holly King. "He's near death."

The queen laid her hand on her son's chest, still wrapped in Chance's and Liesl's blankets. She closed her eyes and her hand glowed, and the low glow moved from the queen into The Oak King, melting into him.

"When we found him, they'd transfigured him,"

Chance whispered. "They were draining his power as soon as he generated it."

The Holly King glanced at Chance, then all of us behind him, and nodded, turning back to his brother.

The door opened, and Jess appeared. "I have the tinctures here, my queen." She walked up to Titania and dropped to one knee.

"Thank you, my dear," said Titania, taking the ampules from the lacewing faerie. She turned and began unstopping each one, dripping them into her son's mouth. With each passing minute, more color returned to the weak old man. After a long time, the queen returned the empty glass bottles to Jess, who dropped them into the leather pouch tied to her belt.

We stood and watched Titania minister to The Oak King, and I fervently wished for his strength to return.

After an hour, Titania nodded and turned to The Holly King, and hugged him. There were tears in both their eyes.

The queen sat in the chair next to the bed and suddenly looked solid.

The Holly King turned and stepped close to us.

"She will remain. We can go," he said softly.

I looked over at the queen, who was so regal and at the same time, my grandmother and therefore so comforting. She smiled at me.

"I will take care of him," she said softly.

I felt a calm come over me. The Oak King would be okay. We didn't know how long he would take to recuperate, and from the looks of him, it would be a long, long time before he regained his health. But he would live.

We all walked out of the tree house and into the woods.

"Where are we?" I asked.

"This is the forest of Tir Na Nog," said The Holly King. "It is a hidden realm within the Faerie Realms," he said as he walked.

When we had stepped a few dozen feet from the Queen's tree house, Father waved his hand in the air, and a door appeared. He stepped up to it and opened it. I could see another forest beyond. The Holly King led the way, and we all walked through the door. I blinked, and we were back at school: The door had deposited on the edge of the forest surrounding Titania Academy.

Chapter Thirty-Eight
# The Living Sight of War

"But Father," I asked as we walked across the lawn to the steps leading up to the school's front door. "Don't you want to stay with The Oak King, to make sure he's all right, to... to help him or something?"

"Holly, my daughter." The Holly King stopped and put a hand on my shoulder. "So much has happened in your absence. It's been more than three weeks. Three hellish weeks."

*THREE?! So long!*

"I... I had no idea, Father," I said quietly.

"Turn around," Father said, gently pushing my shoulder. I swung around to face him, but he turned with me and indicated the forest to the north.

I gasped.

The sky was blackened. Smoke curled up from the forest, and there were the signs of blackened trees across great swaths of land.

In the distance, we could hear bombs going off.

"Father?!" I exclaimed. "The forest! The Fae Folk Lands!"

"They've broken through, Holly," The Holly King said. "Five days ago."

Titania Academy and the forest surrounding it was sealed off with a magical dome that penetrated the earth.

*It's a full globe around us.*

Father was incredibly busy protecting different areas, transporting displaced families, and warding off the northern borders that hadn't been breached yet.

Laura's parents were waiting at the castle for her.

"Laura!" Tam cried, laughing and running to meet his sister.

As we walked up to meet our friends and teachers, I felt exhausted.

Mrs. O'Bambury came to meet us, carrying Lucy, who was grinning widely.

"I missed you, Holly," she said.

I kissed her cheek, "Oh, I missed you too, Munchkin!"

It was a good homecoming.

An hour later, after we'd had a chance to shower and eat, we met with The Holly King and the headmistress in private.

I was still exhausted, but the shower and food had energized me.

Renée, Liesl, and Laura sat next to me, all looking tired but refreshed.

*That's how I must look.*

Chance had gone straight to a private consultation and had barely had time for a quick four-minute shower before they convened this meeting. He sat next to the king, a hearty beef sandwich in his hands. He was in the midst of wolfing it down.

I looked around the room and saw every teacher was there. Several dozen people stood in the background.

"Okay, everyone," The Holly King said in a loud voice. "The first thing I must announce is that, as most of you know already, our team has recused The Oak King. He's at an undisclosed location recuperating, and is in the best of hands. Now, this helps us in two ways. First, The Faction no longer has his power source. This cuts them off at the knees. And second, as soon as The Oak King has fully recuperated, he will be able to join the fight."

Everyone cheered, it was a happy, jovial sound.

I smiled. I had thought it would take a long time for The Oak King to recuperate, but I was glad Father thought it would be soon.

Exhausted as I was, and I think I would need a week to rest, I loved hearing the cheers.

"Now," The Holly King continued. "As most of you know, The Faction forces were able to cross our northern border five days ago. Luckily, our army has recently received reinforcements: We now have an alliance with not only the centaurs, but also the giants. With their help, it may even be enough to push them back north. And speaking of the north, we have completed the rescue operation to help the Elfen Kin to safety.

"Many of the Fae Folk families have opened their

homes to these Elfen refugees, and for that we thank them. Selfless gestures such as these are what we need if we hope to win this war. You never know who you might shelter, and those living in your home for a short while may become lifelong friends and allies. Or even our next Faerie heroes."

There was a commotion, and a young man hurried into the room; he rushed over to Chance and whispered in his ear, giving him a sheaf of papers.

I saw Chance's face go white.

*Oh, no.*

"One moment, please," The Holly King boomed out amid the chatter that had arisen at the young man's entrance. "We may have some new information." He bent his head close to Chance.

They spoke for some moments.

I saw Father's face go white and tears form in his eyes.

*What's happened?*

The Holly King stood up. "My friends, I have some devastating news." He paused and looked down at the papers Chance had given him, clearly trying to collect his thoughts. He looked up again.

The room was pin-drop quiet.

The Holly King cleared his throat. "The Faction... has broken through the barrier between the Faerie Realms... and the..." He looked down and seemed to choke up, then raised his head once more. "...between the Faerie Realms and the Human Realm."

The room erupted in barely controlled pandemonium.

I felt my stomach roil.

Later that hour, Chance, Renée, Laura, Liesl, and I stood on a tall hill with Father, the headmistress of Titania Academy, Professor Farryn, Brendan, Jess, Ned, and Mrs. O'Bambury.

We looked to the west at the setting sun. The sunset made the sky looked like it was on fire. Pinks, oranges and yellows mixed into blues and purples as the black of night began to unfurl across the heavens.

"It's beautiful," I murmured, holding Father's hand.

"Now it's time to turn around and see," he said. We turned as a group to face the east.

The sky facing east was full of color, and it was beautiful as well. But a large jagged hole, ringed with magic, had been torn in the sky. Through this hole we could see a busy metropolis: The lights and sights of the city, cars moving along the highways, a great flowing river lined with buildings, some stretching toward the sky.

"That's Dublin," The Holly King said softly. "The breach looks directly out on their city. Over a million people."

"Do they know the danger?" asked Laura.

"I'm going to meet with the president tomorrow," said The Holly King. "Minerva will accompany me." He sighed sadly. "I will fully inform them of everything, but they may already have an inkling of the imminent crisis before them." He pointed to the large rip in the sky. The edges looked like they were on fire. "You see, they can see that breach as well as we can, plain as day."

The Faction's plot was laid bare now for all to see. Their purpose was to conquer the world.

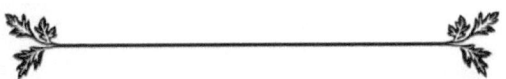

*Dear reader~*

I'm so glad you read Faerie War and I hope you loved it. I do hope you'll consider leaving a review. It means so very much to hear what you think.

Get book 5 of the series!

Faerie Devastation
Coming out September 2020!

Here ends Faerie War, the fourth book of the Titania Academy series. The fifth book will be called Faerie Devastation.

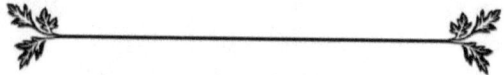

# ABOUT THE AUTHOR

Samaire Wynne grew up in a lot of different places, and now happily resides on the East Coast, laboring away at writing stories every day. She is an animal lover with far too many pets, yet she still muses how she'd like to add even more. A lover of all things night and gothic, she also loves to read and reread her favorite books. Owned by a cat named Tyrion, she can be found haunting the shadows and mists that hang low over the hills of southern Virginia.

www.ingramcontent.com/pod-product-compliance
Lightning Source LLC
Chambersburg PA
CBHW020633020726
47494CB00001B/167